★

WATCH OUT FOR BLACK CATS

I stepped even harder on the accelerator. I rounded a curve and the headlights picked up something small and dark and stirring on the highway. I jammed on the brakes and leaned on the horn. The damned thing didn't move. I hopped out and went to look, and found myself eye to eye with a half-grown black cat. I bent over to pick the poor beast up, my back to my own buggy, when it blew.

My car, I mean. It exploded into space and knocked me flat on my face, right on top of the cat. Somehow I had enough wit to stagger to the side of the road before sinking to the ground again, the cat and I still hanging on to each other for dear life. The two of us lay there panting until a patrol car drew up.

★

A
VINTAGE
YEAR
FOR
DYING

FRANK ORENSTEIN

WORLDWIDE.

TORONTO • NEW YORK • LONDON
AMSTERDAM • PARIS • SYDNEY • HAMBURG
STOCKHOLM • ATHENS • TOKYO • MILAN
MADRID • WARSAW • BUDAPEST • AUCKLAND

For the next in line—Jenna and Eric

A VINTAGE YEAR FOR DYING

A Worldwide Mystery/March 1996

First published by St. Martin's Press, Incorporated.

ISBN 0-373-26196-9

Printed in U.S.A.

My thanks to Richard and Valerie Eldridge
of New York's Brimstone Hill Vineyard both for their
own fine wines and for giving me the knowledge I
needed to pursue my own criminal ends
with that magic brew.

ONE

IF SOME ANCIENT GOD had stepped out Saturday night and hung one on, if he had awakened Sunday afternoon, hot, sticky, and in a rumpled bed not his own, if a thousand kettle drums had been beating out a dirge inside his head, if he somehow knew that his stomach had been stretched from Mount Olympus to Bucyrus, Ohio, tied around a tree and twanged like a ukulele, and finally if he had opened a wary eye, that sorry blob of living jelly would have looked like the sun hanging over Appleboro one August afternoon—angrily red, full of pain and venom, and glaring with hatred at the despairing earth below.

The suffocating air that boiled beneath those spiteful rays had itself oozed up from the Gulf of Mexico to cover the prostrate eastern states, picking up stagnant fumes from the shores of the Gulf, noxious swamp gasses from Florida and Louisiana to Virginia, and industrial poisons from Delaware to Pennsylvania and New Jersey.

Life of all sorts in Appleboro, animal or vegetable, flora or fauna, was miserable. Scarcely worth the bother.

I trudged over to the air conditioner in my small apartment-cum-office over Harriet Lorimer's garage. The old machine clanked and wheezed and reluctantly put out a thin stream of cool air. This was getting to be a habit: first I stood with my back to the thing, plucking shirt and T-shirt away from my clammy frame to let the fingers of cold air grope their way through. Then I turned and gave my front the same treat. While I wiped my forehead with the back of my forearm, I looked down at myself, but nothing had changed. Even if I weighed only a handful of pounds more than I had forty years ago, still in my twenties, the pounds had shifted. I don't know, maybe they were bored with the old arrangement, but for whatever reason they had taken a hike from their youthful hangouts and huddled all around my middle. Probably interested in getting closer to the food supply.

Enough. I don't fascinate myself sufficiently to keep that up for long, so I turned my eyes to the great wide world beyond the window, and there, I am sorry to say, I saw Florene Beasley slogging down the road, holding one child by the hand and carrying another one in her arms. I squinted to look at the infant. Was that yet another one? There was a theory in Appleboro that Florene had babies twice a year so that her husband, Al, could take time off from the classes he taught at the state university at least once during the spring and fall semester. It almost seemed possible. The Beasleys hadn't been married much over seven or eight years, nobody had actually counted more than three or four kids, but when they were all assembled, shouting or crying, demanding attention, eating whatever they didn't plaster over their faces, their clothes, and each other, and when Florene appeared to grow more shapeless diurnally, it seemed as if the accumulated spawn had to total at least a dozen.

I hoped she wasn't turning in toward my door. Unfortunately, she was.

"Hi, Florene," I said. "What're you doing in this neck of the woods?" Florene and Al lived in what the real estate developers had tried to call the Apple Dell section of town, while the locals had persisted in staying with the area's God-given name of Swamp Bottom. Anyway, what with the bursting of the real estate bubble there hadn't been much building, and nobody much cared what it was called, including the banks that were stuck with the remains.

"I've come to see you," Florene said, explaining all and nothing as she shifted the latest of her gifts from heaven from one arm to the other.

"Okay, grab a seat." She squeezed herself with a couple of grunts into the visitor's chair next to the desk. I remembered her as forgettably pretty when she married Beasley not so many years ago, and thought of how little time it had taken her to fade, if adding thirty pounds could ever be called fading. Her face, once fair and delicate, was now fair and blotchy, the red patches on her cheeks uneven and making a matched set with the spots on her forehead and chin. All in all, her complexion looked more appropriate for a girl in the throes of adolescence, and her body looked as if only the straining fabric of her dress kept it from puddling down over her shoes and onto the floor.

Poor Florene. I wish I didn't think that way about her. None of it is her fault, but in my simple-minded way, I find myself vaguely annoyed each time I look at her. This makes me feel more than a little bit guilty, but of course, I end up blaming her for what is clearly my own problem. I have to keep telling myself that there's a decent human being who can be hurt, somewhere deep down inside that tub of lard. (There, I've done it again, damnit.)

I waited for her to settle down and talk, but her fingers stayed restless. Five of them clutched the baby while the others picked nervously at her thigh, scratched her ankle, rubbed her chin, and generally wandered aimlessly over the uninviting terrain.

I made an effort to be pleasant, though the normal human instinct, of which I am frankly ashamed, was to be repelled. In fact, the woman's husband, Al, was himself locally famous for his skill at being repelled by Florene. "What is it, Florene?" I finally asked. "What can I do for you?"

"I've come to see you," she repeated. "About Al."

"What about Al?"

"I want you should find him. He's dead."

"Whoa, now, dear. Is Al missing, or what? You kids have a fight? Are you sure you shouldn't talk to the police? You know I can't take over their business, so let's take it real slow. Tell me: What's happened?" I reached in the desk and found some gum drops that Harriet had failed to confiscate as part of her campaign to turn me back into the lissome youth I never was. Florene plugged her face with a few, gave one to the older child, and stopped the baby's mouth with a pacifier. All three munched quietly and stared. A trio of moo cows.

"I been to the cops. They don't want to help. So I come ta see you." She settled back, satisfied that all had been clarified.

Florene was a woman of few words, possibly because profligate distribution of a commodity she held in such short supply would have been spendthrift. But if her words were rare they were nevertheless not at all precious. To the layman's eye she was a dull normal, and this condition I found, in spite of myself, a source of irritation.

It's that Harriet Lorimer got me into this, I thought as I forced a deep breath. "You've got to tell me more than that. Now, when did Al disappear and why do you say he's dead?"

"Yesterday. He went off yesterday. And I know he's dead."

"Did you tell this to the police?"

"Yeah."

"And what did they say?"

"Oh, heck, they said one day he doesn't come home doesn't mean a thing, and they asked me if he ever went off by himself before."

"And what did you tell them when they asked that?" It was like trying to extract some sense out of an eight-year-old, never one of my strengths.

"I said lots of times he'd go away, even for three, four days."

"But this is only one day, honey. He'll be back this time too! You know that," I scolded gently, my voice a parody of sweet reason.

"No. Not this time."

"Why not?" Surreptitiously, I pushed the buzzer on my phone three times. It connected to another phone in Harriet's kitchen, and three times meant she was to call me out on a very important case. An emergency.

"'Cause we was supposed to have a party the other day and he gave me cash to take the car in and shop for things and when I got back he was gone."

"Maybe he was called away?"

"No."

"Why not?"

She looked at me as if I were an idiot; maybe she was right. "'Cause Al would never miss a party. That's how I know he's dead."

The phone rang. I sprang for it as a man on a sinking ship springs for a life preserver. "Hullo. Hugh Morrison speaking.... What!... I'll be right there." I slammed the receiver down and put on my defender of the republic face, all granite chin and grim determination. "Florene. I'm sorry but I've got to leave. An emergency. We'll talk later if you want. But you'll see. Al will be back in a couple of days, just like always. You'll see," I repeated as I got up and put a hand on her arm, prepared to drag her out of the chair if she didn't get up by herself.

"No," the woman said, but she stood. "He's not coming back. Like I keep telling you, he's dead. You deaf or something?"

TWO

I WATCHED Florene and brood ooze down the road in the heat. Then I iced some of yesterday's coffee and waited for Harriet. She'd be only half dressed over in her house, what with this damned weather, but curiosity would soon goose her out of slow motion. After a three-buzz signal she'd be in misery until she knew what it was all about.

It was all her doing, anyway. What in the name of common sense was I doing living over this woman's garage in the first place? I had retired from the state troopers, taken the engraved clock the boys had given me—as much for making room for a younger man to move up as to express their undying love for an old comrade—and gone back, moderately content, to my trailer home to pass the days eating canned chili and whittling sticks down to matchbook size without their turning into art objects. It may have been pointless, but God knows it was peaceful, even ideal for an old widower; all I had to do was open the door and let the wind blow the dirt out once a week or so. And I didn't have to talk to people I didn't want to talk to, much less take any guff from indignant citizens who think the cops are there to be blamed for every kid that smokes a joint in the abandoned outhouse behind the Methodist church.

Then Harriet Lorimer, herself a widow and a dear friend, had said, "Hugh, you've got to get back to work."

"The hell I do. Why?"

"Because a man goes to pieces if he doesn't have something to do."

"I've got plenty to do. Whittling, opening cans of chili, opening sardines, soup, tomato juice, tomato sauce, tomato ketchup, toma—"

"Don't be funny, Hugh."

"Don't be bossy, Harriet."

It was a standoff, each of us daring the other to speak. As usual, I gave way. "Seriously, I've got my pension, I don't need much. What the heck would I do, going back to work? I hate work," I think I grumbled.

"Well, I've been thinking." (That was what I was afraid of.) "I think there'd be a place in this town for a friendly, neighborly, part-time investigator. You know, somebody wants to know where his kid is getting marijuana, the jewelry store needs someone around when they get in something pricey, weekenders want someone to watch for the vandals that trash their cottages while they're down in the city, somebody's lifting the goodies from the liquor store. The police are too overloaded for all that. You know that yourself."

"Oh, Harriet, I just quit the force. Why start the same thing up again?"

"But don't you see? You can take a job or not, work three days one week, none the next. You'd do it when you felt like it. Word would get around, and people know you in Appleboro. And I'm sure a few extra dollars would come in handy. And...."

"And what?"

"You could get out of this awful trailer and move into the apartment over my garage. I'm a chubby old widow, Hugh, and I'm lonely. And so are you. I could even be your secretary when you needed one. I was pretty good at that before I got married."

"Yeah? Sit on the boss's lap, did you?"

"Of course." She sighed. "Though these days, it'd be easier all around if the boss would sit on mine."

I think I know Harriet Lorimer pretty well by now, and I figured she was fishing for a compliment. Besides, it might deflect her from this ridiculous notion that a man needs to go to work. "Now, none of that, you hear? First place, you look terrific. Second place, you hadn't changed a bit since, since—"

"Since the first time I got old, you mean?" She pointed a quizzical eye in my direction. "And don't try to change the subject."

Harriet knew me as well as I knew her.

So I went back to the subject. "I don't know, Harriet," I said. "I'm kind of tired. Don't they call it burnout? And the doctors tell me I've got the beginning of cataracts," I said, just for good measure. It was the only excuse I could drag up on short notice.

It didn't work. "Oh, pooh, everybody over sixty has the beginning of cataracts, and most of the time they don't amount to a damn. Besides that gives me an idea for a name for this new little business."

"Which is?..." I braced myself.

"The Clouded Private Eye. Pretty classy, huh?"

That did it. Within two months, I was installed in the microscopic apartment over the Lorimer garage, living room and office combination, bedroom, small kitchen, bathroom, two crotchety air conditioners, framed private-investigator license on the wall, and small sign out front with my name on it. Harriet kept the books, such as were necessary. I paid her a nominal rent plus a contribution toward the four or so times a week she put together dinner for us, and every gossip in Appleboro was in a transport of delight over what they were sure was the randiest, raunchiest pair of sinful seniors in the entire Hudson Valley. Which didn't hurt our little business in the least, seeing as how people feel sneaky about contacting private investigators and hence welcome the opportunity to look down on the hired help.

There was a knock on the door. "Come in, Harriet."

She did, and on her handsome face was a look of eager expectancy generally found in people half her age. Her blue eyes were opened wide, her lips slightly parted, and her silver hair, usually so meticulously tortured into position, was in slight disorder. "Oh, Hugh," she said, rushing to station herself in front of the air conditioner, "this weather is murder." The amenities observed, she quickly added, "What in the world did Florene Beasley want?"

I told her, leaving out the observation that she must have been watching out the window to have seen Florene, and added, "I'll hold her off a couple of days until Beasley comes back all by himself and she forgets about it." Harriet nodded her agreement. "I don't understand, though. Maybe you can tell me. How the devil did Al Beasley, professor of English and Pee Aitch Deed up to the kazoo, ever get married to this sad little girl whose cultural life must have peaked with Bugs Bunny? The poor kid's not much more than a baby machine!"

"You should know that for yourself. You've been in Appleboro almost as long as I have, and you're a cop. But since you don't know…Florene was never a beauty but she was lush and curvy, the kind that looks so awfully good for a couple of years until it melts like a butterscotch sundae in July."

"And did it ever!"

"Well, she was working the counter in the faculty cafeteria down at the college, and Al Beasley saw her, and decided to sample some of the sweets behind the steam table that weren't on the list of daily specials. It was easy, I expect."

"What a louse."

"I agree. But he overlooked several details. First, Florene's head may not have functioned very efficiently, but she was good at making babies. And second, her daddy was, and is, a security guard at the college, with old-fashioned notions and guns to back them up with. So we had an honest-to-God shotgun wedding right here in little Appleboro."

I chewed on that, and then asked, "Tell me, just out of curiosity, why did the girl's parents give her a name like that? Florene. Somewhere between too fancy and completely ridiculous."

"They didn't. Her name's Florence. That was Beasley again. Trying to gussy the girl up, I suppose, make her into something classy. But once a Florence always a Florence. You have to feel sorry for the child. Beasley can't stand her, and he's made her life miserable. Her father should've kept that shotgun home, and let the girl have her baby. There's worse things these days than being an unwed mother."

"Like being married to old Professor Beasley?"

Harriet nodded. We observed a moment of silence to consider the insanity of two people locked into a miserable marriage in order to achieve something called respectability.

"Harriet," I said, "as far as this town goes, you've got a memory bank that'd put a mainframe computer to shame. How the hell do you do it?"

"That, my friend, is a trade secret. All I'll say is that IBM and the Japanese are bidding for it."

"It's one helluva talent. Maybe you can tell me one other thing. Florene's a Kingston girl, isn't she? Family comes from up there?" Harriet nodded. "What I'd like to know is, why do Kingston girls always have such outsized butts? It's not normal."

Harriet was enough of a feminist to bristle automatically. "I really don't know, dear," she answered sweetly, "probably for the same reason old detectives always have such outsized gut-buckets. And if that's all for now, come on over for a glass of ice tea."

I thought of that coffee I had iced. Then I thought of the cookies Harriet would have with that ice tea, and the rest was easy. "Good idea. And maybe this'll all go away before the girl stops scratching her fleas long enough to think of it again." It was an ice tea kind of day anyway.

THREE

BUT IT DIDN'T ALL GO AWAY. Two days later Florene toiled into the office again, dragging the same load of juvenile impediments. "Al's not back. He's not coming, either. I told you, Al's dead." She was irritated, either with Al for being dead or with me for not believing it.

"Now, Florene, don't get upset. There's no reason to talk like that. You'll see, he'll be home soon, like always. I'm sure there's nothing to worry about."

She looked at me as if I were feebleminded. "Hell, I don't give a damn about Al. Whatever happened to him, he had it coming. But I can't get his insurance if you don't find the body, that's all. The insurance guy said something about some stupid law. I gotta wait years. Might as well be a couple of centuries. Bunch of crooks."

The girl was as persistent as the heat. I was weary, and I sounded like it. "I'll ask around, see what I can turn up. Okay?"

"Look, Mr. Morrison, don't do me any favors. You find Al, you'll get paid. But you don't find him, me and the kids, we starve to death. I already had to ask my dad for money. And those louses who came over for Al's party, they didn't even leave a dog biscuit in the place. Some of them're still around, spaced out in front of the house. Like mice. Cockroaches. Rotten example for the kids."

Her father must have said something about examples for the kids. "Yeah. I'll call the police myself, see where I can get with them. You go home and relax."

Her face told me she had her own ideas about which one of us was the dummy, but nevertheless she started to go. At the door, she turned and asked, "'Scuse me, but you got any more of those gum drops?" I gave her the rest of the bag, first palming a lemon one for myself, and scooted her out. The lemon turned out to be pineapple, which I hate, but I ate it anyway.

I lumbered over to the window for a cool-air bath, and looked out. Would the heat never end? The leaves on the trees were still green, but a black green, the color they turn when every living thing has been seared by the heat. They hung limply, anticipating the day they could surrender and drop off. Florene walked out of my sight, her head hanging. Once again I had to remind myself that that aggressive front she put up was her armor against a pretty shabby hand she had been dealt by fate, life, and the late or not late Professor Al Beasley. Maybe, I thought, I'd call one of the guys on the force, show her I was doing something, cool her off until her old man decided to sashay back in the front door.

I wouldn't charge her, because that was the unexpected way my little hobby shop (as Harriet called it) had developed. I had turned into the godfather of Appleboro. Anything go wrong? Call Hugh Morrison. Hugh would fix things, maybe even for free if your wallet was lean. And he could do things the cops couldn't, like not turning in the Laski boy when he found out the kid was selling marijuana. Instead, he'd get the name of the boy's source and turn *him* in. As for the kid, there'd be a personalized Morrison probation depending on his staying clean and getting his grades up to where they had been previously.

I didn't charge for that sort of thing, either. What the hell. In that case it worked out anyway, because the boy's father, who owned the best deli in the area, kept Harriet and me in mascarpone, buffalo mozzarella, and pickled eggplant for months. If I'd still been on the force I couldn't have ever handled it that way, but sometimes being the godfather works out for everybody.

If it seemed called for, I'd charge, but I never knew how much until I said it out loud. Harriet would sometimes scold, "You can't keep doing this for peanuts, Hugh. If you don't make 'em pay they won't respect you. You perform a necessary function in this town, getting people justice without their having to put up with the injustice of the law."

"Huh?"

"Oh, shut up. You know damn well what I mean."

I did. That is, I knew and I shut up and I obeyed.

It was lunchtime. Ambling over to the side of the driveway, I kept in the shade of the maple on Harriet's back lawn and went into her place through the mudroom. "Harriet," I called, "it's too hot to cook. Let's drive over to the diner for a salad. Ice tea. Whatever."

"I'll be right down," Harriet called down the stairs. "No dessert, though."

"Nothing?"

"Maybe a fat-free yogurt."

"Could we maybe talk about it?"

Harriet came down into the living room. "No. Well, if you do something for Florene, maybe a sherbet. I may have a martini; it'll help me nap better after lunch."

"Yeah, I'll bet. I'll call Pinky down at the station house after we eat. Find out what he makes of all this. Were there any calls while I was out yesterday afternoon?"

"A couple. I'll tell you over lunch."

"That'll kill my appetite, all right."

"All to the good. But listen, Hugh, do me a favor and don't put off that call to Pinky too long. Everybody in town pushes that poor girl away. I know she doesn't look as if she's capable of being worried, but she is. Please?"

"Sure. I never could refuse a pretty face."

"Well, thank you."

"I meant Florene."

FOUR

"HEY, SANDY," Harriet called after the retreating waiter, "bring the dressing for Mr. Morrison's salad on the side, will you, please? And let me have that martini before you bring the food."

"You got it, ma'am," the waiter sang.

I sniveled. "Three drops extra of blue-cheese dressing isn't going to put ten pounds on me."

"True, but it isn't going to take ten ounces off, either. Now, while we're waiting, I'll tell you about the calls. Two came in yesterday. I said you'd be in touch."

"Let's have it." I watched while Harriet dug into her bag and took out a pad of paper she had purloined from a hotel room in Key West years ago. The top of each page featured a drawing of a fisherman hauling in a whale-sized marlin. "Some day," I said, "they're going to get you for petty larceny."

"It's worth it. I always knew these things would come in handy sooner or later. Now, let's get to business. Harry Spellman called. He's getting a big liquor shipment in next Wednesday he wants you to check."

"Look, I've already told him that if the stock is disappearing and he's not drinking it up himself then it's one of the clerks."

"One of the clerks is his mother, Hugh."

"Okay, so if the old lady's not a crook, then it's the other clerk. What's he need me for?"

She held fire while the waiter brought over the martini; if you talked in front of anybody in Appleboro, possibly excepting the bodies on display in the Compassion Heights funeral parlor, the whole town had the story the next day. "Hugh," she finally said, "will you just look at that martini! If they served it in a thimble it'd be bigger. I keep forgetting about this place and— Oh, the hell with it." She sipped her drink and sighed.

"Anyway," she said, "back to Harry Spellman. Look, the clerk's been with him for years. She manages the place when he's away. She's got this new baby, her husband's construction business is going well, she's a solid-citizen type. She'd never be stealing. Besides, how's she going to make off with a couple of cases a week, stick 'em in her brassiere?"

"She could do worse."

"Don't be vulgar. What do you want to tell the man?"

"Harriet, if we took that job I'd end up sitting in my car in the mall all day, broiling in the sun, watching to see who goes in or out. Or else I'd be on foot, disguised as a trash can. Who needs it? Hell, Harry's only looking for professional help on the cheap. Tell him no; tell him to try an agency in Kingston and leave me out of it."

"That's what I figured you'd say. I'll get back to him and tell him probably no, but if you find you've got the time, you'll be in touch. (Harriet could never give an unconditional no to a potential client.) "You got one other call, but I'll save that for after lunch."

The salads arrived, my chef's salad ("Easy on the cheese," Harriet had instructed the waiter), and Harriet's good-health special—alfalfa sprouts, bean sprouts, and shredded carrots on lettuce with a garnish of under-cooked broccoli florets. The blue-cheese dressing was on the side, and Harriet ladled two teaspoonfuls onto my plate. "You think I could lick the spoon?" I asked, no hope in my voice.

"Maybe. If you behave."

The waiter broke in. "Another martini, ma'am?"

Harriet gave him the old fish eye. "No thanks, Sandy. I'll just take the rest of the first one, when you get a chance."

The boy grinned. "I know what you mean, ma'am, but the bartender's got his orders. If I was you, I'd do my serious drinking at Hogan's, over in Highland." He winked. "Big ones at Hogan's ma'am. Whoppers." He left.

Harriet was openmouthed. "Now, what do you make of that?"

"At last," I said. "Something about this town I know and you don't. The kid's father owns Hogan's, but doesn't want his boy working in a bar and grill. That's why he's here."

"Oh. Well, getting back to things, if you're not going to do anything about Harry Spellman you can get right to that call for Florene."

"I said I'd call Pinky. Don't you trust me?" No answer. I munched in silence on the semiarid grass for a couple of minutes. Then I asked, "Now, what else came in?"

Harriet looked at her notes and shook her head. "Oh, Hugh, if you didn't like the call from Harry, you're going to hate this. Mrs. Delavergne called."

"Oh, no."

"Oh, yes. And she refused to speak to me. Insisted you call her. Post haste, she said. Her very words: Post haste. She doesn't speak to the hired help, only to the top man. Like Queen Elizabeth doesn't get on the phone herself to tell the plumber the john is plugged."

"That woman's offensive. I'm not calling."

Harriet shrugged. "Be practical. If you don't call she'll only make a nuisance of herself, call you every hour on the half hour, write letters to the paper about irresponsible tradespersons like she did last time, and pound on your door." She sat back and mused. "You know, I think she even said 'tradespersons' in that letter."

Harriet was right. "Okay, I'll call. I'll hate myself for it but I'll call."

"And then there's one other thing. Don't forget you promised to go to Woodstock to the concert next Sunday."

"I did?"

"You know perfectly well you did. Marie-Jeanne Corrington is playing the harpsichord in a Bach concerto, and I want to hear her. You promised. Besides, it'll be good for you."

I feel about listening to Bach the way I feel about eating carrots. I like them both, really I do. But I'm pretty sure my pleasure would be greatly enhanced if people didn't keep assuring me that they'll be good for me. "Oh, well, if it'll be good for me, by all means, we'll go. Now let's get out of here before I find out about tofu and me."

I stood, grabbing the last slice of bread as I did so, and mopped up the few drops of salad dressing still on the plate. Sadly, I eyed the rest of it in the nearly full paper cup. "Listen, sweet bird, you think maybe I could ask for this stuff in a doggy bag?''

"You *can* ask," Harriet said firmly, "but you *may* not. Thomas Alva Edison once said a healthy man always gets up from the table while he still feels he's got room for a little more."

I said, "Thomas Alva Edison is dead." And he was, too.

FIVE

BACK AT THE OFFICE I went directly to the refrigerator and constructed a monster ham sandwich. As a gesture of submission to Harriet, I put it on 100 percent whole-wheat health bread, and as a gesture to myself I slathered it with whole-egg nonhealth mayonnaise. I smiled happily at the gourmet treat as I called the station house. "Hi, Pinky. Hugh Morrison here."

"Not *the* Hugh Morrison! Not the old gent who solved the mystery of the purloined Mrs. Herbert Hoover rose bush!"

"The very same. How are you?"

"Same as usual. You?"

"Likewise. Listen, pink stuff, I know that Florene the beauty queen has been down to see you, and now I got her around my neck."

"That's a lot of weight for a boy to have around his neck, son."

"You know it. Can you give me any help?"

"What can I say? Everybody's sorry for the girl, honest. I mean, we've all known her since she was a kid, before she married this guy, but he's got this habit of taking off every time he can't stand the sight of her, which is not entirely unreasonable, given the sight of her. We tried to tell her he'd be back, but that's not what she wants to hear."

"That's right. What she wants to hear is that there's a corpse somewhere she can C.O.D. to an insurance company so she can collect. Matter of fact, she's been sitting on their doorstep baying for the goodies."

"I didn't know she was that bright. Anyway, I don't know a thing that could help you find the guy or get rid of her. He'll be back. Try to calm her down."

"Fat chance," I said. "It'd be easier to find her a corpse."

"You do that. Then we can give you a hand. Okay, then, gotta go. Keep in touch, old buddy."

I put the phone down. Two groans and I picked it up again to call old lady Delavergne. If I could stop her motor from racing, and if Beasley still hadn't shown up, I'd get back to the Florene business, let the girl see me in action. It wouldn't do any good, but what the hell, maybe it'd cool her off for a while, seeing me on the trail of the missing husband. Delavergne and Beasley . . . Thank the Lord I wasn't in this for the money.

"Hello, Mrs. Delavergne? Hugh Morrison here. What can I do for you?"

Elsie Delavergne sniffed, putting all of her one hundred pounds and eighty-five years behind it, the better to pack her words in ice before hurling them over the wire. "First thing you can do is return my calls when I make them. Suppose it was a matter of life and death and I needed a policeman? What would've happened then?"

"Well, Mrs. D., then I suppose you would have called a policeman."

"Don't get fresh with me, young man. I'm still a taxpayer and I'm paying through the nose for your salary and for the other layabouts on the force, and I'm entitled to a little courtesy."

"Once again, I'm not on the force. I haven't been for years. You're not paying my salary."

There was a pause, but no Delavergne had ever surrendered, not in the French and Indian War, not during the Revolution—they were on the British side—and not during the Civil War—they were on the Union side, but only to hold the country together, not because they had any muddled-headed ideas about freeing slaves. "Well, young man, if you're not on the force, I'm sure I'm still paying for your fat and possibly not entirely reasonable pension."

I did the surrendering. "I won't argue with you," I said quickly, before she had a chance to howl 'Checkmate!' "What is it you want to talk about?"

"My Persian cat is missing. I know somebody's taken him to sell to one of those animal labs, and I want them caught and prosecuted. Prince Albert is a very valuable animal."

"Caught and prosecuted," I repeated slowly, as if I were writing down her words. "Got it. And do you want the cat back at the same time, or is that secondary?'' I tried to sound earnest, in an innocent sort of way.

"Don't be impudent. You know perfectly well what I want."

It was time to stick it to the old bat. "Okay, ma'am, you know that'll be twenty-five dollars a day."

"What!"

"Plus fifteen cents a mile for any driving around I have to do in connection with the job."

A growl, rather like a drumroll, rose from the Delavergne throat. "That," she said slowly and emphatically, "is an outrage. And you know it."

"Yes, ma'am. And it's whether I find the cat or not."

"I'll let you have half that, twelve-fifty a day, plus ten cents a mile for travel that I expect to be verified as necessary. For one week, and then we'll see."

All alone though I was, I grinned. "Okay, we'll give it a whirl. And out of consideration for your family's position in the community, I'll make it twenty a day, but no less. You going to be home for a while? I'll drive out now, if that's agreeable."

"It's hardly agreeable, Mr. Morrison, but under the circumstances I agree."

"Good." It occurred to me that Harriet might enjoy this. "My assistant will be with me, of course. Mrs. Lorimer. Harriet Lorimer."

"Hm. She's new around here, isn't she?"

"That's right. Only moved up maybe twenty-five, thirty years ago. She gets thrown in free with the twenty a day."

Mrs. D. knew when she was being had. "Well, get on over then," she snapped. Then she hung up.

SIX

ON THE DRIVE to the client's house, Harriet accessed the part of her memory bank that was devoted to the old families of Appleboro and explained the Delavergnes. "Old Huguenot family. Seventeenth century, I guess. Most of them have left the valley by now, but Elsie Delavergne and a few others have stayed around. She was a Delavergne before she was married, though her husband was only about a fifth cousin, so there's no juicy scandal there. Elsie's the family nut-burger, looks on you and me as either useless intruders or incompetent retainers. I expect I'm the former and you're the latter."

"Sounds delightful."

"Well, it won't be dull. And incidentally, her cats have been notorious for years for running away."

"Oh?"

"Yes. To Madam Elsie self-denial at the table, and probably in the bedroom as well, is one way of developing character. She just about starved her husband to death, so that if he wasn't happy when he died, at least he died happily, and she extends the same courtesy to everybody, including the family pets. In her young days, she's supposed to have had the Roosevelts, Franklin, Eleanor, and Franklin's momma Sara, over from Hyde Park and they say she counted the fruit that was left after the cheese and apples were served. The next morning she staged a recount and found she was a couple of apples short. The household, family and staff, was lined up for the third degree. The story is that her husband confessed, not because he did it, but to bring the inquisition to an end."

"She sounds like a match for Sara, from what you hear."

"Hell, Sara probably copped the apples herself. Anyway, in the course of explanations to the family cats that getting up from the table hungry builds character and is good for the digestion—just like Thomas Alva Edison—generations of the little creatures have abandoned the comforts of their fur-lined litter boxes, wrapped their belongings in a bandanna, slung on sticks over their shoulders, and left home. The whole county is crawling with the descendants of Delavergne cat escapees. You may allow for some slight exaggeration in what I've said, but in principle that's the story.''

''Sounds like fun,'' I said as we drew up in front of the lady's house, an early eighteenth-century stone-and-mortar pile that the British had failed to burn during the Revolution. Two wooden wings had been added to what was once a pioneer cottage, but the pivotal point was the old stone structure, built to withstand anything and everything until the last trump sounded. And upright in the doorway was the only bit of iron and steel in the entire compound, ramrod straight and looking capable of outlasting the stones themselves—Elsie Delavergne, née Delavergne, herself.

She stood in what was easy to recognize as the classic Delavergne pose—head to one side, chin out and tilted upward as if to avoid a noxious odor. It was something that worked on strangers and first-timers, suffusing them with guilt for having offended those aristocratic nostrils. But it didn't work for long on the locals, who thought it was funny. ''Kinda kicky,'' as one of them told me, ''like someone lopped the old broad's head off and then did a sloppy job of gluing it back on all crooked.''

''You're prompt,'' she said grudgingly. ''I'll hand you that.'' She touched her gray hair, triple-checking that nothing had dared move the least bit out of place.

I nodded my humble thanks. ''I believe you already know my assistant, Mrs. Lorimer.'' The ladies exchanged nods, Harriet's head dipping not one millimeter more than the client's, nor did her lips widen into any more of a smile. In fact, the greetings were more an exchange of tics and twitches than a mutual acknowledgment. ''We've met,'' Elsie Delavergne said with genteel disdain.

There was no invitation to enter the house until I asked for a picture of Prince Albert, and we were then ushered into a side parlor. ''I'll expect this back,'' the lady informed her new minions. ''And since your employment starts as of now, I assume your mileage charges will not include this visit.''

Harriet had had enough. "Unless, of course, our tires need realigning after bouncing up your driveway. Really, not getting a load of gravel put down every few years is a false economy, Mrs. Delavergne. Doesn't save you a cent in the long run."

Lips were pressed together like steel springs. "Is that right? My family has been managing this driveway for some hundreds of years, and as far as I know yours is the first complaint. Perhaps we buy sturdier machines. Tell me, Mrs. Lorimer, where are you from?"

Harriet hesitated, but only for a moment. "Adam's rib," she said triumphantly. "How about you?"

Her opponent had been through this before, and it was honey for the bear. Her lips relaxed into a dangerously pleasant smile. "Oh?" she said. "That's nice. But I meant before that!"

We left so quickly our departure would have registered as impolite if it hadn't actually been a rout.

On the way home, I cackled—deliberately. "You sound like a hen," Harriet said angrily.

"I'm sorry, but let's face it, the old girl's a better fencer than you are."

"You think so, do you? We'll see who has the last word. She makes me so damn mad! Thinks she's the queen of Appleboro. You know, every storekeeper in the area's scared stiff of Elsie Delavergne. She doesn't introduce herself to them, but sort of presents them to her, if you know what I mean. Shorty Olsen at the Old Mill Tavern told me once he was afraid that instead of paying she'd say he could advertise himself as restaurateur by appointment to the queen!" With no transition, she abruptly commanded, "Hugh, drive me to the vet's."

"The vet's? Doc Hingle's?"

"You heard me. Doc Hingle's. Is there any other vet?"

"Okay, but don't take it out on me." I tried to maintain a hurt silence but curiosity took precedence. "What's up?" I asked.

"I'm not sure yet." She opened her mouth to say more, but clamped it shut instead. "Just keep driving."

"If you find out, do let me know."

"Don't be angry, Hugh. I think it best you don't know. Not yet, anyway." After a minute and a half of not talking, she changed her mind, at least in part. "Listen," she said, "maybe you could come with me after all. I still want to talk to Henry Hingle in private, but you can sit in his waiting room while he and I talk. It'll only take a few minutes and then we can go on home. All right?"

What could I say?

It wasn't office hours at the vet's, so Harriet sailed in, yoo-hooing like a demented hoot owl. "Doc? Oh, Doc! It's me. Harriet Lorimer!"

A thin, gray-haired man walked in. "Hello, Harriet. Hugh. What's the excitement, girl? You wanna be wormed? It's not office hours, you know."

"You'd like that, wouldn't you, you old pervert. No, I'm going to make you even happier, I think. With a little luck that is. Let's go inside; no need to bother Hugh with this."

Doc, a gently sexist piglet, looked at me as if to share male consternation at this dotty female. "Okay, if Hugh doesn't care, who am I? . . ." He ushered her through a door to his office.

Five minutes later they were out, and Hingle's merry face had dissolved into a frown. "I don't know about that," he was saying. "Could get ourselves in trouble."

"Oh, come on. Nothing will happen, and it'll all be for a good cause."

Hingle pursed his lips and considered the situation. "It's a temptation. I'll hand you that."

"Well, come on, then. What's to lose, for heaven's sake?"

He sighed. "Only my license. Okay, I'll tell you what. I'm with you, but—"

"Good!"

"—but I reserve the right to think about it and let you know in a day or so. Gotta talk it over with Helen, and that's the best I can do."

"That's all I ask," Harriet said, and she prepared to go. "And listen," she added, "why don't you and Helen come over for dinner with Hugh and me this Saturday?"

"Love to. I'll check with her and give you a buzz," Hingle said. "And you sure you don't want to be wormed?" he called as we started out to the car. Harriet's only answer was to wave a hand over her head without looking back.

SEVEN

BACK HOME, Harriet and I went into our separate establishments, no doubt to the disappointment of the Appleboro snoop brigade. I picked up the mail, and since I still frequently pine to be whittling rather than working, I sat down to read it all, from the discount back-to-school sale to the congratulatory card informing me of the absolutely free diamond-and-sapphire pendant I had won, would I but dial the following 900 number (at a cost of $7.50 a minute).

I sneaked a look at my watch. There was still time to follow up on *l'affaire Florene,* so naturally I found myself grabbing up a lumber-store ad to devour the preseason sales on storm doors, an item for which I managed an intense, if fleeting, interest.

But duty called, and though it called until its throat was hoarse, I finally heard, damnit, and I went out again, getting into the car to head for Apple Dell and Florene. For one brief moment I considered the advantages of changing my name and moving across the river to start life anew as a gas-pump jockey. The notion was appealing, but somehow I knew that one day Harriet Lorimer would pounce and drag me back by the ear to Appleboro and duty. I started the car. Ho, for the open road and Apple Dell, a.k.a. Swamp Bottom.

There was only one road into Apple Dell, and it went through a few miles of boggy lowlands on both sides until attaining slightly higher ground where the earth was substantially dry. And there was only one house on the road, just after the turn-off from the main highway. Timmy Young lived alone there, and Timmy is worth a few words.

Maybe twenty years ago, Georgie Young, a former Appleboro boy, came back to town a widower, bringing with him a boy of fifteen. That was Timmy, and Timmy was retarded. We called it feebleminded back then, Appleboro being behind the times. But Appleboro takes care of its own. It's no saintly paradise, and it has its built-in crime just like the big city. Drunken driving, for one thing, is practically a religious observance up here, with its attendant fights, crippling accidents, and even deaths, and we've got burglaries and vandalism and both petty and grand larceny—but we still take care of our own; our neighbor's troubles are our troubles.

Anyway, Georgie bought this little cottage, free and clear, and set up a trust fund to keep Timmy going on his own, letting everybody in town know what it was for and why. Then, a few years later, Georgie died. It turned out he had known that was going to happen, which was why he had arranged for the whole of Appleboro to be Timmy's foster mommy and daddy.

Just one example of how it worked: Timmy was instructed to do his food shopping at one of the small groceries in town, not, Lord help us, at the big supermarket in the mall. Timmy would go in and take, without paying, whatever he wanted—usually canned tuna, the grocer would add whatever else he thought the boy should have, and keep a record for settling up monthly with the trustee. Sometimes Lew, the grocer, would say, "Hey, Tim boy, you don't need that stuff. Here, take these cornflakes instead. And these carrots—eat 'em raw. Prevents cholesterol buildup. And have a bag of jelly beans on the house." Timmy may not have known what cholesterol buildup was, but he had probably heard about waxy buildup from watching TV, so he was agreeable to the suggestion. Timmy was always an agreeable kid—now almost a middle-aged man—and the system had worked well for many years. Two places had him sweeping the sidewalk in front of their stores, which gave him a little occupation and a little pocket money. There was even a relief trustee waiting on the bench for if and when the original was no longer around to do trustee things like paying property taxes and keeping both Timmy and the house in good repair.

I saw him on his little porch as I made the turn off the main road, and I drew up. "Hey, Timmy, how you doin'?"

"Fine. Mr. Morrison. Just sittin' here lookin' at things, you know?"

I knew. Looking at things was a never-ending source of wonder to the boy and God knows it was as good or better than what most people did with their time. "Great! Listen, what's the name of the people in the house right next to Mr. and Mrs. Beasley up in Swamp Bottom? You know?" Timmy would never have known the area as Apple Dell, but he did know just about all the names in town and where they belonged. I think it made him feel secure to have every living being sort of nailed into place.

"Oh, sure. That's Mr. and Mrs. Parker. His name is Elroy, which I never heard of before. They're home now. Mr. Parker drove by from work a little while ago." Proudly, he consulted his watch. "Twelve minutes ago." Then his face brightened. "You could phone if you want. I got a phone now. You want to phone before you go up?"

"No thanks, Timmy. I'll just drive on up." He was deflated; I should have used his phone, but I thought of it too late. "Thanks a lot, though. I'll be seeing you. Take care!" I drove off; the side-view mirror told me Timmy was watching me go. I might have been the first person he had talked to all day, but what the hell, I think he was reasonably happy, and who wouldn't want to have a day once in a while without talking to a single living being?

Slowly, I bumped along the potholed road through the bog to Apple Dell. At the last fifty yards, the ground rose a few feet, lifting itself out of the muck to support the handful of houses that had been thrown up before the housing market had gone sour. On the road in front of the Parker place was a mailbox Pennsylvania Dutched up to the eyeballs with cutesy tulips and daisies, and past that, a flagstone path led to a modest white colonial. A healthy lawn, clearly fed and tended with love by its owners, fronted the property. The shrubbery on both sides of the entry was thoughtfully planned—low, spreading yews, a miniature rhododendron, the kind that wouldn't grow to cover the windows, and for asymmetrical contrast two upright arborvitae on one side. Even the shrewdest planning must fail to defeat the ravening deer population of Appleboro, however, and the lower branches of the arborvitae had been chewed back to the trunk, leaving the elegant trees looking as if they had been subjected to a poodle cut.

As I walked toward the front door I stopped several times, as if looking at the grounds, and turned toward the Beasley manor, hoping Florene would see me at work. Even without staring it was easy to see that the Beasleys had done nothing to enhance local real estate values. Their place needed paint, several windowpanes were out and replaced by cardboard, and the front lawn had a brazen sign mounted on a post and carelessly hammered into the ground at an angle—"KEEP OFF! EXPERIMENTAL CRABGRASS STATION!"

My knock was answered by a man whose expression clearly indicated that he had no intention of buying either aluminum siding or swimming pools, signing petitions, or ponying up for a disease he had never heard of and which might have been invented for the occasion. I introduced myself, flashed my license, and explained, "Mrs. Beasley next door thinks her husband may be missing, and she's asked me to help her look into the matter."

Elroy Parker, that was his name, relaxed. A sardonic smile crossed his face. "The only thing that'd help that poor woman is if you could arrange to keep him missing. Ordinarily I wouldn't tell things like this to anyone— Could I see your private-investigator license again?" He looked at it carefully. While he did, I studied him and saw a mildly good-looking guy of maybe thirty, six feet, 175 pounds, fair, medium-brown hair. I filed his face and form in my head, a habit you get into on the force.

"For one thing," Parker said, "he smacks her around a little too often. Yeah, I can see what you're thinking: Even once would be a little too often, but I mean once or twice a week. When he's high on something, and I doubt if it's anything as innocent as alcohol."

He warmed to the subject. "You see that house of his? Single-handedly the man has managed to bring down the neighborhood. Right now, since you say he's missing, it's quiet, but almost any day, to add to the bucolic charm of that tumbledown shack they live in, the lawn is graced with spaced-out kids. Students from the college, dropouts, hangers-on, I don't know which, but it's nonstop partying, garbage never picked up, and for a special treat the occasional rutting on the lawn!

With sound effects! We've called the police a couple of times, but after two days of peace it starts all over again. Nobody else in their right mind would move in on this road, and we're stuck." He shook his head. "No, I've got to say I'm delighted to hear he's missing. I only hope it lasts."

I cleared my throat. "Well, you see, sir, that's the trouble. Mrs. Beasley insists he's dead."

"You're kidding!" he said, adding, "Well, I wouldn't be surprised. Even if I don't want to hear about anybody dying, even that lout, I sort of half hope for her sake that he really is out of the way. She'd be better off."

"She gives me the impression that she thinks somebody killed him."

Parker considered that silently. "Come on in, won't you? Have a seat while I call my wife in on this. Honey," he called, "would you come in here a second?"

A pretty young woman came out of the kitchen. She pushed a strand of hair back in place, smiled at me, and turned to her husband. "Yes, Roy?"

After the introductions Parker said, "Just as a for instance, Cynthy, what would you say if I told you that someone had killed Squire Beasley?"

For a split second, there was silence. The young woman's eyebrows went up and her forehead wrinkled as she shot a questioning glance at her husband. He signaled a negative reply, shaking his head lightly and quickly from side to side. Her shoulders relaxed. The unspoken conversation lasted only a split second, but I tucked the scene into the back of my head for later consideration.

The woman grinned. "Heck, that's easy," she said. "I'd say, 'I'm glad the son of a bitch is dead.' But you're not telling me that, are you? That's all I ever get—promises, promises." She eliminated the smile after her husband explained the situation.

"You see what I mean?" Parker asked me. "The man's unbearable. But if he's permanently gone," (Ever notice how people avoid saying the naughty word—dead?) "for that poor woman's sake, how can we help? I can't stand the sight of her, but it's not her fault, and if there's anything we can do—" He spread his hands.

"Tell me more about these parties. You say that it's heavy with young people from the university, and I gather there's some serious druggies in attendance."

"That's right. A couple of times one or another has gotten pretty uncontrollable, and some of the others have had to sit on him—"

"—Or on her." Cynthia Parker put in.

"—Or on her. One time we found a hypodermic syringe on our lawn, though to be honest that was a couple of years ago. Maybe this year's drugs of choice, like crack, don't need needles."

"We can't let the baby go outside," Cynthia said. "We're frightened. All the shouting and screaming."

"Not to mention the sex."

As if on cue, a small child tottered in and stood close to its mother, hanging onto her skirt and looking suspiciously at me, the way kids always react to my presence. Sometimes I think that kids, all of them being natural criminals, can smell a cop, even an ex-cop, from a distance of fifty yards.

Parker walked over and picked the child up. "How's my little fella?" he asked, kissing the boy on the head. "Say hello to Mr. Morrison."

The boy turned his head away, threw his arms around daddy's neck, and prepared to cry. "Okay, kiddo," daddy crooned, "maybe next time. You go play." He put the boy down and patted his backside to start him walking out of the room. Parker looked at me and grinned proudly. I sensed a man who was happy with life, with himself, his wife, and with the child they had produced. It was refreshing.

I brought us back to Beasley's fun and games. "Don't the police do anything?"

Parker shook his head. "I don't know what goes on. I think they try. They've taken people away, once they even shoved Beasley into a police car, but nothing ever sticks. So far as we know. And there's never any evidence. I think they hide it pretty well before the party takes off."

"Or else they somehow find out the cops are on their way," Mrs. Parker added, "and get rid of it."

"Any serious fights over there?"

"It sounds like it, God knows, but we don't know what goes on inside the house," Parker said. "As I told you, the woman gets smacked around, but I don't know if you could call that a serious fight in the sense of being life threatening."

Mrs. Parker spoke up. "And the way he speaks to her! She does have some dim sense of propriety, and once in a while it surfaces. I heard her say to him one time that he needed a shave, and he spun around—they were out at their mailbox— and screamed, 'So do you, bitch!' And, oh, the noise and shouting when he starts in!"

"Sometimes I think he's going to win out," Parker said, "and we'll be the ones to leave. Come over here. Look out this window. You see that pond?" I nodded. "Look at it. He hired someone to dig it out, and then lined the bottom with truck-loads of clay. It's being filled by the spring in back of the house. The land here is just above groundwater level. When it's filled, it's going to be higher than our lawn, so all that'll stand between us and a bible-size flood is a miserable dam of earth and rocks that that idiot threw up himself! We've got a lawsuit going, but those things take years.

"Then," Parker went on, "just last week, the worst happened. He extended the dam, made it bigger, pushed it over onto our property. Our property! He's over the property line by six feet! The arrogant son of a bitch simply appropriated our land so's he can put in Lake Goddamned Ontario, and before we get him through the courts we'll be breathing underwater. Through straws, if we're lucky. And the crazy thing is, I always thought he was a nut about observing the property lines. Told me once that when I wheeled out my gas grill I went over his land, for God's sake. And never, far as I know, has he crossed over to our side even once." He snorted. "You explain."

"That's awful," I said, telling myself I'd better keep out of this one, "and I wish you luck. Well, I won't keep you folks any longer. I may ask you to let me talk to you again, though. The police think that Beasley has only taken off for a few days, and at first I agreed. But now I'm beginning to wonder. I don't know what's going to happen over there if he's off the scene for good."

"Gosh," Cynthia Parker said, "those poor kids. Is there anything we can do?"

"I don't know of anything in particular," I replied, "but I'd be willing to bet that a pot of thick soup wouldn't be out of order. And let me know if you think of something. Anything. Or if something develops I should know about." I left. After a momentary hesitation I went directly to the car instead of turning toward Florene's, the way I had intended. I don't want to get involved, I said to myself, and I think my lips were moving as I said it. And a helluva detective that makes me.

Foolishly, I glanced toward the Beasley estate and saw my client sitting in the window, looking straight at me. My conscience wrestled me to the ground. I reversed course and trudged reluctantly in her direction.

EIGHT

I'VE GOT TO ADMIT ONE THING: as I slogged through the cigarette butts, sodden papers of doubtful provenance, bits of fabric, the broken aluminum frames of two folding chairs (plus shredded webbing), and an assortment of nameless horrors, there wasn't a single sardine can in sight. Everything else, but not that. I couldn't imagine how they had overlooked the decorative potential of oily metal cans. As an ex-cop I knew that people whose lives are too disordered to clip recipes out of *Good Housekeeping* almost invariably keep going on sardines, but this area had been cleaned up. Well, practically cleaned up. (Later, when I began to feel ashamed of myself for thinking that way, I decided it was Florene, not wanting the kids to cut themselves on any sharp edges.)

The lady herself was standing in the doorway. "I thought you weren't coming over. I saw you at those Parkers." She spoke accusingly, a presumed reluctance to visit making me as derelict in my duty as if I had ducked out altogether. She shifted the baby from one arm to the other and added. "Well, come on in."

I entered. Sardine cans would have been an improvement. It wasn't so much that the place was shabby, but more that it was weighed down by a sense of defeat. Even the air was dingy, not entirely an effect of the dust, which was in ample supply. A convertible couch had been opened and its stained mattress projected far enough into the room to block the path to the kitchen. The padding in an overstuffed chair was making its escape through worn places on the arms, while the springs were burrowing out the bottom toward freedom. A parchment shade on a bridge lamp hung at an angle, as if its neck had been wrung; the several scatter rugs looked as if they had grown fur coats, dull and gray. The only sense of life was provided by a ray of sunlight glinting on a tin can that probably served as an ashtray.

Curiously, there were lace antimacassars on the backs of the couch and chairs, though it was even money that a head laid back would be permanently stuck in place. Florene saw me pondering the possibilities, and spoke. "I know what you're thinking," she said. "Those things were my grandma's, and Ma gave them to me when I got married." Her voice trembled. "I thought it would be nice with Al. We'd have a nice home and everything. Fat chance, huh?"

I felt awkward. "Now, Florene," I said, which means nothing, but is supposed to sound comforting.

She didn't hear me. "You see that lampshade there?" She pointed at the bridge lamp. "That was mine, in my room when I was a kid. It's got that picture of a little house in the country on it and when you turn on the light, the house, it stays dark, but the light shines through the windows. I used to play with it when I was little, and Ma said I should take it along for luck, maybe I'd have a house like that some day."

She took her eyes off the lamp and looked at me. "That's a big yuck, huh? The shade's busted now, and anyway the bulb's burned out and I don't wanna put a new one in. What the heck, why bother?"

"I'm sorry, Florene."

"Not your fault. Look, Mr. Morrison, I know what I look like, and everybody around here thinks 'cause I look like this I got no feelings. I don't want Al should be dead, I don't want my home to be this way, and, gee, I don't even want to be this way myself, but I am and I can't help that!" Her voice broke. "I sort of loved Al, once."

The baby looked up at mommy and joined in the tears. The two of them wailed together. And there I was, Hugh Morrison, tough cop, torn in two directions at once. To the eye, the scene was repellent—dirt, smelly baby, runny noses, shapeless flesh—but who could stand there without offering some comfort, some small comfort, to this poor soul? I stepped over and put my arms around her, letting her moisten my shoulder. "There, there," I said. "It'll all work out, you'll see. I promise you that, Florene. Now you stop crying and see to your baby, and then we'll talk. Okay?''

She nodded her agreement and tried to follow orders. But first, now that the floodgates were open, some more had to come out. ''My ma,'' she said, ''my ma, she used to say to me all the time that beauty is only skin deep and that character is more important. 'Florrie,' she'd say, 'that's what you got, character, and never you mind those girls at the school chasing after boys. Those short skirts and everything.' Well, you know what, Mr. Morrison? Maybe Ma was right, but sometimes I wish things was the other way around. You know what I mean?'' She looked at me anxiously.

I knew what she meant. Her mother may have meant well, but if Florene had ever had any doubts about her looks, old ma had resolved them, had let her daughter know for sure that she'd been badly shortchanged somewhere along the line.

I couldn't say anything; I just patted her on the shoulder. But from that moment on, Florene and I were four and a half people every time we were together. She alternated between the gross creature who would lash out at people before they had a chance to do the same to her (''I hate you first, so there!'') and a sad, defenseless young woman who couldn't understand what had happened to her.

And I was a guy who wanted to kick her behind just for being so unappetizing to look at, and another guy who felt like crying himself when he could get an occasional glimpse of a confused girl wondering why she had been dealt such a dirty hand. The half person was also me, standing on the side watching himself be tender with Florene and at the same time hoping that no one he knew, particularly the cops he used to work with, would ever see cynical I've-seen-it-all Morrison weeping away with Florene Beasley.

We talked, finally, but only in the usual circles. Florene insisted her husband was dead, and I insisted he'd probably come back soon but that nevertheless I would work hard at finding him. And this was the real start of our yo-yoing back and forth in the tangle of our four and a half personalities for many weeks, variously hot and cold on the trail of the late or not-so-late Professor Alfred Beasley.

NINE

ALL NIGHT LONG thoughts about Florene and her problem had been rolling around my fevered brain. I still clung to the notion that her gallivanting husband would come sauntering through the front door within a few days, if not to see his family at least to change his socks. But I wasn't sure.

And another problem to keep me tossing and turning was the worry that Harriet and Doc Hingle were up to some kind of nonsense that would end with old lady Delavergne thrashing me soundly with her umbrella and dragging my battered bod to the village ducking stool. For certain, Harriet was up to something and I wasn't sure I liked it. Every once in a while she fell into what I called her Cleopatra syndrome, involving some kind of kinky plot that she was sure she could bring off, and almost never did. Suddenly I had a vision of comfortably sturdy Harriet loping around the palace with an asp in her cleavage, putting the whammy on lusty Roman warriors. That got me wide-awake and grinning, and I hopped out of bed for a yawn and a scratch and the business of the day.

The air felt cooler, and a quick look at the thermometer outside the north window verified the fact. The heat had broken, and that lovely stuff from Canada had poured south to creep into all the limp corners of the valley and turn the dew into glitter dust.

The first order of business, after shaving and dressing, was to huddle over coffee and a buttered bagel, only it was a margarined bagel because Harriet would issue orders about what was good or bad for my diet and I would gripe and sulk and comply. As a matter of fact, with my peasant taste buds, I couldn't tell the oleo from butter, but the rules of the game were that I had to moan and groan about the sacrifices this domineering woman was forcing on me.

The second order of the day had to do with Harriet's secret huddle with the vet. She had issued the command that I was to go to the liquor store and pick up some wine for the dinner with Hingle and his wife. "The doc likes his hooch," she had said. "Ask Harry Spellman for something good that'll go with broiled trout."

At nine-thirty, when the stores in the mall rolled up their shutters, I was there, walking into Village Wines and Spirits. "Hi, Harry," I said, "how's it today?"

"So-so. Business is lousy." (Was there ever a small shop-keeper who said business was good? Were they afraid of offending the gods?) "And Harriet says you can't help me with this problem I got."

"Sorry, but it's not the kind of thing I can take on. Needs a staff and lots of time to keep watch on who goes in and out of your place." I had to change the subject fast. Nobody understands that a retired cop with a part-time occupation that's somewhere between a hobby and a business might not be available for every job that knocks on his front door. Like expecting a psychiatrist to put a Band-Aid on a scratch because he's nearer to your house than the druggist and might let you have the Band-Aid on the cheap. "Uh, Harriet wants me to pick up a couple of good bottles of wine for dinner tonight. She's got this broiled fish thing for company, and she's trying to wheedle something out of a guy who knows his wines. She figures she's got to soften him up with vino, melt his mind, cloud his judgment. I don't know." I waved my hand in the air in a gesture of dismissal of whatever Harriet was up to, and Harry and I went into the male-bonding mode for a couple of seconds.

"I know what you mean. Sometimes I think a wife's job is to let her old man know what his job is without letting him know what it's all about. What I'd like to know is—oh, hell, I keep forgetting you and Harriet aren't married, but it's kind of like you were, and—oh, shit, I'm getting in deeper. Sorry about that."

"Relax. It's okay. Makes me feel so young. But back to business, and what about this wine? Something classy for broiled fish."

"Sure. How about a nice chardonnay? There's some great stuff they're making right here in the Hudson Valley. We use it ourselves at home."

"Oh, I think I read about that. Didn't DeWitt Vineyards pick up a couple of medals a year or so ago?"

Spellman's shoulders went up and down. "Listen, for every time they stick a cork into a bottle of wine at a vineyard a medal drops from the sky. There's a medal for everything. Doesn't mean a damn thing. But medals aside, no dealer around here will touch DeWitt these days. They used to be the best in the valley but nobody'll carry them anymore. Last year they sent out their prize-winning stuff and it turned out to be moose piss even the local winos brought back. We lost some good customers over that swill."

"That so? Sounds like my kind of wine."

"I'm not kidding. I'll bet they're out of business in another couple of years. The hot local one now is Clarendon Chardonnay. Clarendon's what you want."

"That the place down the East Dorp road?"

"That's it. Don Tupper's place. He makes it with a little help and a lot of interference from his dad, old Clarence Tupper. Clarence, Don, Clarendon. Get it?"

"I get it. And I'll take a couple of bottles." I thought about Doc Hingle. "Better make it three."

TEN

BACK AT THE HOUSE I found Harriet resting on the patio, charging her batteries for the dinner that evening. "Hey, babe," I said, "I got your wine. Where do you want it?"

"In the kitchen, please. With an expert like Henry Hingle I wouldn't dare put it in the fridge more than an hour before dinner. I hope you told Harry Spellman we were having guests who know their stuff. The last bottle you brought home I wouldn't use for mouthwash."

"That's funny. I would, and did."

"Well never mind about that. Florene Beasley has called four times. She's upset about something. I think you'd better get right out there."

"Heck, it'll be lunch in another hour. Florene can wait till this afternoon."

Harriet shook her head in disbelief. "I never knew a copper could ever work so hard at walking away from things. Like a mountain climber who's afraid of heights. Suit yourself, but you know if you don't get to her soon she's perfectly capable of shuffling down here to corner you where you can't get away. Then let's see you disinvolve yourself, Officer."

"Lamb pie, I'm one of those sensitive cops, like the ones in the movies, only difference being that they're all thirty-two years old and more gorgeous than Rudolph Valentino." Harriet's eyes rolled up to the heavens, praying for patience. "Okay, okay, I'm off to never-never land. What time you want me for dinner tonight?"

"The Hingles will be here around seven. Suppose you come at a little after six and give me a hand."

"Will do." I made a great show of weariness as I dragged myself off to the car. To tell the truth, I wasn't all that reluctant to visit Florene, especially after that little show-and-tell session we had had the day before. I had permanently gone a little soft on the girl, but I was too embarrassed to let it show in front of Harriet.

It was a pleasant drive on this bright and shiny day. The sun was glinting on the Shawangunk cliffs, making them look as white as if they had been scrubbed with a widely advertised and expensive detergent. A fresh breeze was tickling the aspen leaves into their quivering act, and the utility poles and wires were hosting excitable conventions of redwing blackbirds.

I made my turn onto the Apple Dell road and waved cheerily to Timmy, who was seated on his porch, and continued on to bump my way along the potholes to the Beasley manor. Once again I figured it for a blue ribbon in the county fair for rural housing, slum division.

Florene must have been watching for me, because she was out the front door by the time I had the ignition turned off. "Gee," she said, "thanks for coming, Mr. Morrison. And I know you told that Mrs. Parker to bring over some soup. You shouldn'ta, but I'm kinda glad you did. It was good." Gratitude came hard; she looked uncomfortable.

Me too; I looked uncomfortable. Closeness didn't become either of us. "Oh, heck, it's nothing. And really, people like you, Florene. Mrs. Parker wanted to help, that's all. But tell me what you wanted to see me about."

"Oh, boy," she said. "You're not gonna like this one little bit. Come on and see what I found. I told you so. You didn't believe me, but you wait and see. None of you ever believes me." Resentment flooded her face, and the red blotches got blotchier. The sulky Florene had surfaced.

"Hey, calm down. Just show me, and then we'll see."

A wicked grin displaced her resentment. "Oh, we'll see, all right. Come on." She waved me along and the two of us walked single file, like a couple of low-slung ducks, to the back of the house. A few times she looked back as if she expected me to bolt for the car and zoom out of her life.

We drew up at the earthen dam around the partially filled pond. Like everything else about the Beasley manor, the pond was a dispiriting sight, a combination of muddy puddles and watery mud. Unless the spring that was supposed to be feeding it was planning a surprise, it looked as if it would be many a moon before there'd be lebensraum for more than a couple of minnows. It went well with the house, though; they belonged together in a brotherhood of despair.

"Looka there," Florene commanded, pointing at a spot across the pond site where the dam had been disturbed and now looked as if it might be considering a total collapse.

I looked, and I looked again. My stomach flipped, no mean accomplishment in my case. There are some things even a city cop doesn't see too often, and that goes in spades for a country cop. I couldn't believe it, and the bright and shiny day I had been revelling in felt, for one awful moment, cold and harsh. "Is that—? Florene, is that—?"

"Uh huh," she told me, cool as frozen yogurt now that somebody finally had to believe her, "it sure is. It's him. That's his ring on the finger." She jutted a gaggle of chins toward the hand that was dangling out of the embankment perhaps a foot down from the top. "And that shoe," she explained like a museum guide, pointing at a wing-tip leather oxford gracing a foot sticking out of the earth three feet from the hand, "that's the special kind he orders from some place in London. You don't see so many of those around here, I can tell you." Her voice was flat, without emotion, until with a shade less cool she added, "I could feed my kids for a month on what those shoes cost." Her words were bitter and resentful, yet strangely free of either sorrow of panic.

For a moment I couldn't move. I don't know which was worse, the discolored, shredded flesh in front of me, or Florene's matter-of-fact droning like a tour guide pointing out the same dreary site for the thousandth time. It was clear that the newer section of the dam that the Parkers said had been thrown up on their property hadn't had time to settle down before someone had found it a simple task to deposit the late Professor Beasley beneath its surface. And it was equally clear that some animal—or animals—had found it just as simple to scratch away at the dirt on the trail of unaccustomed delicacies, possibly even enjoying a bit of exercise before getting down to dinner.

The Parkers never would have seen it because the body parts were on display on the inside of the dam, facing away from their house. Only Florene had a ringside seat. Maybe I should call it a graveside seat.

A raccoon, normally in its lair during daylight hours, had been brought out by the scent of an interesting treat. It moved cautiously along the top of the dam to examine the merchandise, turning its sharp and foxlike face occasionally toward Florene and me to keep a watchful eye on the intruders. An obscenely dainty paw reached out to bat its quarry gently, and the dangling hand responded by swinging back and forth as if to beat time to some silent dirge.

The bile rose in my throat. I hurled a stone at the creature and spun around toward my guide. "Florene, for God's sake, have you called the police?" I was afraid I already knew the answer.

She didn't say. Instead, she complained, "I told you so, din't I? And din't I tell the police he was dead? Nobody believes me, not ever."

"Listen to me, forget about that. You've got to call the police, and now. Want me to do it for you? Remember, I'm on your side."

Florene was supremely disinterested. "Do whatever you want. I can't think no more. And I've got to feed the kids; it's past their lunchtime." She blew out a breath. "At least now I can afford it, once I get the insurance money." Something between a laugh and a cry came out of her throat, but then her mouth twisted bitterly as she said, "You wanna buy a pair of good English shoes? I could let you have some real cheap. Hardly used at all. Only came last week." Emotionally drained, she turned to go back to the house, dragging along as if she were a prisoner encumbered by heavy chains.

"Hey, hold up! When did you find this—him?"

"What's the difference? I dunno. Like maybe the day before I came to see you for the first time." When she saw the disbelief on my face she turned defensive, for the first time realizing that someone might possibly think she had done something a little bit wrong. "Heck, who was going to believe dumb

Florene if I said I found him and I didn't do it? I wanted the cops to find him, and then I wanted you to find him, but you're all so damn smart you wouldn't listen to a dummy like me. Well, you're the dummies, yes, you are!'' she shouted.

"Hey, wait a minute!" I shouted back. "We're supposed to be friends, remember?"

She blinked. "Oh, yeah. I forgot. I'm sorry. Anyways, it's done, and I'll get that insurance money that Mr. Smart Professor thought he was going to collect on me. But I guess I shouldn'ta yelled at you, Mr. Morrison. I'm glad you're helping me. Honest, I am."

What could I say? "Forget it. Let's get back to the house and make that call."

"Sure, if the phone company hasn't cut us off yet. They said they would, Al's so late in paying." She giggled. "Now he'll be even later, hey?" She was spinning so giddily from sad to bitter to giggly that I was getting as dizzy as she was.

The phone was working, and I called the station. Fifteen minutes later the phone rang. I picked it up but whoever was on the other end hung up as soon as they heard my voice. Maybe six or seven minutes after that the cop cars drew up.

Florene was strangely pleased at what she was able to show them, acting something like a fine English lady taking the garden club on a visit through her botanical triumph, pointing out the cunning and creative surprises waiting around each turn, basking in their admiration and jealousy. I realized that at some level the girl felt relief; she was handing her problem over to someone else. Let the other guy carry the heavy load. Little did she know.

The cops stood around flapping their arms helplessly, not knowing what to do anymore than I had. Then one of them thought of calling more cops. At this point, I gave them my deposition, and since more or less all of them knew me as a former member of the club, they raised no objection to my staggering off. I told them all I knew, and that was precious little more than what they themselves knew and had known since Florene first entered the station house a week or more ago.

On the way home I waved to Timmy again. After making my turn onto the main road I resolved not to spoil Harriet's dinner party by saying anything about the novel approach to landscaping at the Beasleys until the Hingles had left at the end of the evening.

ELEVEN

DINNER THAT NIGHT was a merry affair, as it always was when the Hingles were on the scene. Henry Hingle was approximately fifty-five years' worth of fun and frolic, and he looked like the drawing of a leprechaun in a kid's book of Irish folk tales. He was fairly short, about five foot seven, I'd guess, weighed nearly as much as two-dozen gnats and at that, most of the weight seemed to be in his large, pointy ears. While I'd never been one to believe that eyes could actually twinkle, Henry's light-blue ones gave the lie to my lack of faith.

I'd suggested one time that an ancestress of his in County Clare must have wandered into the woods with one of the little folk a couple of hundred years ago and come back not particularly sadder but nevertheless a good bit wiser. At the time he seemed pleased by the idea.

"Yes sir," he was saying at the dinner table, "smartest damn thing I ever did was to go in with the old vet here in town and take over after he retired."

"Well, it wasn't as simple as all that," Helen Hingle protested. She was as bantam sized as Henry and of an equally smiling disposition, so that the two of them looked more like brother and sister than husband and wife. "Fifteen, twenty years ago, his patients ran to cows and sheep and pigs in labor. You weren't all that fond of being hauled out of bed in mid-January to take charge of a difficult lying-in at the dairy farm, and you know it."

"True, love, true. But the town has changed, just the way we knew it would. It's dogs and pussycats now, and I don't make house calls. The occasional horse, but I get along with horses, so that's just fine."

"You get along with all of them," Harriet said. "Sometimes I think you speak the language."

"Oh, I do," Hingle replied, "and they appreciate it. I'm fluent in seventeen dog and cat tongues, including Norwegian elkhound, if you want the truth."

"Uh huh," Helen said. "Fourteen, if you want the truth, and two of them pretty badly."

"Would you believe sixteen?" Hingle asked.

"If I'd believe that I'd believe anything," Helen said.

"Hold it," Harriet said. "Time out for more wine, anybody?" She was really laying on her class act, urging more wine on the guests, which she had never done for me, and I wondered once again what she was up to. The table had been loaded with the loot that her generation had been able to haul back from Europe when the dollar was the only currency worth mentioning, and we were eating off English china, Irish linen, and French crystal. The silverware was Danish, real sterling, as I had personal reason to regret, since the woman had me polishing the stuff before each of her major blowouts. Once I had accused her of moving me in over her garage in order to keep the slave labor conveniently at hand; she had only smiled and let the accusation stand.

At any rate, the Hingles weren't shy. They both shoved their glasses forward. (So did I, though I couldn't see what was so special. But then I'm a beer-and-pretzel type—domestic beer, and plenty of bad-for-you salt on the pretzels.) "You bet," Henry said. "This is damn good stuff Don Tupper puts out." He took the bottle and inspected the label.

"It sure is," I said, not adding that at those prices it ought to be damn good stuff. "Funny thing, though," I added, oozing expertise, thanks to Harry Spellman, "up to the last year or so the DeWitt Vineyard people had the best chardonnay in the state, and all of a sudden it went bad for them. That's when Clarendon moved up."

Harriet cocked a cynically lifted eyebrow in my direction. "Hugh, I never knew you cared. Such sudden depths!"

"He's right, though," Henry said. "And it was strange. Even stranger was watching a fourteen-carat phoney like Herr Professor Beasley switching wine barrels in midstream."

"What do you mean?" Harriet asked.

Helen Hingle broke in. "Oh, it was a riot, my dear. Beasley bills himself as a wine maven and somehow he gets away with it. He used to be in the DeWitt Vineyard ads as the former director of the local chapter of *Les Copains du Raisin—*"

I broke in to explain to a puzzled Harriet, using the remnants of my high school French. "That means the buddies of the grape, sweetheart." That, I figured, would pay her back for that crack about my sudden depths.

"That's right," Helen agreed, "only there's no such outfit. It only sounds like the real one, which is *Les Amis du Vin.*"

"That means—" I started to say.

"Thanks," Harriet said sharply, "but I know what it means. I took Norwegian elkhound one-oh-one in school and that was part of the first lesson."

Henry was used to intervening in cat fights, so he hopped in to divert the participants. "Anyway, what Helen's getting at is that Beasley did a quick change and came out as Clarendon's local spokesman without even blinking!"

"That was after DeWitt went downhill." Helen explained, "and after that—"

"Downhill!" Henry nearly shouted. "Hell, they hit the ground so fast they dug themselves a six-foot grave before they stopped."

Helen put a hand on his arm. "I'm talking, Henry. After they went downhill, it took only until the very next edition of the weekly paper that Beasley was in the Clarendon ads saying that *Les Copains du Raisin* was of the opinion that Clarendon Chardonnay was the only respectable local wine for the cultivated enthusiast. I think if the paper had been in color his face would have been red. A complete switch."

"A real phoney," Henry said.

I felt awkward, knowing what nobody else at table knew about the late and apparently little lamented Alfred Beasley. So I turned the topic slightly to one side. "Tell me, Hank," I said, "what does the dog in the street vote for, drinkwise?"

"Well," he answered, "that's a very good question. I can't answer drinkwise, but smellwise they prefer dog piss three to one. Except for the Norwegian elkhounds; I've tried to ask them, but I can't make out what the hell they're saying."

Helen looked annoyed. "Henry, you may talk that way around your patients, but not at table, you understand?"

"Yes, Helen. I keep forgetting that other people aren't as broadminded as my clientele. Sorry, Harriet. And incidentally, before I forget, I've decided to go along with you on that deal we were discussing. In fact, you might even say the deal has already been consummated." He looked terribly pleased with himself.

"What deal?" Helen and I asked together.

"We've solved a difficult problem. We can't talk about it yet," Harriet said, "but you'll both know in time."

"What's the matter, cat got your tongue?" I asked.

For some reason this sent Harriet and Henry into gales of hoots and giggles and foot stomping, plus an exchange of knowledgeable glances. Whatever was going on between those two was somehow connected to the unwritten agenda of the dinner party, and once they had reached an understanding, it was as if a spring had been released. The laughter subsided, and the party was over, coasting gently to its conclusion.

The Hingles soon took their leave. As they stood at the open front door Helen turned to me. "Don't worry, Hugh, I'll find out what it's all about. I'll listen in when he's seeing a patient. He tells them everything."

"It's true," Hingle agreed. "A dog may not keep his mouth shut, but the only thing that comes out of it is his tongue. Dogs are very discreet people, much more than certain wives I could name."

As the couple walked toward their car, Harriet, who was watching from the steps, saw Helen Hingle turn toward her husband and let her tongue loll out. She panted, and the two of them laughed, walking closely side by side with evident affection.

"What a lovely couple they are," Harriet observed as she and I were clearing the dishes. "And they're not very impressed with our Professor Beasley, are they!"

"No one we know is."

"And speaking of that, did you talk to Florene? How is the girl, and what's the latest out there?"

I finally opened up and told her. "And it looks bad, awfully bad. The damn fool woman sat there in her house for days with her husband nine-tenths buried in mud, asking me and the police to find him. I tell you, she's nuts."

"Oh, Hugh, that's dreadful! What's going to happen now?"

"What's going to happen now? Hell, I don't know." I picked up a wine glass and wagged it at Harriet like a school teacher. "But I'll tell you one thing: If I were still on the force, there'd be a wee bit of suspicion that we ought to think about popping Madam Beasley in the pokey for knocking off her old man."

"Oh, no!"

"Oh, yes. Knocking off, killing, offing, however you want to slice it. My God, she was practically on her knees begging someone to find him because he was dead. And then adding that she didn't want him back, but only, if you don't mind, please pass the insurance money."

"Do the police know that?"

"They know. I'm afraid they heard it from me when I called Pinky to find out what was up. Damn!"

"Oh, Hugh."

"Oh, Harriet," I echoed glumly.

TWELVE

THAT NIGHT I was knocked out of a sound sleep by the telephone, and with a mouth full of cotton wool I managed to grunt something in Zombie.

"It's me, Harriet. Got a minute?"

I cleared my throat. "Do you know what time it is? No, I don't got a minute, not at this hour."

"I'm sorry, but the birds have started in and there's some light in the sky and I thought ... Hugh, we've got to do something about Florene."

I mulled that one over for at least three seconds and then said, "I am doing something. I'm going back to sleep."

"I'm serious about this."

"So'm I." With all the chatter the last possibility of continuing to talk without waking up was finally stolen from me. I cleared my throat. "For Pete's sake, what can we do at four in the morning? You say 'do something.' How about going back to sleep?"

"I'm sorry, but you know the police are going to say that that poor child murdered her husband. Don't you just know it? Do you really think that confused lump of a girl is capable of anything like that?"

"Um, yes. Maybe only thirty percent yes, but still yes. She's stupid enough, God knows, even if she's also probably too inept to bring it off. Now listen," I interrupted as Harriet started to object, "no more. Nothing's happened yet and nothing I can do now is going to change what's going to happen next, if anything. I promise you I intended to look out for the girl, but for now, let me get back to sleep—if I can. Cool it for a couple of hours. Then we'll see."

"But—"

"Go to sleep. Look, I'll check with Pinky tomorrow and let you know. G'night."

At nine-thirty I was rapping on Harriet's screen door, still in a foul mood, and when she came to let me in I started scolding. "I've told you a dozen times, Harriet, you can't go to bed with just the screen door shut. You've got to shut both doors. Anybody could stick a hand through this damn screen, open up and walk right in, the way you leave things at night."

"Oh, I always forget. Besides, who would come in, for heaven's sake?"

"Who wouldn't come in? Appleboro isn't the Emerald City of Oz anymore, if it ever was, and you better believe it. So you keep your doors locked at night. *Capeesh?*"

She sighed. "You're right. I'm sorry. But tell me, did you speak to Pinky?" She looked at me anxiously, and I could see that she hadn't had much sleep, worrying the way she was over Florene. Harriet looked tired and old. Her eyes were bloodshot and the hollow in her throat was somehow deeper and more wrinkled.

How could I stay angry? I put a hand on her shoulder. "You're a nice person, Miz Lorimer. Maybe a nut-case, but a nice nut-case. But you've got to simmer down. Pinky said nothing's happened or even going to happen yet. The cops need more than an insurance policy before they put the cuffs on Florene. And they'll go slow. They all know her, they know she's got seventeen kids, and they'll be very careful about anything they do."

I wondered briefly if I ought to admit to the change of heart I had found myself developing for my client. I opted for honesty: "To tell the truth, Harriet, after my talk with Florene the other day I've grown a little bit fond of her. Frankly, I'm not sure whether it's my head or my heart that's gone soft, but that's the way things stand. I'll do whatever I can for her, and you can count on it. Okay?"

I could feel her relax under my hand. "Okay, Hugh. And thanks."

"Sure thing. Now, what've we got cooking for today. Please God, no more problems."

"I think you'll be surprised. Let's go into the television room. There's something there I want you to see." She led the way into a basement room that held two well-used armchairs, a comfortably shabby couch, a table-tennis table left over from more active years, a small but ominously snarling refrigerator with the enamel worn off the corners to expose the black metal underneath, a bridge table (with folding chairs stacked against the wall), a twenty-one-inch television set—and a cat purring nearly as vociferously as the refrigerator as it lay with arrogant indolence on the larger and more comfortable of the easy chairs.

I had never seen an animal with a more communicative expression on its face. It looked at me with disdain, as if to let me know I badly needed a bath plus an extra-strong man's deodorant, like they say on TV. "Supercat," I observed. "Where did this come from, and why?"

"Ultimately from Elsie Delavergne, since you ask," Harriet explained, "and because it was hungry and was looking for a decent meal."

"You're kidding! This is Prince Albert?" I looked at Harriet, fearing the worst. "Come on, I want to know what's going on."

"Well, it's only that I figured since you introduced me to the old bat as your assistant I might as well work on the case while you were busy with other things. At least you were supposed to be busy helping poor Florene."

I knew that trick; Harriet had done something she shouldn't have, and she was larding me with a little guilt to keep me off balance before she confessed. "Go on. Just how did you work on the case? Do tell."

Prince Albert yawned, bored in advance by Harriet's story.

"It wasn't all that much work. I told you the Delavergne cats have been fed worse than Oliver Twist for generations, and it's been no different with the Prince here. He's run off before, and he knows the cuisine at Doc Hingle's is tasty." She shrugged. "That's all there is to it."

"Uh huh. How's he know about the chow at Hingle's, from one of the other cats about town?"

"No need for sarcasm. He knows because whenever madam goes on a trip she boards the poor thing with Henry. And cats may be stupid, but when it comes to getting enough to eat, they can figure things out."

"All right. For the moment I'll buy that story, so let's cut the cackle and tell me what you've been up to."

"You're a real spoilsport, you know that? Look. Twice before Al—I call him Al—"

"'Zat so? You two related? I should have known."

She ignored that. "The first time he padded over to Doc's, Doc brought him back home, but the Delavergne practically accused him of trying to steal a valuable animal and then getting cold feet. What he told me was that he could've stuck the woman's gratitude in his eye and never even felt it. Henry was furious, so the second time Al came around begging for a few crumbs he kept the poor thing until it got dark and then dumped him over the hedge back to his loving mommy." Harriet smiled. "Right into the flower bed, it turned out, which Al tore up in a rage as a sort of editorial comment on how he felt about being back in the slammer. I had a hunch that the same thing had happened again, and I was right. That's all there is to it, Hugh, honest. I knew he'd be hanging around at Henry's." She opened her eyes round and wide and failed miserably at looking innocent.

"And?"

"And what?"

"And why is the dear Prince here, lording it up on your easy chair? Throne being renovated?"

"Oh, *that!* I thought you'd understand. I've kidnapped him. Catnapped? No, that doesn't sound right. Kidnapped. I wanted Doc to keep him, but he couldn't afford to, in case the caper went sour. Not in his position. On third thought, maybe catnapped is better."

A veil was lifted; sometimes, when Harriet does something she knows is wrong, she gets silly about it, and catnapped-kidnapped was the clue. I think it goes back to her childhood, well before the age of feminism, when she probably saw her mother and her aunts and maybe her old granny able to rule the roost only by pretending, without even realizing it, to be foolish, helpless females, naturally dependent on the intellectually superior male. Harriet, tough as Arnold Schwarzenegger and twice as bright, isn't like that at all, but once in a very great while when there's no other way out, she reverts. And, boy, she knew she was out of line on this one, snitching fancy pussy-cats.

I have to say that these moments only make me even fonder of her than ever. I can't say they make me love her more, because years of being alone in that trailer after my wife died, living on canned chili, left me too numb for all that. Or could it be, I don't know, that there's something in canned chili that drains the love factor out of a body. Garlic, maybe? But I had to be stern. "Are you out of your mind?" I asked. "What next, ransom notes?"

Giddiness having failed, Harriet switched to indignation, which was more like the woman I love, if you'll pardon the expression. "Are you being deliberately dense?" she demanded. "What's the matter with you! We're going to hang onto the beast for a few days and wring as much money out of that woman as we possibly can. What're you charging her? Twenty a day?"

"Plus expenses," I added, "you crook. What the devil has got into you, acting this way? You can't do this, Harriet." I flopped down hard in the chair that Prince Albert had opted against staking a claim to and slapped the arms. Dust rose up, and the animal turned to look at me, blinking with contempt at my elderly antics.

"Yes, you are dense," Harriet said, answering her own question. "Of course we won't keep the money. Don't you see? We'll give it to the animal-rescue league or the SPCA. But we'll let it sink in on Elsie Delavergne that we know why puss takes off from home and that we'll let the whole world in on her dirty little secret unless she shapes up. Doc will arrange that; we've got it all worked out."

"Do you, now?"

"Naturally. First, you and I 'find' Prince Albert. (She made quotation marks in the air with her fingers.) That's what we were hired to do. Then we rush the poor thing over to the SPCA in Kingston because he seems so feeble and Doc's not available in Appleboro. They certify that he's suffering from long-term malnutrition, and they threaten to remove him from his owner unless the old girl reforms. Doc has already spoken to his buddies there, and they'll cooperate. And of course all of Appleboro, which is Elsie's whole world, would know her shame. See?''

"I can't believe this."

"Try." Harriet sat on the couch and crossed her legs, trying to look debonair and long legged like a Hollywood bad girl. (She failed.) "And by the way, I've taken an ad in the weekly asking for any information, no questions asked, that may lead to Al's safe return, and I gave your telephone number. Now don't you forget to include the ad as a job-related expense, dear.''

"How could I forget? You're crazy, you know that?"

"I'm crazy? Unh unh. I'm creative, that's all."

"Harriet, I'm getting out of here before the Prince banishes me. I think I'll hop back into bed and have a nightmare. It'll be more restful."

"Oh, go ahead and sulk, if that's what you want, but remember you've still got Florene Beasley to worry about, so don't sleep too long.''

"I stand corrected. I may have two nightmares. And never get up, damnit.''

I left. I did not, however, go to bed. I had two fried eggs, bacon, and buttered toast. Then I waited around until the matinee at the movies in Newburgh, and I hid there for half the afternoon. It only costs a buck for seniors in the afternoon, which helped me conquer the guilt my mother had instilled in me for going to the movies in the afternoon instead of playing outside in the fresh air.

THIRTEEN

I GOT OUT OF THE MOVIES a little after four. It slowly seeped into my addled brain that I had only the vaguest idea of what I had seen. People had been shot and stabbed and I think someone had been decapitated with a nail file, but I hadn't been able to follow the action the way I did years ago. You'd think that murder followed by a manhunt and then by the triumph of justice ought to be easy to keep track of, but they complicate things these days. Why, when I was a kid and went to the movies. . . .

Hey, wait a second. There I was, babbling happily about how much better the world used to be, instead of trying to find out what was bugging me so badly. Part of it was Harriet's acting like a nut burger over this miserable cat, all on account of Queen Elsie D having got the better of her in a battle of the forked tongues. It showed a vulnerable spot in her that I didn't like one little bit; I needed the woman to be reasonably invulnerable so that I could be the nut. No fair.

And then there was *l'affaire Florene.* I was all wound up and ready to spring to the rescue, but it wasn't at all clear that rescue would be called for. Getting emotionally involved with a client's problems isn't the smartest thing that can happen to a gumshoe, especially to one like me who hates going to work. The fact is, I truly and sincerely hate work. Honest. I hate work. There, I've said it.

Under such circumstances, the only sane course of action is inaction. Fill up the time and maybe everything will go away. So I drove to the shopping mall to look for a sport shirt, which I needed in case I happened to grow an extra torso and didn't have a thing to wear. I should have known better. There's nothing like a shopping mall to make a fellow feel like a non-person, especially if he's leaning in that direction to begin with. Every mall is a plastic clone of every other mall in the whole wide world and if you're not careful you might start wondering whether you were in New York or Ruanda. You might even forget your name, if you happened to have one that day. A mall is a mall is a mall.

I started looking at shirts. I've learned to read the laundry instructions ever since I was awarded the use of Harriet's washing machine, because I'd been horribly trapped by mistakes in the past. Some shirts want a hot-water wash. Others demand warm; some say cold. Add to that regular cycle versus gentle versus permanent press. "Wash with like colors." Press with warm iron or drip-dry or tumble dry regular or tumble dry low. What the hell, one fine day you're going to need fourteen washes to do seven pairs of socks, or else suffer the wrath of an outraged Hong Kong tong in control of the men's socks monopoly.

I yanked out maybe eight shirts and tossed them all back. A clerk came over. "Can I help you, sir?"

"Yeah. I'm looking for a sport shirt, something without laundry problems. Maybe you've got something that says 'wash in warm Perrier, no ice'?" Why'd I have to take my troubles out on this nice kid? I smiled feebly to take the nastiness out and said, "Sorry. I can't make up my mind. I'll have to let my wife come back and do it for me."

I slunk out and drove home. On the way I stopped in Spellman's liquor dispensary. "Harry, let me have the best champagne you've got for a special present." I don't know why, but I felt I needed something nice for Harriet and me to cool down with.

Spellman grinned and went into the back. "Here it is, bo." He held up a bottle that looked as if it belonged in an art-nouveau museum. "After you drink it, you can stick flowers in the bottle. It'll only run you a hundred and twenty bucks. It's an economy in the long run."

"Tax extra?" I asked. "And you can do the sticking, friend. This is for a present, not a seduction."

"Cheap, cheap," he said sadly, like a canary in mourning. "So try this one here for twenty-five bucks." Harry was no fool; if he had started with the second bottle I would have segued down to the fifteen-dollar level. But this way he got twenty-five out of me, the sly dog.

I drove home with the precious cargo and shoved it into the refrigerator, settled down with a beer, and turned on the answering machine. Pinky's voice poured out. "This is me, buddy," it said. "I got some news about your client, and never mind which client because I'm not about to put this on tape on account of Richard Nixon, God forbid, maybe should be listening. And if you get this message late, don't call me at home. It'll hold till tomorrow and Natalie doesn't like me getting cop calls at home so's the spaghetti gets cooked to where you could mash it. Ever try mashed spaghetti with tomato sauce? Looks like cow plop. It tastes—don't ask."

Fortunately, Pinky's time on the machine ran out. He was enjoying himself too much, knowing I'd be hopping up and down with impatience for his news. But what are friends for, I suppose, if you can't drive them off their rockers, just like Harriet and me.

There was a second message on the machine, from Harriet. "If your teeth aren't set on plunging into a can of tuna for dinner give me a buzz. Benjie Zimmerhaus gave me a couple of trout right out of his pond, and you can do them on the grill." I had to smile. Harriet subscribed to the reverse-discrimination notion that if it was cooked on the grill, boys did it better than girls even if they wore funny hats while they were at it. And her call meant that she was planning a sideways apology as much as I was, which made me feel great.

I pushed the little buzzer button and when she answered I said, "Give me fifteen minutes and I'll be over after I grab a quick shower. With some rosemary from that pot on the windowsill and a bottle of fizz."

Dinner was eminently satisfactory even more for what those dreary psychologists who give lectures to police departments call interpersonal relationships than for the eats. We made up without having to talk about it, and Harriet condescended to serve me a dessert loaded with whipped cream, customarily a forbidden delight. For my part there was the half of that bottle of champagne I poured into her glass. Well, maybe slightly under half in her glass.

After dinner we settled back and talked. She was so nice about not nagging me to fly to fair Florene's rescue like a superannuated knight of the round table that to my own amazement I brought it up myself. "When I got back home this afternoon, there was a message from Pinky on the machine," I said.

Harriet lifted her eyebrows, saying nothing but waiting for me to go on.

"He said there was news about Florene. Something's developed in the case, but he doesn't want me to call him at home. Natalie gets into a snit if he doesn't quit working when he quits work. I can catch him at the station first thing tomorrow."

That was too much for her. "Oh, why don't you call him tonight, anyway? Maybe it'll be good news and we can forget about the whole thing."

"And ruin one of my sources? We need Pinky there on the force, you and I. No point in getting him mad."

"Listen, sugar, I'll handle Natalie. Let me call. Okay? Hugh, I asked you if it was okay."

"Go ahead, but make sure she understands it's your idea, not mine. If it works, fine; if it doesn't, not fine."

She jumped for the phone. "It's a deal."

For ten minutes there was nothing but the sound of the two women restocking their internal computer banks with the freshest and finest Appleboro dirt. I didn't hear anything for the first five minutes except Harriet clucking "Oh, my!...You don't say...Isn't that just like the man?...I knew that would happen sooner or later...I'm glad I'm not in her shoes...I wish I'd been there...Don't worry, my lips are sealed."

For the next five minutes again I didn't hear anything specific, because it was Harriet's turn to enter data into Natalie's computer, and she turned her back to me, hunched over the phone, practically swallowed the mouthpiece, and whispered. In fact, the only thing I caught was Natalie's voice shrieking, "Why, that's a hoot! I love it!"

Then my Machiavellian friend, having softened up the opposition, said, "You know, Nat, poor Florene Beasley's in such trouble over that rotter's death, and Hugh and I are trying to help however we can. Anyway, Hugh tells me that Pinky has some new information on the case, but Hugh doesn't want to bother him at home. Men can be so damn stuffy sometimes. I'm sitting here wondering if maybe you've finished your dinner, we could put the two boys on the phone and see if there's any good news for the girl... You're a dear. I agree, they're good at making all sorts of excuses for not getting off their butts after they leave work... You're right, that's why we have to take over once in a while to get things done. Talk to you soon. And thanks.''

She turned around and with a superior smile handed me the phone. "Here," she said. "Pinky's dying to talk to you. That's how these things work, sonny.''

"Yeah, if you want to compromise your integrity. All right, let me have it." I listened to Pinky, asked a couple of questions, and ended by saying, "It's lousy news, all right, but at least it gives me something to go on. Thanks, bud... No, you cannot have my color photograph of J. Edgar Hoover, but I might consider slipping you Nelson Eddy as a Royal Mountie... You, too, and without vaseline. 'Bye now.''

I turned to Harriet. "It's hit the fan. I'm sorry, but they've booked Florene.''

"Booked her? For...."

I nodded. "That's right. For murder.''

"But how, what happened?''

Pinky says they found a pickax. On the side of the pick there's Beasley's hair and the right blood type. And on the handle there's one clear set of prints—Florene's, all by themselves. Period. Some minor smudges that don't mean anything, except a couple are small enough to belong to one of the kids, and one that just might be Beasley's.''

Harriet waited. I said nothing more so she added, "That's it? That's all?''

"That's it. Except for her prints and Beasley's on a shovel that she could've used to dig a hole in the dam, tuck him in, and cover him up. No other prints. Not even the kids. Just Al and Florene together again. For the last time. Look good, it doesn't.''

Harriet got up and went to the sideboard to take out the cognac she keeps there for special occasions, of which this was one. She looked for a place to put two snifters down so she could pour, but the clutter of ornamental plates, knickknacks, souvenirs, and photographs filled up the available space. She picked up a pink seashell and said, "I don't know why I keep these damn things! They look so pretty when you pick them up while they're still wet, but now I can't even remember where I got it." Her voice was choked, and suddenly, to her surprise as much as mine, she slammed the offending shell into the fireplace like Cy Young sending one over the plate in a Series game.

You might say she was upset.

"Harriet," I said as she handed me an impressively large slug of cognac, "I'll do whatever I can. Honest. No promises, but I'll try. First thing is to make a couple of calls and get them to set bail as low as possible. Nobody could possibly think Florene is going to skip town with all those kids plus a hundred and sixty pounds of flab to wag around. Not to mention that she probably doesn't know how to buy a bus ticket anyway."

"Thanks, Hugh."

"Uh huh. And her old dad will be able to make bail for her if it comes as low as I think it will. Then we figure out who else could've done it. Maybe the neighbor Beasley's been driving crazy, and maybe not." I drew a deep breath and blew it out again. "Tomorrow I start, first with Florene's father, find out what he knows or thinks he knows, and then there was that talk of drugs. After that, we'll see."

I shook my head sadly. "So I go to work, goddamn it all to hell, I go to work."

Harriet looked awestruck at the sight of me saying I was going to work, as she damn well should have.

FOURTEEN

WE DECIDED, Harriet and I, that the place to start would be Florene's family, mother and father. Beasley had maintained Florene as a combination bed warmer, housemaid, and punching bag, and if she had talked to anybody about it, it probably would have been her parents. A couple of calls and I learned that Wednesdays were a day off for Ed Weller. He agreed to see me that morning, along with his wife, Leona, Florene's mother.

Life as a security guard at the university had left Weller in a state of permanent suspicion. If it moved and if it lived within a twenty-mile radius of the campus it was probably the enemy. There's no blame attached to this. It's a simple fact, and to understand it you have to know a little about the area around Appleboro. The school isn't in our town, but it's the biggest industry around, with the possible exception of IBM up in Kingston and over in Poughkeepsie, and that makes it a major fact of life for all of us.

There are three different worlds around here, and they're like three schools of fish, each swimming separately in the same pond without the slightest interest in contacting or even in acknowledging the right of the others to exist, sliding through and past each other without even a blink. We've got the local folk, that's the townies; then there's the students; and finally the weekend people from the city with their cottages and A-frames in the woods or on the edges of the rivers and ponds. The townies look on the weekenders with the amused contempt quite reasonably reserved for people who can't fix a leaky toilet without calling a plumber. They dislike the students for cluttering up the traffic in the area, slopping along Main Street in various stages of undress, and for not paying taxes. They view the security guards as incompetent and lazy fools who do little or nothing to restrain the student body from breathing in public. The townies eat steak and potatoes and use the least expensive oils in their cooking.

The weekenders see the townies, with affectionate superiority, as happy peasants who charge less for fixing leaky toilets than city workers, but who are incapable of doing anything that requires a broader view of the world than that available from a toilet seat. They disdain the students for being too young to be interesting and they wonder if these are the ones who break into their houses during the week, steal the liquor, and vandalize at random. With a generally liberal approach to the fires in other people's backyards, they are prone to regard security guards as minor instruments of oppression, good for little except swinging nightsticks, but fortunately too stupid to do much damage. The summer people eat broiled salmon and this year use Spanish olive oil for cooking. (Last year the gods of fashion had decreed Greek olive oil.)

Retirees are a subcategory of weekenders, being weekenders fifteen years late who have moved up permanently. More about them later.

The students have no use for either the townies or the weekenders, both groups being too far over the hill to be anything other than irrelevant to the real world. (With a wonderfully creative disregard for the English language many of them called us oldsters "irrelevant," which somehow pleased me more than it should have.) The area has, for them, a certain natural beauty, but they have no stake in it, since after graduation they intend heading for California or the seats of power in industry, the professions, or government. The security guards at the school are classed as barnyard animals, sometimes harmless but often not, planted in their midst by a jealous older generation bent on denying them the rights and prerogatives of youth to trash those aspects of the world they have no interest in maintaining. Since they live on pizza, students do not cook, and hence use no oil at all. In fact, they prefer to think—and do not confuse them with an overly literal, plodding adherence to fact—that any use of oil at all, Spanish, Greek, inexpensive, or petroleum based, is a deliberate rape of the planetary resources that should by rights be theirs to inherit and, frequently, trash.

Small wonder that Ed Weller's dominant emotion was leeriness. His wife, Leona, supplied a faithful echo. She stood next to him when I came into their house, but slightly behind, half in hiding. Maybe she had some not quite conscious thought that if a visitor started blasting with an automatic assault rifle, at least one of her arms and shoulders would be shielded by her man's similar but beefier appendages.

"Come on in," he said. "This is my wife, Leona." Leona and I nodded at each other. She did not fully emerge from behind her husband's shoulder.

Ed Weller and his daughter Florene, or Florence, looked alike except that the looks sat better on a man. He was overweight, too, and big, but a proud, important sort of stomach on a security guard gives him a look of authority. He was clean shaven, though the existence of a dark, heavy beard gave a certain definition to his face that kept it from the blobbiness that was poor Florene's lot.

"Florence didn't do anything," Leona said to me. "She's a good girl." Mrs. Weller was a surprisingly dainty woman, thin and pretty. Her gray eyes and partly grayed brown hair, matched with a long thin nose and fair skin gave her a delicate look, and a life of hard work had kept her figure trim. I would have bet that she had split some of the wood that went into the airtight stove I saw in a corner of the living room.

"Yeah, Leona," Weller said, "the man knows that already. What we want to do is help." They were seated side by side on the couch, the missus still shrinking back, seeking safety by receding behind her husband. He took her hand and held it. He turned to me. "What can we do? What do you want us to tell you?"

"Well, look," I said. "I don't think Florene—"

"Florence," Leona said.

"—Florence killed her husband anymore than you do. And we all know he wasn't the nicest guy on earth—"

Weller snorted. "You can say that again."

"—and there were a lot of people who didn't like him. I want to find out who they were, anything and everything you can tell me, and I'll take it from there. One of them killed him."

Dead silence. "How the hell would we know? He didn't let Florence have us over, even," Weller said.

"We used to go over sometimes when he was out of town," Mrs. Weller added. "Bring something to the kids. Sometimes I'd cook up something decent for them to eat. Living in that shack."

"How much is this going to cost us?" Weller asked. "I'm not a rich man." He waved a hand around the room. I saw the cheap colonial furniture that fouls every discount store in the nation, all maple with chintz cushions that fade after the first six weeks of supporting family behinds. And these had been sat on for more than thirty years. The place was clean and dusted, there were no ashtrays, no books, and *TV Guide* was the only magazine. The pleated parchment lampshades—Leona Weller was big on pleated parchment—had had all the grime brushed out of the pleats, and they lacked the lopsided, drunken tilt shades usually get from sitting on top of inexpensive lamps. It was a decent house, even if a few artfully placed vegetable crates might have made it more attractive.

It was time for one of those instant decisions of mine that so often infuriate Harriet. "That depends on how much I have to do and how much insurance Florene—pardon me, Florence—gets. If she gets little or nothing, that's what my charges will be. Only expenses, and if they go over two hundred bucks, I'll check with you first. If she gets a lot, maybe up to a thousand, including the expenses. But don't worry, I'm in this because my assistant, Harriet Lorimer, and I want to help the girl. We know her, and we think she's innocent."

"Uh huh," Weller said, "I heard about you." He grinned, but in a friendly way. "A lot of people around here think you're nuts."

"I am," I admitted. "It's a privilege of age."

Meanwhile, Leona was thinking. "The people next door, they hated him. Florence told us. He was flooding their land. Maybe they?..." She looked hopeful. "And those parties he had all the time. Liquor and drugs...." She faded away, as if she herself didn't believe this could be very helpful. She was, unfortunately, right. It was quite possible I wasn't going to learn a thing from the Wellers.

Ed changed the approach. "Look, the bastard used to hit her. She had welts on her back, bruises on her face!"

"He hit the kids, too," Leona added. "Florence isn't a very brave girl, but she told us one time he hit the boy so hard that she picked up the big kitchen knife we gave her and told him she'd slit his throat if he ever again...." Realizing what she was saying, she stopped, and her gray eyes overflowed.

Ed put an arm around her shoulder. "You know what he said to her? He said she didn't have the brains of a guinea hen. Florrie isn't the brightest, but he had no right to talk like that, did he?" I didn't answer. "Well, did he?"

I cleared my throat. "No, he didn't. No one does."

"Damn right no one does. And he said to her she had a face like a damp cushion somebody sat on too long so's it couldn't spring back into shape. She cried when she told me that."

He warmed to the recital. "And that maybe she'd look better if she got her ass lifted. All the time like that. We know the girl's no beauty, but nobody's got the right!"

Leona protested. "Before he came along, she was a nice-looking girl, as nice looking as any of them, even if she wasn't any movie star. Besides, I always told her that beauty is only skin deep and she had something better. She had character, and the world respects a girl with character."

"Yes, ma'am, I know. Florence told me how you used to tell her that." (And thereby managed to batter what little ego strength the poor kid might have had. The things we can do in the name of love, even innocently!)

"He told her she ate too much," Weller said. "He said he'd put her out in some field with the cows, that she'd fit in like one of the girls, get all the hay she could hold. What the hell else can I tell you?" He stood up and walked out of the room.

"It's been hard on Ed," Leona explained. "It's hard on me, too, but women learn how to put up better than men. They have to."

I wanted to tell her that women didn't have to learn that anymore, not these days. But it was too late in the day for Leona Weller, and besides, that wasn't why I was on the premises. "Mrs. Weller," I said, "I know it's rough on you, but I'm going to be doing all I can. And if you or Mr. Weller can think of anything, anything at all, that might help, please give me a call.''

She nodded. I left.

That night I said to Harriet, ''They weren't any help at all. What it looked like to me was maybe Ed Weller himself thinks Florene stuck it to her old man, and he's building up the picture for a plea of self-defense.''

''Isn't that a little too sophisticated for a man like Weller? All that plotting and planning?''

''I don't think so. I don't know what kind of training security guards get, but he's bound to have picked up some knowledge of how the law operates. Hell, just from watching TV, he could learn enough.'' I hesitated. ''There's another possibility, though.'' I stopped.

''Which is?''

''Maybe Weller did it himself. Maybe he wants it known that a father will spring to the aid of his child when she's threatened. Maybe, if it comes to that, he's looking to reduce a jury to weeping and wailing and deciding they'll do the same thing in his place.''

''Maybe. Maybe you could ask Timmy if he saw Ed Weller going down the Swamp Bottom road. I'll make a note of it.'' She got out her pad, and started writing. ''Incidentally,'' she added without looking up from her writing, ''I thought I'd look in on Florene today, see how she's doing.''

''Oh? And how is she doing?''

Harriet shook her head. ''Who can tell with that one? She can only think of one thing at a time, and right now it's the insurance money. No idea of what she's going to do with her life, how she'll get along. She's got this notion that once she gets that money, she'll be forever rich. And probably young, underweight, and beautiful. It's hard not to lose patience, and I kept having to tell myself she's not very bright.''

''That's the understatement of the month. And incidentally, how much insurance money is there?''

''That's another thing. She doesn't even know.''

I shook my head. What else could I do or say? If it weren't for this feeling I had that Florene couldn't have killed her husband, that if she had tried she would have jumped into the makeshift grave herself in the confusion, I would have dropped the whole thing then and there. But it was like having a hungry puppy show up on your doorstep. It breaks your heart, and you have to give it something to eat, even when you know the damn thing will never go away after it finishes licking the bowl.

"There's one other thing," Harriet said. "While I was there, the police showed up again. Pinky, too. They asked Florene if they could look around, and she was delighted. No one's paid that much attention to her in years."

I said, "Huh. I wonder what they were up to. The lawyer her old man took on ought to put her on a short leash. She shouldn't let the cops in any time they say pretty please. Any high school dropout knows that. You don't know what they were looking for?"

"Not an inkling. They stayed inside the house and ploughed through Beasley's desk, poked around a little more, and then left."

"I'll see what I can find out. Maybe I can lay a guilt trip on Pinky for poking around without a warrant because he knew the girl would let him in anyway. Anything else happen?"

"Not a thing. The phone rang once. Florene answered, but as soon as she did, they hung up. I thought it was some kind of troublemaker out to harass the girl, but when I asked her she said that there's almost never any calls like that."

"There was when I was there," I said. "Happens all the time though. Even to me. Probably doesn't mean a thing."

FIFTEEN

THE WIDOW BEASLEY HERSELF, her mum and her dad, her neighbors: No one so far looked on the dastardly deed as constituting anything near an irreparable loss. Time had healed their hurt in something less than ten minutes. I needed the help of somebody a bit more sympathetic to the corpse's point of view, and I figured the university might be the place. Beasley had hung on there long enough to gain a full professorship and academic tenure, so someone must have had a reasonably decent opinion of the man.

I called the school and got the name of the head of the English department. Fabian Cribbs—it sounded like the name of the head of an English department. I had visions of a latter-day aristocrat, all fine nerve endings, who would say things like "It is I," and "To whom am I speaking?" and who knew whether "I shall return" was more or less imperious than "I will return," and could explain why. It turned out I wasn't far from wrong.

I called the man, or I should say the doctor, since the average academic would sooner leave the house each morning without his pants than without his degrees. Fortunately, his secretary was Sandra Laski, a local woman, aunt of the kid I kept from messing up his life with drugs some time back.

"Hey, Hugh," she said. "Well I'll be damned. You thinking of coming back for an education?"

"Think you can teach me anything?" I asked.

"Plenty, but my husband wouldn't like it. Besides, the question's academic, meaning you can't afford me. Anyway, what's up, Hugh?"

"I'm helping out your Dr. Beasley's widow, who, as you probably know, is halfway in the soup."

Sandy was impressed. "No kidding. You want to talk to my boss, I guess."

"That's it. Does he have any time today?"

"How about nine-fifteen tomorrow? He generally functions better in the A.M., before the students fry his brains. That do you?"

I said that would do me fine, and Sandy suggested I come in fifteen minutes early for a briefing on Cribbs that she promised would be both useful and scandalous. I agreed.

Five minutes to nine the next morning I ambled into Oostdyk Hall, a crumbling incompetence, political corruption, and a pathetic desire to be mistaken for Oxford University, despite having been slightly reminiscent of Oxford, except that it looked too old and decrepit. Since it was raining out, there was a pail next to Sandy's desk, and our conversation was punctuated by the soft plonk of water coming through the roof. The state does everything in style.

"Got your water wings at the ready?" I asked her.

"Rainy days. I use 'em for a bra," she told me. "How are you, Hugh? How's Harriet?" Sandy was one of the few townies who could ask about Harriet and manage not to snort or turn purple.

We brought each other up to date on one thing or another and then she said, "Look, we haven't got too much time before his lordship gets in, so let's get right to it. First off, he was pretty thick with Dr. Beasley, and he should be able to tell you a lot about the man. But he's running scared these days and if you make him jumpy he'll clam up and shoo you out."

"What's he scared of?"

"Some things I know, some I don't. But I can tell you that for one thing he's worried about hanging on. The man's pushing seventy, and I don't think he's kept up with his field. It used to be that Shakespeare was Shakespeare, the same one century as another. Now they've got something called deconstruction theory, which I don't understand, but I gather it means you can make Shakespeare mean anything you want if it fits what you care about four centuries later."

"Huh?"

"That's what I say, too. Like, so help me, I think you could get a Ph.D. by writing about *The Merchant of Venice* and proving that Shakespeare was an antifeminist fascist because there's a lady lawyer in it in the days before lady lawyers, and this Portia, she goes around persecuting old Shylock. Which proves that there shouldn't be lady lawyers and if there are, they're nothing but a pack of bums. You get it? What the hell, neither do I, and the big problem is, neither does Dr. Cribbs. The students dismiss him out of hand, and he's worried. So don't frighten him, okay?''

"Cross my heart."

"I mean it, Hugh. He's a nice man, only he got into the wrong century. His idea of an English professor is someone who can pour tea and talk about elegant rhyme schemes at the same time without spilling anything. He knows from nothing about this other stuff. And by the way, you'll know if and when you flunk out."

"How?"

"If he calls me and asks what time the faculty meeting is— something like that—I'll answer that it's in ten minutes in the Vandergelder pavilion and that he'd better hustle his bustle over posthaste or he'll be late. You got that?"

I got it. I sat down to wait, and at nine-fifteen on the nose, Fabian Cribbs itself tottered in. His paper-thin, ashen skin was stretched and wrinkled as if a rubber kitchen glove had been pulled clumsily over his head, and the general effect confirmed his age. But his absurdly full and completely black head of hair, glowing with health and arranged with a surreal precision, belonged on someone fifty years younger. In fact, it looked as if it had been heavily lacquered, removed from its housing, and baked in a 350-degree oven till done. (Later, Sandy confirmed that my feeling wasn't far off the truth and that the hair was another frantic and unsuccessful try at remaining current. It was about as convincing as if the unhappy clown had demonstrated his youth by telling his students that Shakespeare was the cat's pajamas or the bee's knees.) Poor Doctor Fabian Cribbs.

He ushered me into his cubicle and waved me into a seat next to his desk, where I faced a wall of books. None of them were less than three inches thick. There were, however, several slender volumes of poetry on Cribbs's desk, arranged so the titles were easy for me to read. I figured they were strategically placed to awe impressionable students. Anyway, I know I was impressed, since "Trees" by Joyce Kilmer is about all the poetry I can understand, except, of course, for certain raunchy limericks.

We chatted generally for a few minutes, circling each other and sniffing in a terribly genteel fashion, like a couple of highborn wolves. He learned about me that I had only attended Brooklyn College, and I learned about him that he thought that Brooklyn College meant I'd be easy to handle. Little did he know.

The opening minuet concluded, I explained the purpose of my visit, and asked for his impressions of Beasley.

He smiled, then shook his head sadly. "A terrible loss. An absolutely brilliant scholar and a fascinating instructor. His classes are—were—oversubscribed. I'd say that almost single-handedly he did more to revive interest in the eighteenth-century English picaresque novel than anything since they made a cinema of *Tom Jones*." He giggled nervously. "A universally admired man and scholar," the good doctor concluded, his expression dissolving to the appropriately pious.

"Well," I said softly, "under the circumstances, I think the admiration must have been a little less than universal, and that's what I need to know about. Don't feel you're being disloyal to Dr. Beasley," I urged, "but I need to know the negatives if I'm going to be of any help."

"But haven't the police ascertained that Mrs. Beasley? . . ."

"Yes, that's true, but there's some opinion that that may not be the right decision. What do you think about Mrs. Beasley, yourself?"

"Ah, well there you've touched on the sore point. Alfred Beasley, to put it plainly, had a randy streak, I'm afraid, and it got him in trouble. In fact, as I'm sure you know, Mrs. Beasley was one of the troubles he got into. It was a sort of counterbalance to the finer qualities of his nature, the ones that made him so elegant a scholar. I'm sure you're familiar with the work of the psychoanalyst Carl Jung?" I looked blank. "With his theory that the aspects of our personalities that dominate our early lives, in Beasley's case the intellectual approach, have an opposite aspect, the more animal urges, that invariably seek release in the middle years?''

He looked at me, pretending to be waiting for me to answer with something about good old Carl Jung. I suppose I'm pretty stupid, but not completely so. The good professor was doing a number on me, the way he would with the more naive undergraduates. He was zapping me with scholarship, and encouraging me to pretend I knew what he was talking about so that I'd back off and try another tack. So I didn't; I thought maybe we were getting close to something useful, and I met the problem head on, the best I could.

"Okay, let's say that's the case, though I believe that Freud himself didn't think too much of Carl Jung." (I had heard that somewhere.) "I understand Dr. Beasley often had wild parties out at his place, and that there were students high on the guest list. Alcohol, even drugs. Do you know anything about that?"

His hand twitched, and he picked absently at some nonexistent lint on his trouser leg, rubbing it off his fingers over the wastebasket. I think I was the lint, and I wondered whether old Carl Jung would agree. He giggled again, but the pitch of his voice was a nervous four tones higher than the last eruption of mirth.

"Oh, I couldn't begin to credit talk like that! You know the academic world is rife with jealousy and even malice. There are people on this faculty who are probably just as learned as Beasley, but lack his flair with the students, and that's what starts the gossip." He looked at his watch—prominently, so I could see him do it.

"It's a little more than gossip, I'm afraid, sir. The neighbors have told me something about the parties at the Beasleys', and I thought for sure you'd be able to add a bit more."

"I wish I could help you, but I'd scarcely have been there myself, would I, now?"

I sat still, blinking, like a bullfrog, but saying nothing. This generally encourages people to feel guilty and to think they have to elaborate, especially when they're trying to keep from saying anything meaningful.

He finally opened up a bit. "The fact is, I've been reluctant to say it, but I did have to talk to Dr. Beasley on several occasions about these stories. Drugs, you know. That's not what parents send their children to the university to learn about, is it? I told him I didn't want to know about it, and that it would have to stop."

"It sounds like you thought the stories were true, then."

"I expect it does, and perhaps I shouldn't have put it like that. To you. Or to Al Beasley either, I suppose. The thing is... Oh, my goodness, it's getting late!" He swiveled his chair about and called out, "Sandra, my dear, what time is the faculty meeting?"

Sandy's voice came floating in. "I was just about to remind you, Dr. Cribbs. You've only got a couple of minutes, and it's over in Moore House."

"Oh, dear." He turned to me. "That's over on the other side of the campus, so I'll have to rush. Sorry. It's been a pleasure to talk to you, Mr. uh..."

"Morrison. Mind if I come back for a few more questions later on?"

"Not at all. Of course, the fall semester starts very soon and I'll be frightfully busy, but why don't you call my secretary and we'll try to squeeze you in." He nodded at me, edged me out of the room, and took off, shot from a cannon. I think I felt a rush of wind. Squeeze me out, would have been more like it.

Several milliseconds later, when he was out of sight, I said to Sandy, "You were right. Something I said scared your boss." She smiled, but didn't respond. I took a shot in the dark. "Beasley kept him supplied, didn't he? What was it, cocaine, marijuana, heroin? What?"

"Listen, Hugh, I told you, Fabian Cribbs is a nice man. He's got enough trouble."

That was no answer, I suppose, but in a sense it told me what I wanted to know.

SIXTEEN

ONCE BACK HOME I wrote up my notes on Cribbs, a procedure Harriet had insisted on when we set up shop. I had resisted at first. Years of living in that cozy trailer had restricted my approach to orderliness in everyday life to making sure the cans of chili and soup and tuna in my trailer were right side up on the shelves, with the labels facing out. But she had held firm, and she was right, especially when she instituted the further procedure of ending the notes with questions that remained unanswered and called for further exploration.

In this case, the questions I was left with were whether I had guessed right that Cribbs was dependent on Beasley for drugs, and whether they were relatively mild items like marijuana or heavier stuff like cocaine. And was Cribbs's enthusiasm for Beasley's academic performance part of the price he had to pay his supplier? And speaking of suppliers, what was Beasley's source and did it have anything to do with his ending up a part of the dam behind his house?

When I had finished I reread what I had written. It looked like I had a lot of work in front of me, so with not-quite-all-American enthusiasm for getting on with the job, I sighed deeply, put my worksheets into the proper file folder, poured myself a beer, stretched out for a twenty-minute snooze, got up, rinsed out my mouth, and buzzed Harriet.

"Hi there," I said. "I've been working. All morning."

She tsked. "Will wonders never cease!"

"I sure as hell hope they will, and soon. Any calls?"

"A Mrs. Lafferty called. Her boy had some school equipment in his locker, ice skates and a basketball—"

"What was he figuring on, basketball on ice, or ice hockey with a basketball?"

She went on, ignoring the interruption. "It seems they were stolen from the locker, or so the boy claims. The school says he lost them—I don't think they want to hear about real problems—and that he's responsible. His mother says it's the school's fault because the security in the locker room is inadequate. She wants you to prove she's right."

"No."

"Good. That's what I told her."

"Anything else?"

"Something you're not going to like. Madam Delavergne is demanding a progress report. I told her we were close to a solution and that you'd be back to her very soon."

"Good again. We ought to get rid of that flea-bitten beast anyway before she finds out what you've done—"

"—What we've done."

"Unh unh. You're the one put the snatch on that cat, baby. Not me. And the old bat will probably put out a call for capital punishment, even if she has to plug in the chair at Sing Sing herself."

"They don't call it Sing Sing anymore. It's the Ossining Correctional Facility."

"Like I say, Sing Sing. Anyway, Harriet, why don't you call her back, say we think we've found the cat through a confidential source, and no, we can't tell her who it is. Say that we can't check on it for sure until this evening, and if we release the Prince from the dungeon we'll take him to her tonight or tomorrow morning in a golden chariot drawn by six white pumpkins."

"Roger wilco." Harriet loved playing war games.

"Is that all?"

"One more. I know you'll like this one. Sandra Laski called. She thought you'd be home from her office by then and she could speak to you, but anyway, she left a message. She says she's sorry she couldn't be more help, she hopes you don't plan on pushing her boss too hard, and she suggests you might learn more if you got in touch with the fellow that shared an office at the school with Beasley. She says they didn't get along, and this guy, Jerry Blackman, would probably be only too happy to share his thoughts on the late professor, especially the negative ones. She gave me his number." She read it to me.

"Good. I'll give him a buzz tomorrow morning."

"This afternoon. Isn't that what you meant to say?"

"Of course."

"And I know what you're thinking, Hugh Morrison. Not at four fifty-nine this afternoon, but at one-thirty, when he ought to be back from lunch. School hasn't started yet and at best it may take you a couple of calls to find him at his desk. As a matter of fact, you might not get him at all today."

"Only if I'm lucky. Okay, okay, one-thirty it is."

As luck would have it, Jerry Blackman, Doctor Jerry Blackman, answered my first call, at one twenty-nine. (I'll have to think about what kind of luck that was, good or bad.) He was available to talk right away.

I got into the car, and naturally the storm that had been waiting offstage all morning broke the moment I turned the key in the ignition. By the time I had reached the end of the driveway it was coming down in sheets. Up here in the valley we don't get many hurricanes. They generally veer off to the east as they come up the coast. But every so often some demon, frustrated at just missing us, lashes out with its tail, hurls thunder and lightning, and makes sure we get our share of highway flooding and downed trees even if we escape the full force of the wind. The phones often go out in these big storms too, and if they don't, we lose service on our road anyway. We've still got party lines, and old Mrs. Mintz knocks service out for everybody by taking her phone off the hook. She says it's to keep the lightning from leaping out and snatching her wig, which it's supposed to have done in the early forties.

It took me half an hour to make what should have been a ten-minute trip through rain that was coming down faster than gravity alone could have driven it, but I expected that at least it'd knock some of the dirt off the car. Harriet was always after me to get the thing washed, while I was always resisting these middle-class affectations.

Naturally, as I drew into the lot nearest to Blackman's office, the downpour stopped as suddenly as it had begun. And equally naturally a heavy-duty town truck went zooming past and replastered my long-suffering machine with everything and more that the rain had washed off. It was, of course, a fresh, clean load of dirt, so I was inclined to be philosophical about it.

The man stood up and extended a hand when I walked in. "Hello," he said, "I'm Jerry Blackman." No "doctor": I thought I might like him. He was about thirty-five, with dark-rimmed glasses that he kept pushing up. I learned from his pale skin that he spent his afternoons reading, not jogging under a noonday sun, and though he was tall and thin, the beginnings of a paunch made it clear that he also shunned the doubtful advantages of the exercise zoos his generation was so fascinated by; I *knew* I would like him.

"Hugh Morrison," I answered. I looked around the cramped office. It was nearly big enough for one desk, but it nevertheless held two, one of which presumably was Beasley's. Blackman's was the one farther from the window, which I knew enough to realize signified that he was further down in the pecking order than Beasley. "Nice little place you've got here," I said.

He laughed. "Ain't it the truth. It used to be all mine, but you know what they say, all bureaucracies expand to overflow their allotted space. The English department has grown over the years, but the space hasn't followed suit. We've had to double up. It was adequate when I was here by myself, but for two...." He held his hands up in a gesture of helplessness.

"With you here first, I'd have thought you'd have had squatter's rights on the window," I offered.

"I'd have thought so, too," he agreed. "But exactly one hour after Beasley moved in, looked around, and walked out, I had a visit from Dr. Cribbs. You know him?"

"We've met."

"He explained that the good Dr. Beasley had longer tenure at the school than Dr. Blackman, and besides, Dr. Beasley's eyes weren't the best, and anyway, Dr. Beasley wanted the window, and ten other things he thought of on the spot, so would Dr. Blackman mind too awfully much if—and so on. So Dr. Blackman touched his forelock in all due humility and moved into the shadowy interior. If I had had tenure I'd never have agreed, believe me. And as a matter of fact, I've been

composing the little speech I plan on making to Cribbs if and
when that day ever arrives."

He stopped. "But I go on too much. Let's move over to
Beasley's window. We can talk while I carve my initials in his
desk."

"Fine," I said, and we settled down. I told him about my role
in the affair, working to locate the facts, fairly certain that when
I found them Florene would be exonerated. "The police," I
explained, "are satisfied that she killed her husband. Lord
knows she may have had enough motive, but it's not the way
the woman is made. I doubt they'll be able to convict her, but
there's no reason to put her through all that hell for nothing."

"I never met the lady," Blackman said, "but I'll go along
with that. My office mate was nobody you'd like to see your
daughter dating, not without she was wearing an iron corset
with barbed-wire ties. Ask me whatever you like, and I'll try to
help."

"First off, just tell me about Beasley. What was he like, how
did you get along. Then we'll get to specifics."

"Well . . . I won't start off by saying I hate to speak ill of the
dead, because that would make me some kind of a hypocrite.
So let's say I don't much enjoy bad-mouthing the man, but I
don't know how else to talk about him. First place, just about
every way you look there's something phoney about him. Big
smile, hearty handshake, but you always had to wonder what
the hidden agenda was, when and how he was going to slip you
the shaft."

I had the feeling I might be there for days listening to generalities. "I didn't know Al Beasley, so generalities are lost on
me. Could you hang them on a couple of specifics?"

"Easy. Let me give you a couple of examples. We both spe-
cialized in the English novel. He made a speech about an
eighteenth-century book, *Humphry Clinker,* in which the same
story is told from several different points of view—an old man,
a young girl, and so on. He called it the first seed of relativism
in Western literature. If you don't know what that means, it
doesn't matter, but just look at this." He pushed past me to a
file cabinet and took out a folder. He handed me a typed page,
and pointed at a line half way down the page. "Read that."

I did. It said something about the seed of relativism that flowered in western Europe a century later was first planted by Tobias Smollett in his seminal masterpiece *Humphry Clinker*. I hadn't the vaguest idea what I was reading. "Yeah?" I said. "So?"

"Yeah," he answered, "so I wrote that. It was for a paper of my own. He went through my files and simply took what he liked."

"Did you face him with it?"

"Sure. He smiled sweetly and said it was two great minds with but a single thought; we both hit on the same truth at the same time. I went to Cribbs and complained. You like to know what he said?" I nodded. "So would I. I couldn't understand a word. Some fatuous babble dribbled out about he was sure there was some mistake because Dr. Beasley was incapable of intellectual dishonesty. And of course, the mistake was mine. Cribbs made no sense at all, and he knew it."

I might have looked doubtful, because Blackman went on to say, "Okay, maybe this is just academic infighting. Let me try elsewhere. You know he's our local authority on wine. That's what he always claimed, anyway. I've been saving the ads with his smiling face in the weekly because I know a little about wine myself, and you know what, he cribs that stuff too. 'A staggeringly deep bouquet.' 'A saucy, witty item that will hit you where you least expect it.' 'Liquid velvet in the mouth that leaves an aftertaste of spicy oak.' You got that?"

"I got it, but don't all the experts have to come up with that kind of jazz?"

"Oh, sure, but at least they try to be original about it." He reached for a wine guide, and looked at the page numbers he had penciled on Beasley's ads. "You do it yourself. Compare the lines I've underlined in this guide with Beasley's ads. Word for word. He couldn't even invent his own nonsense!" Blackman's fury was potent enough to propel him out of his chair and over to the window. He turned back to me. "You might be thinking I was in enough of a rage to swat the man myself. You'd be right, but I'm too much of a coward or too much of an honest citizen, depending on how you look at it."

"He was pretty successful, though, for that much of a fake. How do you explain that?"

"A question I've asked myself. I think the answer is what I call the Christmas-tree syndrome. People see all the ornaments and tinsel and twinkling lights and think they're looking at a beautiful tree. And all the while there's this shriveled thing with bare branches underneath the glitter. It works especially well with undergraduates, kids who are naive enough to be fooled by the doodads on the tree. They look at classroom lectures as a kind of show anyway, and if the production is classy they can be led to think the same of the content."

"But that wouldn't explain Cribbs's being taken in by a clever act, would it?"

"You've got a point. I've never been able to figure that one out. There's two possibilities. Beasley has—had—a good act. I've got to hand him that. A good act fills the classroom, and that makes Cribbs look good as chief honcho of a successful department. The other possibility is that Cribbs knows it's all a fake but for some reason he either needs Beasley or is afraid of him. Take your pick."

"But if it was a fake, wouldn't the president of the school know it? And be concerned?"

Blackman gave me a look normally reserved for backward children. "If this was Harvard or Berkeley, where the president is a major scholar, the answer would be yes. But with an outfit like this, the top guy is an administrator and a fundraiser, not a scholar. And an administrator worries about increasing enrollment, the balance sheet, the happiness index of the alumni, professors who generate good publicity, a successful basketball team—and maybe after that secondary considerations like solid scholarship."

That sounded a little strong; this was a bitter young man, and I wondered how severely his problems with Alfred Beasley, Ph.D., had impacted on him. "Tell me," I asked, "have you ever heard any talk of drugs in connection with Beasley?"

"I was coming to that. I only get it secondhand. I don't have any facts I can vouch for, but, yes, there's been talk. As part of the act, like candy canes on this Christmas tree, he's supposed to have had these parties that a lot of the school kids went to where the stuff showered down like manna in the desert. I don't know what kind, I never wanted to know, and that's all I can tell you."

"Is he supposed to have supplied drugs to others as well?"

"Like the opinion poll says—Don't Know, No Answer." He looked at me sharply. "Listen, you know the school protects its own. Well, the faculty all more or less know who the big supplier is on campus, but as far as anybody can tell, it's only marijuana so we keep it in the family. The town cops maybe don't know, or maybe don't care to know, and we're not about to tell them. In fact we don't tell our own administration; a teacher's got to stay on good terms with the student body and that means keeping our noses out of their personal stupidities. If you can give your word this is just between us, I might be able to help you."

"I'm not a cop. I don't want to know any more than I need to. I'm not out to bust any drug rings, though of course if there was major crime involved, I'd feel I had to talk. If it's the way you say, then anything you tell me goes no further. And it might help catch a murderer. That good enough?"

"I'll take a chance, though if you catch the murderer I won't be the one to write indignant letters to the paper if you pin a medal on him. There's one kid, I only know him as Danny, who's rumored to be the big earth mother for the local druggies, and might know about Beasley's source. If," he added cautiously, "the stories about Beasley are true."

"Danny. How do I find Danny?"

"The students will be drifting back to the campus next week for the fall semester. You'll have to figure that out for yourself. One clue: You can't miss him. He's got spikey hair, dyed orange, and the rest of the paraphernalia, like earrings running up the side of one ear. That's all I can tell you, I wouldn't expect him to be around for another five or six days, though."

"At least he ought to be easy to spot."

"Uh huh. I guess so. Orange spikes and four earrings in one ear probably doesn't describe more than a couple of hundred of the kids who'll be staggering back next week."

He thought he was being funny. I thought, as I drove back home, that he was probably right. I also thought that when I wrote up the interview, I might make a special note of the passionate distaste that Blackman had displayed for the chappie who had lately been so furiously crowding both his professional and his office space.

Back in the office, I buzzed Harriet. "Anything to report?" I asked.

"Oh, Hugh, it's awful! Absolute disaster! Can you come over? I mean now, right away!"

SEVENTEEN

I TORE OVER SO FAST that my feet may only have touched ground twice, and I might even have arrived seconds before my stomach got there, though that could be a minor exaggeration. "What happened?" I panted.

"The cat! Prince Albert's disappeared!"

"For God's sake," I said, disgusted. "You know you scared the hell out of me?"

She ignored that. What else could she do? "I thought the storm might have frightened him, but I've looked all over. Under the couch, behind the refrigerator, just all over. The only good thing is that the phone was out so I never did get through to Elsie Delavergne to tell her we'd be able to bring him back soon."

I flopped into a chair. "That's something, anyway. Let's relax. I'm pooped. Sit down and we'll think about it."

For once, Harriet followed my instructions meekly and parked herself timidly on the couch, and that got me suspicious. She was feeling guilty about something. "All right, tell me what happened. It's not your fault," I assured her, "but you did something to upset the beast, didn't you."

She didn't meet my eyes and she didn't talk.

"Didn't you, Harriet?"

"Well . . . the storm. The animal was frightened, and started yowling. Then the lights went out for a few minutes, and there was the phone not working either. And the truth is I just plain forgot to put his food out." She hesitated.

I finished for her. "And we both know how he is about food. All right. Let's think. If you were Prince Albert and you were hungry, where would the nearest McDonald's be?"

"I—Doc Hingle's?"

"Right. Let's call him."

No luck. The Prince wasn't there, but Hingle had a suggestion. "The cat wouldn't come here unless he was literally starving. He'd associate this place with cages and medicines and torture chambers. I think he'd head back home first and see if he could wheedle a few scraps out of the old skinflint. Why don't you try there? If she's out for the afternoon you might be able to pick him up before she gets her mitts on him."

It was worth a try, but first I felt I was entitled to scold Harriet a little for this mess. "You realize, that after you concocted this cockamamie scheme it may damn well fall through. And you know old Elsie won't pay a red cent if she gets the animal back without our help. The only thing we'll be getting is a piece of her nasty mind. Then there's the time we've lost. And the fussing around." I was getting more indignant the more I went on, which wasn't very nice of me.

I think Harriet might have been about to say she was sorry, but I was denied that rare treat when the phone rang before we could get out the door. It was Doc Hingle again.

"I've got an idea," he said. "Stop over on your way. Tell you about it when you get here. If I'm right about him going home, and if the old girl is out, maybe I can save your skin."

We walked into the vet's waiting room and were immediately ushered past assorted Airedales, setters, Manxes, and poodles impatiently waiting their turn. (A Doberman bared its teeth, I think because we were jumping the line. With false bravado, I pretended to ignore the brute.)

Once in the back our ears were assailed with the screams of what I figured for an eight-year-old child being flayed alive. We looked at each other in horror, but when Henry Hingle walked in, he smiled like an angel. "What's the matter, dear hearts? Never heard a Siamese cat in heat before? That's the answer to your problem."

I dimly perceived his notion, but kept my mouth shut. "Now look," he said. "you're going to borrow Ming Toy for a while, and you'd better make it a short while or I'm in bad trouble with her mommy. She'll be in a carrying case—Ming Toy, not her mommy—and if the Prince is waiting around his house, not able to get in, like everybody else in a two-mile radius he'll hear old Ming Toy crooning."

He stopped, and then went on to say, "I think for purposes of this operation we'll call her Victoria. When he hears her, being a healthy young man, he'll come bounding over at the ready. You grab him. There's an extra carrying case for you to pop him in." He smiled. "Simple? I'll say, and maybe a little brilliant, right?"

Harriet looked discontent. "It seems a little mean. Couldn't we let the two cats, just for a little while—"

"Are you insane?" Hingle gasped. "First thing, there's no such thing as a little while when two cats get going. Second place, Victoria here has a pedigree that goes back further than yours, and if she gets herself knocked up I'm likely to be knocked off. So you keep them apart if you value your life."

"Of course we will," I said. "You'll have to forgive Harriet. It's the mother-hen instinct, you know. She can't help it."

What could she say? She clucked.

I took Victoria in her carrying case out to the car, and Harriet followed with the empty case. The howling was loud enough to get every tomcat on the east coast to drop whatever he was doing and head for Appleboro. A few passersby looked at us, but we pretended we couldn't hear a thing. Once in the car I accelerated to top speed in several milliseconds and, leaving the smell of burning rubber behind, we sped out to the Delavergne place.

I jumped out and peeked into the garage. We were in luck; Elsie's car was gone. I raised my hand in the victory sign for Harriet, and she hefted Victoria's cage out to set it on the lawn, where the dear old puss let fly an aria that would have drowned out a platoon of Brünnhildes in full voice.

Almost immediately she was joined by a squadron of Siegfrieds as Prince Albert entered stage left, voice lifted in song, to claim his hairy loved one. He bounded up to the cage to free the captive maiden from her durance vile, and the villain, me, grabbed him. Harriet opened the second cage and I plopped him in and slammed shut the iron gate.

We loaded the beasts into the car while they swung into the tomb scene from *Aida* where the lovers, buried alive, bleat their tonsils out to proclaim their deathless passion. Almost immediately after we hit the road we spotted Elsie Delavergne's ancient Buick heading toward us. With that rare presence of mind for which I shall always love her, Harriet reached over and flipped the radio on, volume up to the limit. The lovers' duet blended in competition with a heavy-metal outfit. I had to hand it to the cats; love conquers all, and they were louder, though the combined effect made it unlikely that the old girl in her car could separate the melded melodies.

Two of the heartbeats in the car, Harriet's and mine, gradually returned to normal. The other two, naturally enough, did not, what with hope springing eternal in the feline breast. But we managed to drop Victoria—once again Ming Toy—back at Henry Hingle's without incident, and we continued on with Prince Albert. The operation over, we hugged each other in an orgy of self-congratulation.

"You owe me," I said, "at least a thick steak."

Harriet nodded. "And a baked potato with sour cream. And I'll join you."

"Good," I said. "I'll cut up the chives."

EIGHTEEN

TIMMY YOUNG TOOK COMFORT in the minor routines of life. Weather permitting, he hitchhiked down to Main Street early each morning (except Sunday) to do the chores the local shopkeepers had set for him. After he had carried out the empty cartons or swept the sidewalk or packaged up the trash, he collected the few kopecks he had earned and did his shopping for the day. Then he'd head back home and be in residence by ten-thirty or so to do whatever amused him from that point on.

Sometimes he'd work the small front and rear gardens his father had put in years ago, depending on the season. Nobody in town had any use for all the seeds that came in the packets of lettuce or peppers or anything else, and Timmy was everybody's favorite recipient for the surplus. Somewhere along the way he had picked up the notion of crop rotation, so that this year the flowers might be in the front garden and the vegetables in the rear, and next year a stately row of brussels sprouts could be flanking the front door. (Timmy didn't like brussels sprouts, so he used to take most of them to the Salvation Army thrift store, leaving them on the loading dock. But he always grew them if someone provided the seed, feeling an obligation to appreciate the kindness that had been shown him.)

Other times he might wander into the boggy area down from the house, counting, in the spring, for instance, the jack-in-the-pulpits, trillium, marsh marigolds, and violets, keeping separate tallies for the white, yellow, or violet violets. And then there was the occasional wild orchid to append to his lists. He was proud of his counts and of his counting, so long as nothing strayed over one hundred. And he never wandered out of sight of the house or the road.

Or he might simply stay home and watch television.

All things considered, it wasn't a bad life, and for Timmy it was even a good one. Some folks around town—including me, at times when the everyday world seemed especially chaotic, would find themselves gently envious of poor old Timmy. They knew there was nothing to be envious of, but that's the way it goes.

Knowing he'd be home or at least nearby by late morning, Harriet and I showed up at eleven. He was seated on his porch with a jigsaw puzzle, and from the looks of it not doing badly at all. Harriet proffered a clear plastic bag of bran muffins.

"These are for you, Timmy," she said.

"Gee, thanks, Mrs. Lorimer." He inspected the thoughtful gift. "And they got those yellow raisins in them! I love yellow raisins." His childish eyes turned expectantly on me.

Fortunately, I was prepared. "Here's a bag of Tootsie Rolls," I said. "Don't eat 'em all at once, you hear?"

"And not at all before your meals," Harriet added.

Timmy frowned. "How long before a meal counts as before a meal?" he asked.

I found the question completely logical, but Harriet was stumped. "Well, don't eat any in the morning, and only one or two in the afternoon. Maybe in the evening while you're watching television," she said, completely failing to answer the young man's question. "And brush your teeth before you go to bed."

"Yes, ma'am," he said in a voice that indicated he had heard that foolish instruction before.

There were a few people I knew I had to talk to on Florene's behalf, but Harriet and I thought that since Timmy was the self-appointed gatekeeper to Apple Dell, we should visit him first. Timmy, we reasoned, would know many of the nonresidents who had visited the development a few weeks ago, when Beasley had been killed. Conceivably time could be saved if I went to see them first. At least it was worth a try.

"Timmy," I began, "you know most everybody in town, right?" He agreed. "And you know that Mr. Beasley was killed two weeks ago, don't you?" Again he nodded his agreement. "Well, poor Mrs. Beasley is very, very worried because nobody knows who did this terrible thing."

"Gee," Timmy said, a mouth full of Tootsie Roll, sounding more muffled than impressed.

Harriet stepped in. "We need your help, dear. Can you think back a few weeks and tell us all the people you can remember who went down the road to Swamp Bottom, where the Apple Dell houses are? It would help a lot."

Timmy looked scared. "Gosh, I don't know. That was a long time ago. And, and, gee, I'm not here all the time. Maybe I don't remember. Pa told me I was, you know, feebleminded."

"Shucks," Harriet said, "nobody can remember everything that far back. Whatever you know would be a big help."

"It'd be like you were a sort of policeman," I said as an inducement. "Like you were helping out the law."

"Would it be all right," he asked, his eyebrows lifted anxiously, "if I couldn't remember the people who go to Mr. Beasley's parties? I don't even know most of them. Is that okay?"

"That's okay. Anything you can tell us would be just great. We'd be proud of you."

Timmy was mollified. He frowned, deep in thought. "Well...there's Mr. Weller, a couple of times. Mrs. Weller, but only once I know about. And Mr. DeWitt and Mr. Mittleman and Mr. Tupper—" The phone rang inside the house. "Excuse me, please." He ran inside. I wrote down the five names he had given us.

We could hear his voice, though from the long silences it was clear someone else was doing most of the talking. "Yeah," he said, "I guess so. No. I don't have any of them, leastways not right now... Oh, sure. That'd be great... Uh huh, uh huh. Sure I'd be interested, read it right off, no kidding ... Yeah, I'll be here then, next Tuesday... Okay. 'Bye."

He came out again. "That was a man calling about some bombs," he explained. "I'm sorry it took so long."

"Bombs?" Harriet and I asked in unison.

"Yeah. I didn't understand too good, but he said somebody was going to have some new thing he thought I'd like. Mississippi bombs or something. He's going to send me about them. Maybe it's a new firecracker, you think?"

"Tell me," I asked, "did he say where he was calling from?"

"Yeah, but it was a big long name." Timmy more or less paraphrased the title of a major brokerage house.

Harriet and I looked at each other. "Timmy," Harriet asked, "do you think he could have said bonds? Municipal bonds?"

"Yeah, that sort of sounds like it, maybe. What's that, anyway?"

"Oh, nothing much that you'd care about, dear," Harriet said. "But you let the man send it on, and if you don't like it you can throw it away."

"Hey! That's a good idea!"

"Could you go back to telling us," I asked, "about the people who went down the road?"

"Sure. Lemme see. There's Mr. Tupper and then a man who I don't know his name but I think he's a teacher at the college. He's kinda old and he has funny hair, like he puts a whole mess of goo on it or something. He goes down the road lots of times. I know Mr. and Mrs. Parker have company almost every weekend because some of them stop here and ask me where their house is, but I don't know their names." He stopped. "That's all I can think of, I'm sorry."

"Don't be sorry," I said. "That's great. I don't know what we'd have done without your help."

"I'm glad," he said simply. "'Course," he added as we were leaving, "there's the mailman and the UPS man and the garbage man," but we were already headed for the car.

After one more warning from Harriet about not pigging out on Tootsie Rolls, we left. Timmy waved goodbye. In the car, Harriet turned to me. "If I'd known you were going to give the poor boy candy I'd have stopped you cold. You should have more sense than that."

"I do, but you've put candy on my proscription list. This way I get a little pleasure knowing that someone else can glom it up without getting a lecture on calories."

"You're awful."

"That's right, and that's the way I like it."

We rode in silence for a while until Harriet said, "You know, it's kind of nice."

"What's kind of nice?"

"Not much, but it's nice to think that a boy as sweet and simple as Timmy can frustrate one of those damned telephone salesmen and get rid of him in no time at all, just by being himself.''

I agreed. ''It is nice.'' I don't remember what life in the big city is like, but out here in the country, they sell by phone. And sell and sell. Bonds while you're trying for an afternoon nap, swimming pools and aluminum siding at cocktail time, fabulous prizes you've already won if you'll only spring for a $7.95 kitchen thingummy, and an invitation to visit, all expenses paid, a time-share colony in Florida, usually while you're watching your favorite TV show. ''Maybe we should all go along with it, like Timmy. Get rid of them that way.'' Maybe Timmy had taken a giant step for all mankind.

Back home we listed the names: Ed and Leona Weller, Florene's parents; John Mittleman, a local hellfire end-of-the-world scold nicknamed Savonarola; Don Tupper, who ran the Clarendon winery; Arthur DeWitt, proprietor of DeWitt Vineyards; and the lardhead from the college, who had to be the eminent professor Fabian Cribbs. Not a bad list, and presenting a lot of ideas. Or, as we used to say on the force, a lot of opportunities for us to overcome.

NINETEEN

SINCE I DOUBTED that John Mittleman, Appleboro's favorite prophet of doom, could have had anything to do with Beasley's death, I thought I'd cover that base first and scratch him off the list. Timmy, after all, had pegged him as one of the Apple Dell visitors, though it was most likely that he had been on one of his salvation safaris, dropping off religious tracts. He usually covered the whole town, neighborhood by neighborhood, in about five days, Monday through Friday, and then rested Saturday and Sunday, needing one more day than God for catching his breath, his job being so much more strenuous than his Savior's.

He hadn't always been that way, but it had come on him some ten years earlier. It was then that his teenage daughter had left home for New York City after she got out of high school. Mittleman was sure that setting foot in Manhattan was in itself on the order of simultaneously violating Commandments One through Ten, and when the girl made a modest go of it as a fashion model, that took care of Commandments Eleven through Ninety-nine. It's true that her picture showed up in a (respectable) magazine featuring an outfit that made a miniskirt look like a Mother Hubbard, but what the hell, she had the figure to do it with.

His poor wife, Jenny, was in the garden when I walked up, cutting what I think were dahlias, though personally roses are the only flower I can identify with any certainty; they're the ones with the thorns that bite. She looked up, squinting into the sun. "Hi, Morrison," she said, "how ya doing?"

"How are you?" I responded. "John around?"

She snorted. Jenny Mittleman wasn't into sin and salvation the way her old man was. "Yeah. Try out back, the Vatican West room. He's polishing this week's thunderbolt for the paper." She was referring to the letters her husband sent to the local weekly with an awesome regularity. One day I expected they'd all be published in a volume thicker than *Gone with the Wind*, under the title SEVENTEEN HUNDRED WAYS TO AVOID PERDITION, and bearing the parenthetical subtitle, AND NONE OF YOU WILL EVER MAKE IT. John Mittleman was certain that whatever was, was wrong.

"Thanks, I'll go back."

"Have fun." She snorted again.

I found the man in a back room off the kitchen that had probably been a pantry at the start of the century, but which now was a cross between an office and a chapel. He was seated in front of an ancient Royal typewriter, one of the big old office models that were made to last forever, barring interference from Satan, banging away with what was, literally, a religious fervor. His dark hair, liberally tinged with gray, hung over his face, but his dark eyes shone through like twin torches, as if to burn a hellfire message onto the paper in the machine.

He stopped and looked at me, his two index fingers frozen in pecking position over the keyboard, his hunched shoulders relaxed not a single centimeter. Not that he was unfriendly; I might have been a sinner, but who wasn't? At least I represented what passed for law and order, if not decency, in a world of depravity. And at one time, before he was called, we had had a casual nodding acquaintance.

"Hello, Hugh Morrison," he said, "what can I do for you?" There was no hope behind his question that I might be asking for his help to find salvation.

He was right; I only wanted to know about his visit to Apple Dell about the time that Al Beasley was killed. I told him that.

His head wagged from side to side with satisfaction badly disguised as sadness. "That poor fool. The wages of sin." A smile as thin as sour milk twisted his mouth a tad. "What can I tell you? I was out there to spread the word. If only one person listens . . . The houses were empty. The women work these days, instead of staying home, having children, tending house, making a home. Contraception, abortion. . . ."

He was heading into a lecture whose relevance for a man in my position was somewhat less than minimal, so I broke in.

"It's his wife, Florene, I'm concerned about. The police think she did it."

"The fools. The poor girl's a decent soul, and I think, I *know,* because I've talked to her, that all these years she has walked in the way of the Lord as well as she could, given the life that man made her lead. Her children, her little babies, her angels...."

Mittleman did nothing but sail off course. I tried again. "Yes. But apart from that, I think it's up to all us, uh, right-thinking people, to help find the criminal, the sinner, and...." I wanted to say something about helping the sinner find salvation, thinking that would appeal to John Mittleman, but while I may be a part-time sneak, I balk at turning into a part-time hypocritical sneak. So I faded out.

Just as well. He got the idea anyway. "Of course. The last time I was out there, and I think it was before the man was killed, at least for a day or two, there was nothing out of the ordinary. She was there alone with the children. The neighbors were off. The backhoe they were using to dredge up that pond was setting quiet." His head jerked up and he glared at me. "There are ponds and ponds in Appleboro. If God had wanted a pond on that land He would have put one there himself! Nature belongs to God, not man, and to arrogate unto oneself that which belongs to God is, is—"

He couldn't find a word bad enough, which gave me the chance to hop in again. "Yeah, it's terrible. But you didn't see anything out of order? Nothing wrong?" I was about to give up; there was no way I could get him off his hobbyhorse and start him thinking about Beasley's murder.

"Not that time. But other times, of course. Oh, yes, indeed. The parties, the wild parties. School kids, eager to be corrupted, spread over the lawn. Coupling under trees, wallowing in shameless depravity. Naked. Two young girls together, hugging, kissing, feeling. Sodom and Gomorrah."

Under the proper circumstances, which these were not, I can enjoy a description of an orgy as much as the next guy. Reluctantly, I was about to deflect him from the hot stuff, when he abruptly said, "And not just the school kids. The corruption has spread like a fungus, a contagion. In July, I was out to

Swamp Bottom when one of those bacchanals was under way, and I saw the wife of one of our local businessmen, there with the rest of them.''

''Oh? Would you tell me who it was?''

''No, I would not.''

I knew he wanted to let me know, so I made a little face of disinterest and said, bored, ''Well, if you won't, you won't.''

''Betty Ann Tupper,'' he said hastily, before I could switch topics, ''that's who.''

''Don Tupper's wife?''

''The same. The man works like a dog at that vineyard, and this is the thanks he gets.''

''Was she, did she?''

He shook his head; I think he was disappointed. ''No, she was off by herself. Fully clothed. But she must have wanted to. She was there, wasn't she! And then I've seen Beasley on Timmy Young's front porch. I don't know what he was up to, but I'm sure he was out to bring corruption into that poor soul's life as well.''

''What makes you think so?''

''I don't think so. I know so. On my way back from Apple Dell I stopped at Timmy's to see what I could do for him, and he told me that Beasley had brought him ice cream. Timmy was happy about that; he liked Beasley. I asked him if that had happened before, and it had. Every week. No one can tell me that that man did anything out of simple goodness of heart. He was after something, something rotten, something he needed Timmy for. You can count on that.''

For a wonder, I tended to agree with Mittleman. Beasley wanted something from Timmy. As directed, I counted on that.

TWENTY

"WHAT DO YOU THINK?" I asked Harriet. "Wife lured into sin and degradation, outraged husband seeks revenge, kills seducer?"

"I think you've been reading too many Victorian novels, and it's given you a brain fever."

It was still summer, at least technically, but fall had sent a coming attraction across the Appalachians in the form of a cool, crisp breeze. And I had found a clump of purple asters on the road, the last spectacular wildflower a boy could count on before the annual ice age set in. So I built a small fire in Harriet's fireplace, more for its looks than for necessary warmth, and we were sitting in front of it, staring into the flames, me with a Scotch on the rocks, Harriet with a Manhattan. (She said a Manhattan, which she almost never drank, sometimes made her think of her young days, sipping a wicked, wicked cocktail in the Rainbow Room on top of Rockefeller Center.)

"Yeah, but nevertheless." I rattled the ice in my glass. "You can't expect Don Tupper, who certainly is over forty, to like it if he knows that his child bride is playing footsie with the Roman-orgy crowd down in Apple Dell. You think he knows about it?"

"I can't give you a simple answer, but—"

"You never can," I said glumly. "But go ahead anyway."

"First, let me give something a stir on the stove. You want another drink? I'll get it while I'm up." She heaved herself out of her chair with a sigh and stood with her back to the fire. That's the trouble with fireplaces; you can only toast one side at a time.

I held my glass out. "Thanks. Just a small one. Need any help?"

"No, you stay put." I watched with affection as she walked into the kitchen with my tumbler for Scotch in one hand, her stemware for a Manhattan in the other. She might not have been so young anymore—who was?—but she walked upright and with grace. Maybe the grace was overlaid with a little superfluous flesh, but Harriet was entitled. I smiled to myself, leaned back in my chair with my eyes closed, listened to the clink of ice and the clank of a spoon, drew in a breath of something wonderful bubbling away on the stove, and I sighed. I have no idea why I was so content, and it occurred to me that I was probably asking for trouble.

"Well, now," Harriet said after she had come back with fresh drinks and settled down again, "about Betty Ann. First, she's not precisely anybody's child bride. I'd say she's twenty-three, four, which I grant you is a long way from her husband."

"What's he, forty, forty-two?"

"I'd say about that. Anyway, in this town, I'd be willing to bet that if Betty Ann has been at Beasley's parties, then, yes, her husband would know about it. But he also knows what she's like, and I doubt that he'd be too worried, even though he might not like it."

"'Might not,' hell. Probably doesn't like it a bit."

"Okay. I'll go along with that. But you have to know a bit about Betty Ann, or rather about her mother and father. Don't get me wrong, both nice people, but he was kind of distant and removed. I hate people who try to be pop psychologists, but I'd bet the girl sometimes felt she didn't have a father at all when she was a kid.

"And momma Lenore was the other way around, always making sure her daughter understood how much her mother was doing for her, and that nothing the girl could do would ever make up for it."

"That's too abstract for me. Flesh it out so a dumb gumshoe can understand what the hell you're talking about."

"Easy. You set the table while we're talking, and I'll get the dinner out."

"Right," I said, as we both got up. "I brought two bottles of wine. Which do you want, red or white?"

"Doesn't matter. No, let's make it red. Red wine almost tastes more expensive, so why not."

"Red it is." I went into the kitchen and opened the wine, and started setting out wine glasses, silverware, and plates according to instructions. I used the plates that had been Harriet's grandmother's, the ones with scalloped edges and small blue and green flowers around the borders. They always made dinner feel cozier, more familylike. I don't know whether they qualified as fine china or not, but I liked them, even if they couldn't be put in the dishwasher. "Keep going," I said. "I can hear you while I'm doing this."

"Well, one example. I heard this from Lenore's cousin, up at the Kingston senior-citizen center. It seems that last year Lenore, who moved downstate after she was widowed, called and asked if she could come up the third weekend in October to see the autumn leaves. Don and Betty Ann were all tied up for some reason and they asked her to come the weekend before. She did.

"Anyway, Don apparently said without thinking that beautiful as the leaves were, they were still a little short of the peak, which would probably arrive in another five or six days. The story is that Lenore sighed deeply, turned her reproachful eyes on Betty Ann and said something like, 'Oh, that's when I wanted to come. You two were busy then, you said. But never mind. This is nice, too.' And looked hurt."

"I get the idea. A guilt trip for the kiddies."

Harriet was warmed up. "Right. And there are other stories. If she bakes a pie for them, she'll let them know she had to travel all to hell and gone to get the right ingredients, but that she didn't mind because she knew how much Betty Ann used to like it as a child. And of course it weighed a ton getting it here on the bus."

"Could I dish up a little more stew for both of us?" I asked. And I poured us each some wine.

"Hugh Morrison, have you heard a word I said?"

"Of course I have. But what's this got to do with Betty Ann at Beasley's parties?"

"My hunch is that the poor girl's been psyched out by her mother, and has to keep trying and trying to make people love her. She married a much older man, maybe looking for her distant daddy's love, and her mother taught her that nothing she can do is enough to equal out the sacrifices that were made for her. So when a slob like Beasley asks her to his house, since he senses something vulnerable about the girl, she doesn't know how to refuse, and when she sees what's going on, she doesn't know how to leave. But she stays clear of the action, just the way John Mittleman told you."

Not entirely convinced, I said, "It's possible, I suppose. I won't argue the point. But how would her husband look on it? Mad at her? More to the point, mad at Beasley?"

"I have no idea."

We sat quietly in front of the fire. I was thinking about what a lot of trouble a man was asking for, marrying a girl half his age. I said as much to Harriet.

A sweet smile settled on her face; she was lost in some fond memory. "You know," she said, "when Joe and I got married we were both in our low twenties. He used to say that if I ever got to be over thirty, he'd have to get rid of me. Otherwise he'd lose face, going around with an old lady."

I played along. "And when you got to be over thirty?"

"Oh, then he'd say that he'd have to get rid of me if I ever got to be under thirty again, what with the young being nothing but problems."

"He had something there, your Joe. I suppose I ought to look into any problems that came along with Betty Ann, huh?"

"I suppose so. But I hope there's nothing in it."

"Me too. I always hope there's nothing in it. That's why I'm such a lousy cop."

"Ah, but you're a good lousy cop. Otherwise I wouldn't have anything to do with you." She pecked me lightly on the cheek.

After we had cleared the dishes away—it was my turn to wash and hers to dry—I sat down at the phone and dialed the Clarendon number. "Hello, is this Mr. Donald Tupper?" I asked.

"No, this is Clarence Tupper, Donald's father. Can I help you?"

"I think I'd better speak to him, sir. Is he around?"

"As a matter of fact he's down in New York for a couple of days, seeing about getting some distribution for our wine. But if you want to put in an order or something. I can take it down, Mr. —?"

"Morrison," I said. "But that's not why I called. You certainly know what happened to Professor Beasley, since he did all those ads for you, and I'd like to speak to your son about that."

"Huh. Thought they fingered Florene Beasley for that. What do you need to speak to Donald for?"

"The thing is, Mrs. Beasley has asked me to do a little investigating on her behalf. It's not at all clear that she's guilty of anything, and talking with your son about her husband would help us get to the bottom of things."

"Hey, now I remember. You're that retired cop asking lots of questions around town." The tone was a tad chillier.

"Well . . . you might put it that way. Or you might say I'm trying to help someone who needs help right now."

"Uh huh. Donnie can't help you, mister. He wouldn't know anything about it."

"I'm sure you're right, Mr. Tupper, but since he had a business arrangement with Beasley, he might be able to give me some useful information. I mean, I know he's been down to the Beasley place, and he might have seen something. Even without knowing it was important. Can you tell me when you expect him back?"

"He'll be back when he gets back. That's all I can tell you, except that he didn't see nothing. Won't do you a damn bit of good to talk to him. Let the boy be." The old guy hung up on me.

I turned and looked at Harriet. "Trouble?" she asked, and after I had filled her in on how Clarence had stonewalled me, she added, "It sounds like he thinks his boy needs protecting."

"It does. Or maybe he *knows* his boy needs protecting. I'll call again day after tomorrow, see if I can get young Tupper. He ought to be back home by then. This is beginning to sound interesting. Meantime, doll, what say you and I get rid of Prince Albert before he takes off again?"

"I look forward to it."

"First thing tomorrow morning?"

"First thing. Roger wilco."

As I walked back to my nest over the garage I heard the phone ringing. I went into high gear and picked it up in time. It was Clarence Tupper.

"Say, there," he said, "strikes me that maybe I was too quick just now. Maybe I can help you before Don gets back. The Beasley woman isn't much to look at, that's for sure, but it's not the plain Janes that cause trouble in this world, right?" He laughed; I didn't.

"Sure thing," I said. "What've you got in mind?"

"Maybe we could meet at Carrie's place? I could fill you in on Beasley. I guess you already know that Don and me took him on board for our advertising. What do you say?"

I said yes. Carrie's place, more properly Carrie Nation's Milk Bar, was the tavern of choice outside the town limits. When the old Middle School was down the road a piece it actually was a milk bar, no alcohol being allowed for sale near a school. One fine day the school moved into a new building across town and the milk bar followed. A tavern took over the empty premises, added "Carrie Nation's" on top of the old milk-bar sign, and opened its swinging doors for business.

Carrie's thrived. It became a hangout for the proprietors and staffs of the local vineyards that were multiplying like rabbits in the valley. The proprietor was shrewd enough to latch onto the growing vogue for wine bars, and the tavern was informally divided into two sections—the wine-bar types to the right, the beer-and-hooch types at the bar and to the left.

Clarence and I made a date for the next evening. He assured me that he'd have a mouthful (as he put it) to tell me, and that some of the other toilers in the vineyards of the devil (if you insist) would probably be there too. They liked to gather to relax, gossip, and bad-mouth each other's output. I could probably meet the bunch of them.

I had the feeling things were going to start to move.

TWENTY-ONE

THE NEXT DAY'S AGENDA was set with la Delavergne in the morning and Clarence Tupper in the evening, and I figured that something would come along and fill in the gap between the two. All I had to do was wait.

We headed out for old Elsie's place bright and early. Our spirits were as high as Prince Albert's were low—and he was traveling in a carrying case borrowed from Henry Hingle, and he liked it not one bit. He swore like a sailor.

"Cool it, boy!" I suggested. "It's home to mother, but take it from an old sinner, you can always disappear again."

The sun was bright and the air was crisp. Harriet put down the car window despite the chill of the morning, and, eyes closed, lifted her face into the wind. Her hair was blown about and she liked it that way. "It tickles," she said. "It's a wonderful day. Let's take time off and spend the money we squeeze out of the old lemon."

"Sure. But we'll be lucky if she settles for enough to buy us each a small cone. Without chocolate sprinkles."

Harriet raised the window and turned toward me. "Seriously, how much do you figure on charging?"

"Hell, I don't know. I'll know it when I do it. And by the way, you crook, I thought we were donating the take to the SPCA."

"Yeah, you're right, copper. But let's celebrate anyway. What the hell. Now, let's see, there's eight bucks for the ad in the weekly, let's say ten dollars for gas, and at twenty a day—God, but you're cheap—how much will that come to?"

"More than she'll pay. Suppose we say we put four days on the job, which comes to eighty bucks. She'll cut it down to forty and we'll settle for fifty. Okay?"

"Gee." Harriet's voice was sad. "Is that all? It hardly seems worth it."

"You can't get blood out of a stone."

"Or money out of a Delavergne, I guess." Her voice was even sadder. She sat slumped in the passenger seat, frowning, thinking. Suddenly my sweet girl sat up straight, turned toward me with her mouth open, but then she closed it again, apparently deciding against letting me in on whatever vile plot she was hatching. She leaned back in her seat. I sneaked a quick look and found an uncomfortably pleased expression settled across her face.

We got to old Elsie's place, and as we walked up the path to the front door, carrying case in hand, the cat bawling its lungs out, I saw a curtain twitch in a downstairs window. I knocked, and no one answered. After the second knock, Harriet and I looked at each other. "I know she's there," I said. "You wait here, and I'll go around back."

In the back, I found the woman who cleaned for Elsie in the garden picking green beans. "Would you please tell Mrs. Delavergne that the people are here with her cat?" I asked.

She straightened up, holding a hand against her back; she was probably as old as Elsie herself. "Poor beast," she muttered to herself. "I'll see if Mrs. D. is in," she added, making the response she certainly had been programmed to give to all visitors.

"In case she doesn't know, tell her she's in. I saw her at the window."

The woman smiled, gave me a what-can-I-do shrug, and went inside. Back in an instant she said, "Mrs. D. says she's lying down with a sick headache. Would you please leave the cat, and she'll settle up with you later."

Harriet caught this last bit, having walked around back to see what the talking was all about. "No," she said, "we will not leave the cat. Please tell the lady she owes Mr. Morrison eighty dollars for his time, eight dollars for the ad in the weekly, and ten dollars for gas. That's a total of ninety-eight dollars."

"She's not gonna like that."

"Tough. Then tell her to come out and discuss it."

"Hey, wait a minute, Harriet," I started to say.

"You stay out of this, Hugh," she instructed. "I handle the books, right?" To the woman she said, "You just tell her that, please."

"My pleasure." She hobbled off, her bandy legs going like pistons. Back in a moment she was smiling eagerly as she explained, "She says she'll give you fifty. That's all she's got on hand." The woman winked broadly. "She says."

"We'll take it," I said.

"No, we will not take it," Harriet said. "Please tell Mrs. Delavergne that we had to take the animal to the SPCA because he was so run down. In fact they said he wasn't too far from starving. And tell her the weekly might be interested in running a story on how an ad in their paper helped find a valuable animal that ran away from home to find a decent meal. They pay for stories like that," Harriet lied. "Maybe the SPCA would be interested in legal action too. Cruelty to animals." She sniffed. "We could look into that. Think you can remember all that?"

"Yeah, but what am I supposed to be, Western Union? Maybe I could get a bicycle and deliver telegrams, running in and out like this."

"People who used to deliver telegrams when I was a girl always got a tip," Harriet explained. "Tell her we'll take eighty, and forget the rest of the expenses."

"Gotcha."

She was back in two minutes bearing a check. It was for seventy-nine dollars. Harriet took it, handed it to me, and smirked in triumph. Then she opened her bag and drew out a five spot. She held it out. "Thanks for your help," she said.

The woman grinned. "It's a pleasure. Anytime." As we walked away, she added, "And I mean that. It's a pleasure!" The last thing we heard was her delighted clucking, mingled with a few outraged roars from Prince Albert himself, though whether this last was a comment on his failure to make time with Victoria or simply disgust at being back in the slammer was something we would never know.

As we neared the car the breeze picked up again, whistling around the house and through the trees. It sounded to me suspiciously like a whistle of near disbelieving admiration, and from the way Harriet was walking, head high and with a happy smile, I think she heard it that way as well, plus the triumphal march from one of those operas she sometimes tries to drag me to.

"Oh, shucks," she said. "I forgot to let her know that the SPCA might be interested in doing a follow-up to make sure the Prince isn't starving to death again."

"Don't worry," I said. "She knows. One tiger can always tell when another is out for blood."

TWENTY-TWO

IN THE CAR Harriet turned toward me. "Hugh, I'd like to drop in on Florene, if that's okay with you. But I want to pick up my camera first."

"Sure. Why? What are you up to now?"

"Nothing, really. But at my bridge game yesterday one of the women was saying how much better Florene was looking these days. Slimming down, and those marks on her face and arms are clearing up. I think, just in case worse comes to worst and she goes on trial, we ought to have some pictures of her looking beat up, before those welts fade away completely. And anyway, I'd be easier in my mind if I could see how she's making out by herself."

We picked up the camera and drove out to Swamp Bottom. Timmy was bending over his front garden as we passed, evidently back from his morning trip to town. I tooted the horn in greeting, and all three of us waved, he with a couple of fresh-killed beets in his hand.

Florene was on her couch when we arrived, eating something. Whatever it was, it must have included an attachment that automatically covered her face with powdered sugar each time she bit down, to the point where she looked ready for a starring role in a Kabuki version of *The Lower Depths*. The two older children were similarly decorated. The house smelled depressingly of children.

"D'ya find him?" she asked.

"Find who?" I inquired, though I was afraid I knew the answer.

"Him!" she said. "The guy killed Al! Who'd you think I meant!" My client was annoyed.

"Not yet."

"I've been borrowing money from my dad, you know, and I need to get that insurance money." She looked hurt, like a child whose faith in the adult world had once again been be-trayed.

"You'll get it," I promised, though without total convic-tion.

"Now, now," Harriet put in. "Don't you two start quarrel-ing."

For a fleeting moment Florene and I were allied. We both looked at Harriet with scorn. I was transported back to child-hood, about to say, as was Florene as well, "I didn't start it; she did!" I sighed instead.

Harriet switched us to another topic. "Florene, dear," she said. "You're looking awfully good these days. Do let me take your picture."

As the woman wiped off her sugared face, I took a closer look myself. She did look good, all things considered. And even thinner.

"Let's go outside where the light is better," Harriet sug-gested, "and leave Mr. Morrison in here for a bit." Florene as-sented, and they were off, leaving me and the kids to eye each other with justifiable distaste.

The oldest one gave me a fish eye. "Ma says you're a cop," he said suspiciously.

"That's right," I answered.

"Yeah? Well, lemme see your gun."

"I don't carry a gun, sonny. You could get hurt with a gun."

Scorn and disbelief flooded the atmosphere. "No gun! What kinda cop're you, no gun! Jeez! You sure you don't have a gun?"

Why do I always end up on the defensive around kids? "Yeah, I'm sure," I said. "And besides, you can't see it, so knock it off, sonny."

My logic may have been a bit wobbly, but he understood, and each of us retired silently to his own corner of the ring.

The ladies came back. There was a smudge on Florene's arm, and another on her forehead. I wondered if they had been playing in the mud. Harriet said to me, "Florene's been telling me about the police, when they were here last. She says they were looking all through the place, going through her husband's desk and the bureau drawers and even the boxes in the closet."

"Do you know what they were looking for?" I asked. "Did they take anything?"

"Nah. They didn't take a thing," Florene said proudly. "I was keeping an eye on them."

Harriet spoke up. "Why don't you tell us what you think they were after? Maybe it'll help Mr. Morrison find out what happened to your husband."

"I don't know what they wanted, but I figured whatever it was it had to be something Al didn't want anybody to have. So it had to be the stuff he hid."

I waited for her to go on. She didn't. My eyes rolled heavenward, seeking help, but I kept my tongue under control. "What did he hide, Florene?" I asked as calmly as I could. "And where is it?"

"I don't know myself what it is." She got shrewd: "And, gee, if I tell you where it is, without I know what it is, how the heck am I supposed to know if I ought to let anybody see it? Answer me that, Mr. Morrison."

Harriet came to the rescue again. Left to my own devices, I might have bopped my client on the snout, helpless young mother or not. "Now, Florene, Mr. Morrison is on your payroll. He's on your side. And if he doesn't find out what happened to your husband he knows he won't be paid." (That wasn't exactly my way of doing business, but I let it go, since the likelihood of there being any profit in this was less than minimal no matter what I came up with.) "So you've got to trust him on this. Besides, I'll be watching things too. And I know what it is to be a mother, just like you, so you can count on me to keep an eye on things."

Florene turned a beady eye on her fellow mother, if I can put it that way. "You're too old to be a mother, Mrs. Lorimer."

I smiled happily; it was Harriet's turn to get tangled up in Florene's logical webs. But she wiggled free like a professional wrestler. "That's true. I'm too old to be a mother. But I used to be a mother. And I remember it very clearly, just like you will when you're older. All right? Now you tell Mr. Morrison about whatever it is your husband kept hidden."

"Well . . ." Florene balanced the pros and cons in her tiny head and came down on the right side. "All right. After the first time the cops were here, when he was here too," she said, pointing at me with a few of her chins, "I figured maybe they'd be back again, so I took Al's secret stuff and you know what I did with it?"

"No," I said dully, "I'll never guess. What did you do with it?"

"I put it in a thermos jug, the one Al used to put his liquor in with ice cubes when he had those lousy parties. Pretty cute, huh?"

"And where's the thermos jug?" I asked. Pulling facts out of Florene was almost as much fun as pulling poison ivy out of a flower bed.

She turned to Harriet. "You sure it's okay to tell him?" For one insane moment I was even sorrier than the kid I didn't have a gun on me. Battle fatigue was canceling out my new-found compassion for the girl.

"It's okay," Harriet said. "I'm here to keep an eye on things."

"I put a piece of rope around it and tied it to a stone, and I dropped it in the pond. There's one spot that was deep enough to cover it, and it's getting deeper every day, practically. C'mon. I'll show ya."

Out back she pointed to a stone about four feet into the muddy pond, just barely visible beneath the surface. "See that? That stone's on top of the jug. Pretty smart, huh?"

"Pretty smart," I agreed, "but how are we supposed to get it?"

She shifted pronouns on me. "We aren't going to get a damn thing. You are. You can wade out and pick it up." She caught the look on my face. "All right, I'm sorry, but there wasn't that much water in the pond when I set it out. It was only maybe a foot from the edge then. I can't help it if the pond's filling up, can I?" She looked at me as if she were about to cry. "Gee," she said, "sometimes it seems like everything I try goes wrong. I can't help it, Mr. Morrison, honest I can't."

Harriet stepped in all brusque and businesslike. "I'll hold your shoes and socks, Hugh, and for heaven's sake, roll up your pants."

I obeyed and waded in. Somehow I knew that fate intended me to end up as either Laurel or Hardy or both, and I did, stepping into a hole that brought the water up over my knees. My trousers, which, after all, can only be rolled up so far, soaked up the muck as effectively as an expensive bath towel. I fished out the stone, and the thermos followed on the end of a piece of rope, an exercise that splattered my upper half as richly as my trouser legs.

Marching out of the pond I stomped over to the car, managing to keep my bare feet off many sharp stones and onto many others. I threw the thermos into the back and climbed into the driver's seat. "I'm going home," I announced to Harriet and the world, "I'm leaving. If you want a lift, get in."

"Hey, ain't you gonna open that thing?" Florene demanded, tears forgotten.

"No," I answered, "not until I get my penicillin shots."

Harriet scurried over and jumped into the passenger seat. I thought she was a little scared of me, but after we got on the road she asked, "Didn't your mother ever speak to you about playing in the mud?"

I stepped on the gas by way of expressing my rage, and made it home in a breakneck burst of speed, probably exceeding forty-five miles per hour.

BACK IN THE peace and quiet of my little apartment, I showered and put on clean clothes. Then I dragged my sodden garments down to the line behind Harriet's and hung them up without trying to get the mud off first. I knew it would be easier to brush them off after the muck had dried and turned to powdery dirt, but the main reason for putting them on display was so that the woman would see those filthy rags in all their glory. I wanted her suffused with guilt every time she looked out a back window.

I made coffee. Instant coffee, which I hate, but I needed something warm to fend off whatever bacterial disaster was lurking after that watery immersion. Seated at my desk, I opened the thermos. I sipped the coffee, looked at it in disbelief, got up, tossed it out, and poured myself a straight bourbon. (In my book, Scotch is for pleasure, bourbon for medicinal purposes.)

At the desk once again I drew out the contents of the thermos jug. There was one sealed envelope and a small ring-binder notebook, about five by seven, rolled up and squeezed inside the jug. Instead of opening them right off I let my better, if more foolish, nature triumph: I buzzed Harriet and invited her over for the denouement. After all, she was the one who dragged some sense out of the monster queen of Swamp Bottom.

We settled side by side on the couch. "Which do you want to open?" I asked. "You pick one and I'll take the other."

"I want the sealed envelope," she said without hesitating. "It looks more exciting. You take the notebook."

The envelope was what I wanted too—but always the gentleman, I handed it over. Harriet ripped it open and drew out the contents. We looked at each other. She handed half to me and we both started counting.

It came to twelve hundred smackers, all in hundreds.

"Well, I'll be darned," I said. "Let's see if the notebook explains any of this."

It did and it didn't. Beasley had been keeping accounts, but in a way that would have driven a real accountant up the wall. Only a few entries were dated. It looked like the mess I used to make (for about five days each time) when some fool magazine article insisted that I could manage my money better if I kept records, which was a lie. There were four columns headed CASH, CASH OUT, BALANCE, and BALANCE OWED. No numbers in any column were higher than eight, and most were smaller.

"What the devil," I said, "he can't have been keeping track of bills for a candy-store account. These must all be in hundreds or maybe thousands, whatever they are."

"Hundreds," Harriet announced. "Look at the last figure under BALANCE. It's a twelve."

"And we've got twelve hundred in the envelope. Beasley's balance. Right. But balance from what?"

Harriet's nature was of a more practical bent than mine. "I don't know. Let's just give it to the girl. Or to her father to dole out to her."

I cocked an eyebrow. "Ever heard of evidence, lady? Think we ought to let the police in on this?"

She didn't have to think. "No. Don't be silly. The police don't need the money. Let them have the book, if you think that's the thing to do, but the money's for the girl."

"We'll talk more about that later. But what's important is what it means. There've been these stories about Beasley and drugs. Drugs for his parties, drugs for Fabian Cribbs, and probably for others that we don't know about. And by the way, let's not forget that Timmy told us the good professor Cribbs, hair liberally cemented to his skull, went down the Swamp Bottom road 'lots of times.' Maybe the BALANCE OWED is what he owes for the drugs—"

"—if it's drugs."

"—and the BALANCE column is what he's taken in from sales, and has left over, you think?"

"Or maybe not from sales. Those figures would be smaller. I doubt that any of his customers would be shelling hundreds at a time for anything. Look, we know that Beasley had these big blasts at his house. He probably bought popularity with free drugs and free love and free drinks. I'm getting dizzy, and if you ask me, I don't think we know what any of this means, or why he kept it hidden."

We ground to a halt. Then I said, "You know what? I think this CASH column is money he got some other way. Maybe something equally as nasty as drugs. And these records don't look like they go back very far, which could mean they're just some shady business he got into fairly recently. No more than a year ago, anyway, and maybe less."

"Where does that leave us?" Harriet asked.

"Nowhere, now that you ask. This is all supposition, any-way." I shook my head. "I'll have to talk to the kid with the orange-spike hair, the campus connection, and see if anything develops."

"This is getting complicated, Hugh. You wanted to speak to Tupper out at the Clarendon winery, too."

"Uh huh. I'm seeing papa Tupper tonight, and then I'll be checking in with the DeWitt Vineyard people."

"Gosh."

"You know, Harriet, you wanted me to take up detecting to keep from rotting away and getting old."

"I know."

"And now, if this starts to get dirty, drugs or even worse, if there is such a thing, it could end up with me not only not getting old, but not even getting older."

"Oh, Hugh. What can I do?"

"I don't know. You might try prayer. Meantime, okay, give the twelve hundred to Weller for Florene; we've got so much to worry about anyway that a slightly illegal transaction isn't going to add very much to the pile."

"Thank you, dear. You're really a good man, Hugh, a real sweetheart."

"Of course. 'My strength is as the strength of ten because my heart is pure,'" I said, quoting some Englishman or somebody else equally unrealistic. "And we'll worry about what my brain is some other time."

I stood to go. "Hey, how'd those Polaroids of the girl turn out? Let's have a look."

"They're fine, Hugh." She sat there.

"Well?" I waited. "How's about a look? If worse comes to worst, her lawyer ought to have them, battered wife being so much in vogue these days."

Harriet didn't move. "That's the idea, sweetie. I'll hang on to them in case we need them." Her fingers wandered guiltily toward her pocketbook.

I waited again. "You're up to something again, aren't you. Okay. Bonnie Parker, let's see those snaps. I know they're in your bag."

She got up. "You were a cop too damn long, Hugh. It's given you a dirty mind. All right," she said, digging in her purse. "Here. Satisfied?"

I looked through half a dozen pictures. "Yeah. These are great. She still bears the scars, God knows. Even looks as if she was plastered with m—" I stopped. "Oh, my God! That girl had mud on her face when you two came back in. Did you maybe just happen a little bit to sort of touch up those blotches just a teeny weeny itty bitty—"

"Never mind the sarcasm. Yes, I did. But all I did was to get things looking like they were when she first walked into your office. It isn't as if I made them seem worse than they were! You're acting as if I was some sort of criminal, Hugh Morrison!"

"You guessed," I said, "and it's time I protected society from you. And," ripping those snaps into pieces, "you from society."

"Yellow belly!"

"That's right. And I may have a sweatshirt made up— 'YELLOW BELLIES DON'T GO TO JAIL' "

I left, carrying with me a strong suspicion that Ms. Lorimer and I wouldn't be talking to each other for a day or two.

TWENTY-THREE

EIGHT O'CLOCK ON THE NOSE, as Clarence Tupper had suggested, I drew into Carrie's parking lot. Business was brisk; at least a dozen other cars were there as well. Entering the bar, I peered through a gloom that was barely penetrated by low-wattage bulbs behind the red-and-purple glass grapes and yellow flowers of pseudo-Tiffany lampshades. Carrie's was, by Appleboro standards, an example of up-to-the-minute chic, though I had once heard a visitor clearly from the big town downstate describe it as deliciously behind the times. Me, I didn't mind it at all, except it was too damn dark. But at least the lights didn't blink or revolve, like they do in the kiddies' hangouts.

Tupper wasn't there. I sat myself at a table, or rather at an artsy barrel for four on the wine drinkers' side and ordered a glass of red. "Anything," I said to the waitress, "as long as it's local." Not that I'd know local from vintage Bulgarian cabernet, but ordering local is politically correct in Appleboro, as well as being cheaper.

I sipped and looked at my watch. Clarence was five minutes late, which I suppose doesn't count. I sipped again and looked up to see Roy Parker, the Beasley neighbor, looking over from a group gathered around the next table. Barrel, I mean.

"Hey," he said. "How're things going?"

"Slowly," I said. "And nowhere. You come here much?"

"Sure do," he told me. "All good wine workers end up at Carrie's. I think I told you I used to be with DeWitt." One of the other faces at the barrel looked up. "This guy, my former boss and fellow wino, Art DeWitt. Artie, say hello to Hugh Morrison, who's looking into the Beasley business for Florene."

"Hello, Hugh Morrison," DeWitt said dully. "Lotsa luck, and take my word for it—don't start looking for motives. Too many of 'em. Prolly find fifteen frigging motives in this room here, I betcha." DeWitt was half sloshed, and his was the slosh variety that got sadder and more passive and mumblier with each successive sip.

"Mind if I give you a call to talk about it?" I asked.

He shrugged. "Sure. Why not?" He raised his glass. "To the late, great Al Beasley," he said, "who will nevermore discover a new and deliciously naughty brew that will gutter your bullet and tickle your fancy. I mean butter your gullet. Wha' the hell."

DeWitt was mocking a Beasley line of talk, and he drew a laugh. One of the crowd asked, "Tickle your fancy *what?* Say, listen, if you gave that guy horsepiss in crystal stemware with a little sugar in it, he wouldn't have known the difference."

"Unless the horse had diabetes," another one said. "Then he would've known."

"Yeah. He'd have liked it better," somebody said.

There was general laughter. Even without my detecting skills I got the idea; Beasley was not much lamented by the local *Copains du Raisin*.

I looked at my watch again. Twenty minutes late was getting to be late. I was on my second glass, and wine gives me a sour stomach when it doesn't give me a headache. Parker left his barrel and came over. "Say, listen, there's something been on my mind since you were over. This isn't the time or place, but I'd like to talk to you about it."

"Terrific. Suppose I come over tomorrow evening, after you're back from work."

"No, not that." He looked uncomfortable. "I'd just as soon we talked without my wife there. Cynthy'd be upset, I think."

"Okay, what say I meet you when you get out of work tomorrow. Maybe you could call your home and say you'll be twenty minutes late. Something like that."

He nodded. "Good. I'll do that." He gave me directions on meeting him, and rejoined his group.

Twenty-three minutes late, a little fellow in blue jeans and a checked shirt came puffing in and squinted through the gloom. He looked the way Tupper sounded on the phone—all bones and no meat, wiry, and with the tensed, flat-bellied stance of a man in his late seventies who insisted on being in his early forties, and the calendar be damned. I waved him over, and he bounced across on the balls of his feet like a bantamweight boxer out to total an opponent. "You Morrison?" he asked, and scarcely waiting for confirmation, he went on to say, "Sorry I'm late. We got a big rush order and I had to handle it myself, what with Donnie down in New York."

"It's okay," I said, even though it wasn't. I hate waiting. "Grab a chair, and let's get to it."

Before we could start, I saw Parker get up, preparing to leave his group. He looked over and said to me, "It's a date then. See you tomorrow." I nodded. "Got a lot to tell you. You'll be interested."

He started out. DeWitt looked up at him. "Hey," DeWitt said, his words slogging bravely through the alcohol, "wha' yuh wanna mess around with the cops for. Wha' yuh want, a medal or something? Jeez, Roy!"

Parker winked in my direction. "Take it easy, Artie," he said to DeWitt, "I'll tell you all about it later." He waved a hand and left.

Turning to Clarence, I explained. "Roy Parker. Beasley's neighbor. He used to work for DeWitt."

"Yeah," Clarence said. "All the wine crowd hangs out here. I know every damn one of them. Buncha bums, you ask me. And you know what, I couldn't point out a one of 'em would have a good word for Beasley."

"So I gathered. But why don't we get to it? You got something you wanted to see me about?"

The man looked down at his glass of wine, pursed his lips, twirled the stem, and got his thoughts in order. "First, lemme tell you about my boy. Why I'm asking you to leave him out of this. Donnie's a high-strung kid, you know what I mean?"

Actually, I didn't know what he meant. The high-strung kid was in his forties—and wasn't I supposed to ask him about a man who had done some work for him? "Listen, Mr. Tupper, I'm not a cop, I'm an ex-cop, and I'm not interested in unstringing your boy or anybody else. I want to talk to anybody who can tell me anything about Beasley that might be useful, and that includes Donald Tupper."

"Hell, I can tell you anything about Beasley that Don can."

"Okay, let's have it."

"First place, nobody liked the son of a bitch. A phoney if there ever was one, didn't know his ass from his elbow about wine but shot off his mouth like a big-time expert."

I looked at the man. "So what else is new? Everybody in town has told me that already."

"They tell you he deals in drugs? Gets these dumb college kids who got more money than brains down to his place? Gets 'em hooked on whatever he's pushing? That's why he got himself knocked off. Some kid's father, I bet."

I doubted that Beasley got anybody hooked from what I'd heard. Old Tupper was gussying up the story to keep me away from his boy. "You saying your boy would have an upset stomach if he told me that instead of you? Come off it. Your son's a pretty big boy, no?"

I could see the muscles standing out in his cheeks. Tupper was furious. Two clenched fists lay on the table, the wine glass between them, and he was staring hard into the glass considering whether to try another line, swing at me, or give up. There was a wild quality to him, and he suddenly looked like the forty-year-old he was trying to be, super macho and dominant, probably adored by the girls so long as they happened to be the type who liked being walked on, just for kicks.

He found the answer in the wine glass, and he opted for trying another line. "Okay, I don't know why I should, but I'll level with you. There's this wife of Donnie's. She's half his age, you know? And Beasley got his hooks into her. Nothing real bad, far as I know, but he was making a play."

"I already know that, my friend," I said, "and I also know that she stayed on the sidelines during those parties of Beasley's. So what? I don't even have to ask your Donnie about that." I'm afraid I emphasized that baby word, 'Donnie,' with just a shade of scorn, which wasn't very bright of me if I was trying to get something out of daddy Tupper. "Anything else you want to say?"

A big theatrical sigh emerged, and the old man became a grieving parent. "Well, I didn't want to say, but... Look, when Donnie—Don—was in his teens he got engaged to this girl. They was both eighteen, but everybody figured it was serious, you know? They was even planning the wedding when they turned twenty and my boy was working with me in my construction business and saving every damned cent. Other kids were smoking, boozing it up, living it up, the movies, parties, trips to New York, and he was staying quiet, working and saving and planning for his girl.''

He raised his hand to signal the waitress, and pointed to his empty glass. ''Well, the upshot was that they both turned twenty and she didn't just back out, oh no, the lousy tart shakes that cute little butt of hers and runs off with this other guy. And you know how rotten young kids can be. Donnie'd go into town and somebody start whistling the wedding march behind his back and there was one thing and another. My boy had this nervous breakdown, is what they said. I'd say he went plain nuts, and small wonder. Wouldn't eat, wouldn't talk, wouldn't leave the house except to buy booze, and then—oh, hell, you know how it goes, he ended up in the psychiatric wing of St. Sebastian's over in Middletown. Three months, he was there.'' He stopped. ''That's it. Now you know. And now he's got his wife again half his age, and I'm plain scared stiff, mister, scared it could happen again.''

''I'm sorry, Tupper,'' I said. ''And believe me, if I should ever have occasion to talk to your son, I won't even think about asking anything about his wife and Beasley.''

''You just don't get it, do you?'' he yelled. ''I don't want you asking him about nothing, you hear? Not about Betty Ann, not about nothing! Goddamn it to hell, you keep your big mouth away from my family, or—'' He choked on his words, picked up his wine glass, and smashed it to the floor. ''Here,'' he said, throwing a ten spot onto the barrel top, ''this is for the wine and the glass. And screw you!'' With that he strode out.

The room was silent.

DeWitt looked blearily interested. ''You fellows have some kinda dishagreement or something maybe? Shun't fight, should play nice.'' And with that he bubbled something between a belch and a giggle and staggered into the men's room.

A newcomer walked through the door; the silence stopped him cold. ''What's with you guys? This some kind of a morgue or what?'' Nobody answered. ''And who did what to old man

Tupper? He come sailing outa here with a rocket up his tail, jumps into his pickup and vavoom! I can still smell the burning rubber.''

Nobody answered. In the dark and quiet of Carrie Nation's Milk Bar we were all too busy listening to Art DeWitt throw up behind the little door featuring a silhouette of a cowboy.

I got up and left.

TWENTY-FOUR

I SET OUT FOR HOME too fast. I was damned mad, as mad as Tupper and with better reason. He had nothing to tell me except that his son Donnie was a sensitive plant and I should stay away. On second thought, maybe he was telling me something, and I decided that a talk with the younger Tupper had just become a high-priority item.

To emphasize my determination I stepped even harder on the accelerator. I rounded a curve and the headlights picked up something small and dark and stirring on the highway. Two eyes close to the ground caught the lights and reflected them back. I hate raccoons, the filthy, destructive beasts, but not enough to mash them with my car, so I jammed on the brakes and leaned on the horn.

The damned thing didn't move. I hopped out and went to look and found myself eye to eye with a half-grown black cat. It mewed, or more precisely it wailed. A hind leg was sticking out at an unreal angle. It had almost surely been hit by a car. I bent over to pick the poor beast up, my back to my own buggy, when it blew.

My car, I mean. It exploded into space and knocked me flat on my face, right on top of the cat. In its terror it dug its claws into my jacket, and in my own terror I clutched the frightened thing in my hands too hard, but as it turned out not so hard as to cause it any extra damage.

Somehow I had enough wit to stagger to the side of the road before sinking to the ground again, the cat and I still hanging on to each other for dear life. The two of us lay there panting until a patrol car drew up. They kept me lying flat until an ambulance made its appearance, but before that they asked me questions.

To all the questions, except for those related to name, address, and general state of mind and body, I answered in assorted variations of "How the hell do I know?" which got us nowhere. Meanwhile I continued to hold the cat, who by now had relaxed sufficiently to unclaw my outerwear and respond favorably to my almost unconscious back stroking and ear scratching. In return, he or she purred reassuringly in my ear. I think we constituted what some fool of a psychologist would call a support group, and we both liked it that way.

An ambulance came and took us both away. (I refused to let the cat go, and somebody got the message that I meant it.) At the hospital I was trundled into the emergency room and a team of doctors and nurses went through the usual dehumanizing procedures of getting my clothes off and poking and prodding my raddled frame. Following that they swabbed a couple of scrapes, gave me a shot of something, called Harriet to pick me up, and announced that in medical terms I had suffered what was known as the mother of all holes in the seat of my pants.

Harriet was greener than I was when she arrived at the hospital. They wheeled me out to her car—hospitals would stick a marble clock in a wheelchair if they had to move one, in order to avoid the possibility of lawsuits—and helped me into the front next to Harriet. You know the seat I mean; it's the one alongside the driver they call the death seat at accident scenes. We drove off.

TWENTY-FIVE

IT WAS CLEAR TO EVERYBODY, the cops, Harriet, and me, that what happened was somehow related to my poking around into Beasley's murder. Somebody wanted to stop me as permanently as could be arranged. It helped take the finger off Florene, and I suppose I could have quit then and there, but I was mad. Besides, it wouldn't exactly without any doubt have restored Florene's good name. (Now *that's* a laugh, Florene's good name.)

From what they could piece together of my poor old car, a bomb had been stuck under the fender with a magnet. Something had been jammed in to avoid activating it until my driving jarred it loose, following which a timing device took over. The theory was that the timing device was in the arrangement so as to make sure that I'd have driven at least a little distance away from the spot where the thing was planted, just to make it tougher for anyone to figure out the who, what, when, and where of it all. When I slammed my foot on the brake, the jamming gizmo took off, and I was damn near wafted skyward without benefit of clergy. All while I was studying the puss—BOOM!

Naturally, I decided to keep my good-luck cat. I named him Lucky Jim, later amended to Lucky Jane, but that's another, more pleasant story.

There was my fight with Clarence Tupper. The cops wanted to talk about that. Did that make him a suspect? Hell, no, I explained. "First place, after he decided I was not his favorite private eye, somebody saw him tearing out and jumping right into his pickup. He didn't have a chance to monkey around with the car. Second place, you think he'd bring along his Louis Vuitton suitcase full of bombs in case he needed one? Besides, that thing could've been set earlier in the day. The day before. What the hell, *two* days before."

So who? they asked me.

That was easy, I told them. "Beasley's murderer."

"Oh," they said, and they went away.

I spent the next day in bed, stiff and achy. Harriet was sweet enough to drive down to the mall and pick up a covered litter box for Lucky Jim, plus a starter bag of deodorizing litter. Jim and I expressed our delight, I by saying so, Jim by initiating the facility.

The next thing I knew I got a call from Mr. Elroy Parker, whom I had clean forgotten about.

"Listen," he said, "I'm awful sorry about what happened. Anything I can do?"

"Yeah, as long as I'm stuck here at home, why not drop around and let me know what you wanted to see me about. You can tell your wife you're off on an errand of mercy."

There was a pause. "That, uh, was something else I wanted to say. It's just as well we didn't get together the other day. I'm sorry, but I've got to call the whole thing off."

"Come on, you know something about Beasley's death, you should let it out."

"I'm sorry. I was wrong. Cynthy and I talked it over and we figured I'd just be making waves and making a fool of myself. It wasn't anything, I promise you."

I was annoyed. Sarcastically, I said, "In the classic words of our times, you mean you don't want to get involved."

He got whiney. "Ah, no. It isn't that. Not at all. The thing is, Cynthy said to me— Oh, all right, I don't want to get involved, if that's the way you want it. I'm sorry for what happened to you, but there's nothing I can do and I was stupid to think I knew anything. Sorry."

The son of a gun hung up. And I had liked the guy. A nice, respectable man, obviously nuts about his kid, trying to make a good home for his family, a solid citizen, and like 87 percent of all solid citizens—he didn't want to get involved. Sorry, he kept saying, sorry.

When a little kid gets beat up by a big one, sometimes he turns around and finds an even smaller one to pound on for himself. I'm a little kid, as many people would agree. I had just been beat up, and I wanted my turn at swatting somebody else.

I didn't know who the bomber was, so old Clarence would have to be my smaller kid. I wanted an eye to spit in, and I wanted it now. I rose from my bed of pain the next morning, kissed Jim goodbye, and drove out to Clarendon, determined to speak to the younger Tupper, just to put his daddy in his place. So there.

There was a pretty young woman in the office with an innocent, attractive face, wearing a not-so-innocent, attractive dress. I pegged her from what Harriet had told me as Betty Ann Tupper. She smiled.

"Mrs. Tupper? My name is Hugh Morrison."

"Oh, I know you, Mr. Morrison. Everybody in town knows you. You're maybe our best-known citizen." She giggled.

Wow. At first glance Betty Ann looked as if she had been elected Apple Festival Queen so often that she had retired the cup. The gray eyes were as wide as a baby's, and here was this hypnotic upper lip, just a tad short, so that it went up and down periodically over dazzling white teeth. Her loose, light brown hair kept tumbling into her eyes and getting itself gracefully brushed back. There was lots of motion about Betty Ann Tupper.

"Why, thank you," I said. "I wonder if your husband is available. I'd like to see him about a case I'm working on."

"You mean about poor Florene? I *told* you you were famous! I'll go get Don. Meanwhile, you can try this year's Cabernet Franc. It is really somethin' else!" She put a plastic glass on the counter and poured. Bent over, she favored me with a view down her dress. It was dark down there, but I could see land: I felt like Columbus, even if it wasn't exactly virgin territory that lay ahead.

At second blush, and the blush was mine, maybe she wasn't Apple Festival Queen material. Maybe she was a Marilyn Monroe variant working on a milkmaid role, only a milkmaid who kept her cows somewhere off Broadway in the Seventies, and mixed one part milk to four parts rum punch in her milk pail. I could see why Beasley needed her to grace his tea parties. Those shiny teeth were sending semaphore signals every time that upper lip was raised or lowered. It was hard to say what the message was, but a boy of ten would have known it was there. I wondered if life was entirely comfortable for a husband almost twice her age.

She smiled again. "Now you set quiet and I'll be back in two shakes." Turning around, she exited the premises, shaking many times more than twice. Harriet had promised me the girl's behavior was only an innocent effort to please her ma and pa, but you could have fooled me.

I sipped the wine. By my standards it was good. It tasted one way in the front of my mouth and another way in back, and it reminded me a little bit of cinnamon. And it left my mouth a little puckered, though without any sense of vinegar. I guess that made it good. I looked at the bottle: Clarendon Vineyards, 1992 Cabernet Franc. I poured another couple of swallows and naturally the girl returned with her husband to catch me in the act.

With as much of a debonair manner as I could muster, I announced, "This is darned good stuff."

"Glad you like it. We think it's pretty good too. I'm Don Tupper." He extended a hand. About twenty years older than his wife, Tupper was a good-looking guy with a clean, youthful chin line that made me wonder (jealously) if he patted it with astringents and wore a chin strap at night. The only giveaway that made me think he might be aware of the difference in their ages was his belt. It was pulled in at least two notches too many, straining toward a waistline befitting one of his wife's contemporaries. Visions of Scarlett O'Hara shoveled into a tiny corset by a platoon of sweating slaves came to mind.

Enough of elderly jealousy, the man was younger than me and he was good-looking, but I really had nothing against him. Nothing else against him, that is.

"I guess you're here about Al Beasley," he said, and I nodded. "It's a damn shame. How's his wife making out?"

"Not too badly."

He raised a cynical eyebrow. "You mean she's probably better off, right?"

I shrugged; when you're investigating, you don't take sides, don't commit yourself. "You might say that."

"I will. The man was a slime ball."

"Is that right? Wasn't he sort of a local spokesman for your outfit?"

"Sure, but that doesn't mean I had to like him. And he didn't know very much about wine. Not really. But he was a good man with the words. Listen, Mr. Morrison, anytime you hear a critic talk about 'a witty wine,' you can bet your ass you're dealing with a phoney."

Betty Ann giggled. "Don!" she protested. "Watch your tongue."

Tupper reached over and tousled her hair. "It's okay, hon. Anyway, I'd rather watch yours." Betty Ann giggled again and looked shy. But pleased.

"How come you used him then, if he didn't know what he was talking about?"

"Well, let me explain. Let me pour you another glass and then we'll go through it."

"My pleasure."

"Until this last year, we were pretty much of a very local operation. Nobody more than thirty miles away had ever heard of us or seen Clarendon wines in the liquor stores. And Beasley had a reputation for knowing wine."

"How'd he get it?" I asked.

"I'll tell you," Tupper said, pouring a couple of inches for himself, "but in a roundabout way. Before I started this operation I worked for, oh, less than a year in the personnel office of this textile sales operation down in Westchester. We'd get new MBA's come in job hunting, and I'd peg them at being worth maybe twenty-five, thirty thousand a year, and they'd say they wanted forty thousand to start, and I'd say to them to have a nice day and thanks but no thanks and they'd leave. Then damned if I wouldn't hear a month later that somebody had taken them on at fifty thousand."

He leaned forward. "The moral is, Mr. Morrison, if you say something often enough, loud enough, fast enough, and with enough conviction, sooner or later, if you've got any style at all, some fool is going to start to believe you." He sat back. "And Beasley had style. I've got to hand him that. He could talk about that witty wine in a way that got people to believe that if they couldn't see the wit in a glass of wet, red alcohol the fault was theirs. DeWitt down at DeWitt Vineyards found that out first, before we did. I guess you know Beasley used to front for them before he came to us."

"Yeah, and that was something I wanted to ask—"

The door opened and in came daddy Clarence. "Don," he said, "those guys loading the trucks are getting nowhere. I could—" He spotted me. "Oh," he said, "it's you." He was underwhelmed with enthusiasm.

"You guessed," I said. "It's me." The younger Tupper was puzzled. I explained. "Your father and I met a few days ago for a talk about Beasley."

"That's right," Clarence said. "I told him you were too busy for interviews, Don. Lot of nonsense. Now about those guys loading up, I figure I can load ten cases in the truck for every one those bums heft, and—"

"No, Dad, damnit! You know what the doctor said. No lifting!"

"But they don't know what the hell they're doing. I can carry them better!"

The son slammed his hand down in exasperation. "How, Dad? How? In your mouth?"

They both looked crestfallen. "I'm sorry, Dad," the son said.

"That's all right, son. I was out of line." Old Clarence sagged into a chair. "Sorry I interrupted."

I got back to the point. "You been down to the Beasley place recently?" I asked the son.

He gave a mock shudder. "God, no! Not in months. I'd just as soon visit the monkey house at the zoo."

"You sure? I heard tell you were there just a couple of weeks ago."

"No, that's not so. Why would I— Oh, wait up. Beasley was late with the copy for the ad awhile back, and the man wasn't the most reliable, so I went over to drag it out of him. I don't think I was there more than ten minutes; that was about as long as I could've kept breathing through my mouth without gagging. How'd you know?"

"Timmy Young told me Mr. Tupper had been down to Swamp Bottom."

"Timmy Young? The kid that lives where the road to Swamp Bottom turns off the highway?"

"That's the Timmy Young I mean. Doesn't miss a trick."

"I'll be damned. That's how it goes in a small town, isn't it; scratch your behind on Main Street at three in the morning and somebody'll spread the word you've got fleas."

"Don!" Betty Ann protested.

"Place is full of snoopers," Clarence announced, having recovered enough to remember he didn't like me. "Don, I'll be outside if you need me." He turned a cold eye on me; it looked like a clam. Then he left.

"I'm sorry about my dad," Tupper said. "He's not generally like that with strangers."

"Forget it," I said. "Me snooping around, it's natural. I get it all the time."

"You see, he had his construction company, worked all the heavy machinery like a man of thirty, until two years ago when he had his heart attack. Had to give it up. Doctor's order." Tupper shook his head. "He shouldn't feel useless, but I'm afraid he does, and it gripes him. He still keeps his trucks and things in a barn down the road, thinks he's going back to work soon, knows he really isn't, and it eats at him."

"No need to explain. One other thing and I'll let you be. Beasley used to work for DeWitt wines, didn't he? I hear that after they went bad he only needed enough time to put his car in reverse before he scooted over here. That right?"

He nodded. "That's it. I was uncomfortable about taking him on, but what the hell, something happened with DeWitt and they were on the skids anyway. Beasley moving to us didn't add a thing to their troubles, I promise you. No more than getting stung on the arm by a horsefly after a copperhead has already stuck your leg."

"You have any idea what went on over there? I mean, is it usual for something good to turn into something bad like overnight?"

Tupper worked his hand back and forth, palm up, palm down. "It's not that simple. You get great wines one year, so-so-ones the next. We've got a rough climate upstate here."

"Uh huh. But to go from the best to the worst practically overnight?"

"That's the problem. On the whole, it doesn't sound right. Something must have gone very wrong, and I don't understand it."

"Could it have been done by sabotaging the stuff in the barrels?"

"Hey, wait up. You're not suggesting that I would—"

"Not at all. But is it possible?"

"Listen, man, you've got me up a tree. Yes, it's possible. No, I couldn't say what might have happened. I don't know. And don't push me further, Mr. Morrison. That's honestly all I can tell you. Whatever happened to the DeWitt wines is very strange but that's as far as I can go." Tupper was annoyed and flustered in equal parts.

"That's far enough for me," I said, "and thanks for your time." I turned to Betty Ann. "Good to meet you, Mrs. Tupper."

She smiled, either sweetly or seductively or somewhere in between—maybe that was her secret. She held her husband's arm close and leaned on his shoulder. As I was leaving, she was rubbing her cheek along his shoulder. Betty Ann pussycat.

I turned back. "Oh, hey, I forgot. Mrs. Tupper, did you yourself know Beasley? I mean outside of seeing him around your shop here."

Betty Ann blushed and let her hubby do the talking for her. He laughed. "Come on, Morrison, you forgot nothing. I'd bet a case of my best against a bottle of Bud that you know Betty Ann went to one of the man's parties down to Swamp Bottom. She told me all about it."

"I only went to be polite," Betty Ann squeaked timidly. "I left soon as I got an eyeful of what was going on."

"That's right," Tupper finished, "and she was crying when she told me. I could have killed the—" He laughed. "So to speak, right?"

"Uh huh," I said. "Thanks for your time." I slunk out, bested at my own game. I was still wondering about one other thing: Young Donnie didn't strike me as the sensitive bloom his daddy had projected. Was he, or wasn't he? And what difference did it make? It was, as some Oriental potentate once observed, a puzzlement.

Outside, old Clarence was hanging around waiting for me. "Hey, Morrison," he said, "hold on a minute, okay?"

I nodded.

"I want to apologize for being such an old fool. Maybe you can give me a lift down to the barn and I can tell you about it."

"My pleasure." Maybe he would tell me something useful for a change. We got in the car and started up.

He was quiet for a moment and then said, "You ever hear of Tupper Construction? Used to be pretty big around here."

"Oh, sure," I lied. "Didn't you put up a lot of the houses that went up around here in the eighties?"

"That's me. And in the fifties, sixties, and seventies too."

"Yeah, sure, I heard of you. Why?"

"Well, I'm temporarily sidelined and it makes me a tad snappish sometimes. No real function when you get old if you work with your back." He looked at me. "You're lucky. You work with your head and that can go on until a fellow drops."

"I guess. You figure on going back to work one day?"

"Damn right." A large red barn came into sight. "That's where I've got my stuff, all rarin' to go. Come on in and take a look."

"Great."

I drew up and we went inside. There were a couple of trucks and some attachments I supposed could be hooked up as needed. There was a crane and a shovel and a plow and a flatbed, and the strange thing was that everything was as shiny as the day it was bought. I was impressed and must have looked it.

"There it is," he said, "just waiting for me." He patted a door and he kicked a tire. A lump of clay tumbled from beneath the fender. "I run 'em regular, keep 'em in shape. They've been settin' here useless a couple of years waiting to get back on the road, just like me. Anyway, that's why I get so testy, checking off the months and the years like hatch marks on the wall—one, two, three, four, five; one, two, three, four, five."

He grew pensive. "I guess these are the babies I got left; now that Donnie's grown, he don't need me anymore. Hey!" he said with a grin, "how do you think old Reverend Hooten would take it if I showed up for burial in my backhoe one fine day? Like those old Egyptians taking their toys into the grave with them. Think he'd shit a brick?"

"Two," I said. "At least two." Then I added, "Look, we all know about getting old. I say I'm a private cop and some people—I can see it in their eyes—they're wondering if I came up against some young nut, how long would it take me to lay down and roll over. That's the way it goes." That wasn't exactly the way it goes, but if it made old Clarence feel better as well as encouraging him to open up a little more, what the hell's the difference?

He relaxed. "Well, thanks. I appreciate that. The young have no idea what it's like. I won't keep you back no longer. Only wanted you to know why I get so darned testy with people. You go ahead."

"I understand. Drive you back to the house?"

"No, thanks. I'll walk. The doctor bastards say I need the exercise." He laughed, not happily. "Exercise, they call it, shuffling down the road like a useless old fart. But you wait; next year this time you'll see the Tupper Construction signs going up again all over Appleboro." He hesitated. "And, uh, by the way, if I was you I wouldn't take too serious anything Timmy Young says about seeing anybody going down to Swamp Bottom. He's a nice kid, real nice kid, but what the heck, he's, you know, kind of off center. Not reliable. You know what I mean?"

"Sure thing. Don't you worry about it." There he went again, the poor guy, protecting his infant son. "And listen, I'll have my eyes peeled for those Tupper Construction signs."

I drove off, sad for Clarence, glad for myself, and convinced I had learned something on this trip if I could only figure out what it was. Did it have to do with Don Tupper saying he hadn't been down to Beasley's in months until I told him I knew better? And was he really all that relaxed about the child bride hanging out with the bad boys? Was it something the old man had told me? And why was it, by the way, that he was so concerned about Timmy placing son Donnie down the Swamp Bottom road that he had to remind me that Timmy wasn't the brightest? Or was it the way Betty Ann Tupper came on like an innocent maid of vast experience?

I scratched my head in wonder and hit a spot still sore from the bombing, so I stopped wondering and drove off.

TWENTY-SIX

BACK IN THE OFFICE I buzzed Harriet. "Hey, babe, have you passed on that twelve hundred bucks to Florene's pop?"

"No, I spent it all on pinups of Cary Grant. Of course I passed it on, Hugh. What did you think?"

"Sometimes I don't know what I think. Just checking, no need to get into an uproar. I wanted to be sure the money was off the premises before I called Pinky and told the boys what we found in Swamp Bottom." I could sense the righteous indignation subsiding, even over the phone.

"Oh. Well, yes, I brought it over to the Wellers this morning. I think they're finding it rough financing Florene and the kids on his income. Not to mention shoveling money down some lawyer's bottomless maw. She cried a little; he looked stunned. How'd it go with Don Tupper?"

"Tell you later. Right now I'd better call Pinky. See you later."

I called the station and got my man. "Pinko," I said, "how's business? Kidney punch any crippled newsies lately?"

"Nah. That's for late afternoon, when I need to get up from the desk and stretch. What's up?"

"Just a social call. I understand you were out to the Beasley place and tore it apart. You want to tell me about it?"

"Not particularly. Should I?"

Whether or not Pinky and I were on a buddy-buddy basis, I was still an ex-cop, not a cop, and he was clammed up until he knew what I was fishing for. I sensed I had a likely clam shucker at hand, so I tried. "Maybe. I though I might help. Private citizen cooperating with our boys on the force, that sort of stuff."

"If more people were like you, sir, the job of the police would be much easier. Your story has touched my heart. I have tears in my eyes. What've you got?"

"Nothing much, but if you were looking for some kind of financial records, I might be able to help."

He sobered up. "Listen, Hugh, you know we figure we've got a good case going against Florene. Yeah, yeah," he said in reaction to my snort, "I know somebody tried to blow you up, but a private snoop could have practically a fan club lining up to help him to that great reward in the sky. Could be lotsa people, no?"

"No," I said.

"Sorry I asked. But seriously, most of the guys down here know Florene. What the hell, some of them even went to school with her and we're open for anything that could help. Like maybe Beasley over his head in something involving dirty money. I'll tell you, his bank account has more ups and downs than a roller coaster, not what you'd expect with a school teacher. If you've got something, come on over. Can you make it now?"

I thought a moment. I hadn't had lunch yet. My stomach voiced its disapproval. "I'll be there in ten minutes."

The sacrifices I make for a client.

I FLIPPED BEASLEY'S cryptic records onto Pinky's desk. "Here it is, Pinko," I said. "All of it, for what it's worth." All of it, that is, except for the twelve hundred smackers I had let Harriet purloin in a worthy cause. The thought flickered past my mind that I might get a light sentence myself if I squealed on the woman. Was twelve hundred grand larceny or only petit? I couldn't remember.

I sat down next to Pinky and watched him look through. The red hair that had provided his nickname was mostly gray, and I reflected that he'd be joining me on the sidelines before very long. However, the name we'd hung on him so many years ago was still appropriate; if his hair wasn't the right color, his nose and cheeks, urged on by a heroic dedication to beer, were rapidly making up the difference. "You make anything of this?" he asked.

I told him what Harriet and I had been thinking.

"Yeah," he said. "Reason we were out there was like I said, his bank account going up and down like a yo-yo, and we wanted to know why. No use asking Florene, so we looked around for ourselves." He looked at me. "How'd you turn this up?"

"Well," I said, "there was this course I took. In the police academy. You know? It was called Detecting One-Oh-One, as I recall."

"Very funny. Now tell me."

"Oh, hell, I asked Florene. You should have tried it. God knows she's not bright, but she's not soft in the filbert, either. In fact, I'm beginning to like the girl. A little, anyway."

"Uh huh. Well, thanks, old buddy. I don't know what this is, but we owe you one. Keep in touch."

I sat quietly. So did Pinky. Then I said, "So you owe me one, gimme one."

He blew a breath out, which, it still being before his lunch, was amazingly beer free. "You're a hard man, Morrison. Okay, for what it's worth, Beasley had a lady friend over in Middletown."

"Surprise, surprise," I said. "That only figures, a creep like that. So what?"

"So what is how she came looking for him because she says they were engaged. She says they were set to get married in the spring. She says he said he was getting divorced. According to her, Beasley said Florene was a junky and he was getting out. She said, he said. What the hell."

"No kidding! Any chance she could have decided she was getting a snow job and got mad enough to do something?"

"Don't know. This one's a lady type. A school teacher like Beasley, only middle-school level. Thirty-fivish. Nice looking. No Florene. As a matter of fact, she went looking for her boyfriend out in Swamp Bottom. She had his address, and all she found was Florene." He looked happy. "Boy, what a scene that must have been. Then she came here."

"She saw Florene? I'll be damned! Florene never told me that."

"Uh huh. I bet you didn't ask her, did you? Maybe you shoulda hung around for Detecting One-Oh-Two, buddy."

"Okay, we're even. Look, any other statistics? Like name and address?"

He looked at me hard. "If you was anybody else...I shouldn't do this, Hugh." But he did, and on a little piece of paper: Mildred Saddler, with a street address in Middletown. "Remember, if you get in touch with her, you didn't get this from me."

"Never heard of you, Pink, I promise."

"Okay. If you turn up anything, we want it, you hear?"

"I hear." I left.

Back home I grabbed a bite of lunch. Starting at the bottom and working up, there was bread, mustard, pastrami, lettuce, bread, swiss, ham, tomato, mayo, bread. It looked too thick. I thought about taking the lettuce out, but decided healthwise that was a bad idea. Beer. Two cans. I'm a junky too, when I feel the need, and I felt the need. I didn't think the Middletown connection would have had any hand in the death and transfiguration of Alfred Beasley, but I knew I had to talk to her anyway. And then there was still DeWitt at DeWitt Vineyards to see, not to mention the orange-spike pusher. Too many potential suspects for one tired old ex-cop to juggle, especially when it could still turn out that his client was the guilty one. Finding lost pussycats, even for Elsie Delavergne, began to seem like heaven.

I did what any sensible senior citizen would do under the circumstances. I took a nap. First I pulled down the shade on the office window that faces Harriet's place. That was the "do not disturb" signal she and I had worked out. I mean, what the heck, we're pretty close, but we don't live in each other's pockets, and every kid needs a private sandbox to play in all by himself, at least once in a while.

I got up about five and showered. Then I poured a comforting double slug of Scotch on a couple of ice cubes, splashed it with a sixteenth of an inch of water so I wouldn't become an alcoholic, and popped open a can of peanuts. With some old show tunes on the turntable from the days when I was a new-lywed, I was able to relax. Gershwin, Rodgers, Kern—I guess for everybody the best music is the stuff that was around during his courting days.

At long last, my nerves quieted and the pain between my shoulder blades diminished, I went out and drove to a steak house down toward Newburgh for my next fix of the evening. Another drink, shrimp cocktail, double pork chop, baked potato (I asked for the sour cream and chives but helped it along with two pats of butter as well), string beans. Salad with blue-cheese dressing. Seconds on the hot biscuits. Apple pie with two scoops. Vanilla, because I'm basically very conservative. Coffee, real coffee and not the cancer-producing kind they muck around with so you can sleep, and sugar and cream. Real cream.

Home again I slept the sleep of the well filled, the fulfilled, the innocent, and the overweight.

TWENTY-SEVEN

IN THE MORNING I paid for my culinary sins. I woke up thinking, fool that I was, that I was refreshed, rejuvenated, and rededicated, but the phone rang. I ran in from the bathroom, face fully lathered and towel in hand. It was Harriet.

"Have you heard the news?" she asked. "On the radio?"

"Just got up. What happened, the Democrats in Congress pass a law against family values?"

"Be serious. They said that Elroy Parker of Appleboro was shot to death by an unknown assailant last night as he was driving home from work."

It took me fifteen seconds to absorb the words, including rejecting the possibility that there could be two Elroy Parkers in Appleboro. I wiped the shaving cream off with the towel and sat heavily in the desk chair. "Did they say anything else?"

"Only that his wife and family are in seclusion, and that at this time the police are investigating but have no leads. It happened out on the main road, before he made the turn to Swamp Bottom."

"I wonder if Timmy—"

"No, I thought of that, but from what they said, it must have been in that empty stretch about a quarter of a mile from the turn off."

"Damn," I said. I thought of Parker and his wife and kid. What the hell was I up to? How much blame for what had happened to this man, this family, fell on me? Sure, Beasley was dead, but nothing could be done about that, and if I hadn't stuck my nose in, maybe the Parkers would still be one happy, hopeful, loving little threesome. Thoughts like this come to every cop sooner or later, and the only thing to do is to push them aside, do what you have to do, don't think too much. But that doesn't mean I had to like it.

"Damn," I repeated. "Harriet, let me finish getting dressed and I'll be right over. I'll bring my bagel; you got an extra cup of coffee?"

She did, and in ten minutes I was at her kitchen table, chewing on a bagel and gulping on scalding coffee.

"I liked that boy," I said. "He was one of the good ones. Decent, wife and kids, nice home. Hell, I wish he'd talked to me. I'm sure he knew something important."

"Who knew he made a date to see you, Hugh?"

"At the bare minimum, everybody in Carrie Nation's bar. Everybody in the wine business in Appleboro and beyond. And there wasn't any secret about it; he could've told other people as well. People with information in a murder case can get excited, feel important, want to let others know."

Harriet frowned, and pushed her lower lip out, deciding to point a finger at somebody even though it went against her nature. "You were sitting with Clarence Tupper then, weren't you? And wasn't he raving mad about something?"

I agreed, but added, "If Parker had wanted to implicate Clarence Tupper even in the least, I doubt he'd have been so open about getting together with me right in front of the man." Another thought hit me. "And, you know, this doesn't look too good for Florene, either. If she had killed her old man, she could have figured that Elroy Parker, living next door, had seen something. Maybe she knew he was going to meet with me. What the hell! I don't really think so, but we've got to consider the possibility. God knows, the cops will."

I mumbled on. "What I've got to do is talk to Cynthia Parker. She made Elroy break his date with me. Was it just the 'don't get involved' syndrome, or was she afraid of something else? Now's no time to do it, though. We've got to give her a little time; she's got enough on her tray, and anyway, the police get first dibs at speaking to her."

I licked a small dab of margarine off my finger, and said, "So what we do now is go ahead with the agenda as it was before this happened, and see about Cynthia Parker later."

"What can I do now? I've got to help."

"Of course. I need you to help. First I'll fill you in on the latest." I told her about Beasley's Middletown tootsie and how he had assured her that Florene was hooked on drugs and that he was signing off on the marriage. And then I told her about Florene grinning like she was up to the kazoo in hot fudge when she said to me that she was going to collect insurance on Beasley rather than the other way around, the way he had planned it. "The way he had planned it, Harriet. You get that? We've still got to act as if Florene is everybody's favorite suspect, and if he took out a big policy on her life, we may be able to build up a case of self-defense for the girl."

"I hate talking like that, but I suppose you're right. What do you want me to do?"

"First thing, can you get yourself out there and see if you can find a policy on her life in his favor somewhere on the premises? It isn't absolutely necessary, because the insurance company would have its own records, but we ought to get a look at it soon as possible."

"You think she might have hidden it around the house?"

"Who knows? If it's tucked in that monumental bazoom you might need a search party to track it down, but give it a whirl anyway. After that, get that no-good lawyer of hers on the ball. Have him get a proper kind of doctor who can give her tests for drugs and who can testify that she's clean, if it comes to that."

"What kind of drugs?"

"Anything. Everything. What the hell, Florene could've been grazing on locoweed out in the fields for all we know. But I don't think they'll find anything."

"Hasn't too much time gone by since Beasley's death?"

"Unh unh. If she was really hooked, she'd still be using. And they'd still find it."

"Okay. What are you going to be up to while I'm out there?"

"I'm off to the school to give oral examinations to a couple of professors, see if Beasley bad-mouthed Florene to anybody else besides his girlfriend. See you back home by eleven or twelve and we'll compare notes."

I was on campus before nine. It's been my experience that the last place you can ever find a teacher after the day gets going is in his office. Get there early, or else they'll be off giving lectures, attending meetings, doing library research, or having lunch. But before nine, unless they zoom right into the classroom with the toothpaste still drying in the corners of their mouths, you can nail them either reviewing their notes, shuddering over coffee in the cup the departmental secretary gave them for Christmas, or else just shuddering.

Fabian Cribbs, in the last category, just shuddering, was at his desk. I think his eyes were rolled back in his head and someone had painted fake irises on the eyeballs. The poor guy was no advertisement for a drug habit; he looked as if he might have snagged his nose in an electric pencil sharpener and it had sucked the rest of him in. I should have wondered why he looked worse than the last time I had seen him, which was no mean trick, but foolishly I didn't.

I kept the prologue short: "Dr. Cribbs. It's me again. Hugh Morrison. I have to ask you, did Professor Beasley ever say anything to you about his wife having a habit, that she was hooked on drugs?"

One of the painted eyeballs tried focusing and failed. "Why, no. Why would he? After all, we were scarcely close friends, you know. Just professional colleagues." He had an afterthought: "And that's a terrible thing for you to suggest."

"You telling me the subject of drugs never came up?"

"That's indeed what I'm telling you." He tried a little humor. "Except of course if we were talking of English literature. De Quincey, Coleridge, and the effect of opiates on their literary output." He smiled; I think the sudden movement of facial muscles intensified his headache. He touched his forehead, very lightly. "Why ever would we speak of such things otherwise?"

"Look, Fabian." (If you're police you learn that slipping into their first names puts them down, scares them without their knowing why.) "You and I both know pretty well why you two ever would speak of such things, as you put it, and I haven't got the time to waltz around, I don't give a damn what you do, what you got from Beasley, or what you're doing to get it now, but I need to know what he said to you about his wife, Florene."

"But I assure you—"

"And I assure you. You cooperate with me and I forget anything I know. But otherwise, maybe I'll remember I used to be a cop and I'll do my civic duty." I shook my head. "All these impressionable young students. A teacher should set an example, don't you think?"

I waited, and he thought. "I don't want to be dragged into anything." His voice grew weak. "I can't afford it." He squeaked. "Can you keep me out of anything that might develop?"

"I don't think anything at all is going to develop. If it should, your only part will be to tell what, if anything, Beasley mentioned about his wife. Just two colleagues talking things over. Him concerned about things at home. That's all."

"Well . . . he did mention that the poor woman had a terrible habit and that it was bleeding him dry. That's why he was forced to, ah, push drugs himself." He looked up at me, doleful as a basset hound.

"You can leave out that last about him pushing drugs. No need to tangle yourself up in that." He looked relieved. "Did he say what she was taking?"

"I didn't ask. I didn't want to know. I didn't want to listen. I swear it."

"That's good enough for me. One other thing and I'm off. I've got this talk of ours on tape," I lied. "The recorder's under my shirt. When this is all over, the tape is yours."

He didn't respond. I got up and turned around to leave. Cribbs got up and came up behind me. He touched me lightly on the arm. "Is it all right?" he asked. His eyes were red and weepy. "Am I going to be all right? I'm at my wit's end, Mr. Morrison. My family is . . . There's just so much trouble. Too much, too much." He trailed off. "I don't understand. . . ."

I looked at him and saw that the man was nearly in tears. Maybe I should have been sorry for him, but I couldn't manage it, at least for the moment; people were dead, widowed, destitute, jilted, and who knew what else, and the state of Fabian Cribbs's precious hide didn't seem to matter much. "Look, Dr. Cribbs," I said, "if it's getting into trouble you're worried about, I've already told you it won't be on account of me. But if it's absolution you're after, you'll have to go to another store." I walked out.

When I hit the outer office Sandra Laski was taking her coat off. "Hey, Hugh," she said, "what're you doing around here, signing up for a course?"

"Not on your life, Sandra. Some things you can learn even better without paying tuition." She looked baffled as I left, her head tilted to one side, mouth slightly ajar. It made her look young. Women should look baffled more often; it can be becoming.

I scrambled down the hall to Jerry Blackman's office as fast as these aging legs can scramble and I was in luck. Blackman was preparing to march off to class as I got there. "Hi," I said, "you got a minute for a couple more questions about your late office mate?"

He looked at his watch. "Not really, but why don't you walk with me over to my class. We can talk on the way."

"Fine. How's things going? You still got the office all to yourself?"

"Damn right. I got the desk next to the window again, and for keeps. Anybody else wants the window is going to have to goddamn get it by climbing outside to sit on the ledge. And Cribbs knows it. Sometimes you get smarter."

We left the building and headed across campus. "You seem to have come out of mourning relatively intact," I said.

He nodded. "You could say that. I got over the sense of loss just fine. So what's on your mind?"

"Mrs. Beasley, this time."

"Okay, shoot. Though I hate to contemplate the lady on an empty stomach."

"Uh huh. That's sort of my point. Did Beasley ever say anything that might indicate his wife was on drugs?"

"Did he ever! About as gently as a vegetarian talking about a two-pound bloody sirloin. With A.1. sauce. I could never understand why he kept telling me about it; he didn't like me anymore than I liked him, and we both knew it."

"Did you let him know you weren't interested?"

"You could say that too. He finally stopped after I told him flat out that if he wanted to tell me his personal affairs I'd return the confidence with an in-depth spasm-by-spasm report on my cat throwing up on the Thanksgiving turkey. Right at table. She jumped up. You wanna hear?''

"Preferably not."

"That's what I figured. It even got through to Beasley, but, now that you mention it, not until he was absolutely certain that the sad tale of his wife's addiction had penetrated my professorial skull."

"That's what I needed to hear. There's a minor possibility you may have to testify to that some time in the future."

"Oh, hey, I'd hate to get that poor mutt of a wife of his in trouble."

"Don't you worry," I assured him. "To the contrary. Even *au contraire,* as you academics might put it. And thanks for your time." I left him at the entry to one of the classroom buildings.

TWENTY-EIGHT

BACK HOME I FOUND a note from Harriet tacked to the door: If I was home by noon I should pop over for lunch and an exchange of information, and she was out of skim milk so we'd have tea if that was okay. That gave me an hour and a half. I went upstairs and wrote up my notes on my morning on campus. Then I changed to a short-sleeve shirt and a pair of khaki trousers. It's a funny thing about living here in the Hudson Valley. Everybody's momma teaches him to fold up the summer stuff after Labor Day and truck it up to the trunk in the attic. Fortunately everybody's too lazy to get to it on time, because September around here can never make up its mind whether it's the end of summer or the beginning of fall. Right now it was the end of summer. Somehow the sun had crawled up to the middle of the sky again, no matter what the astronomers thought it ought to be doing, people were taking a last dunk into their pools, and the Canada geese were signing new leases on the local ponds instead of heading south for the winter.

There was a healing quality to it, and I dragged a folding chair outside, turned my face into the warmth, and, not without a sense of guilt, felt grateful for any truth there might have been in the ominous predictions about global warming. I fell asleep.

I felt cold. I opened my eyes and found Harriet was there, standing between me and the sun, putting me in her shadow. She had my notes in her hand. "These were blowing across the yard," she said. "It's a good thing nobody can read your handwriting."

"What time is it?" I asked.

"Bedtime, apparently," I was told.

"Okay, okay. I'm awake, more's the pity. What's up?"

"It's lunchtime, if you're interested. I've set it up on the deck so we can stay outside."

A cold cucumber soup with a chicken-stock base, two percent milk (instead of cream), a secret combination of herbs that Harriet learned from a witch in the Catskills and is proscribed from divulging on pain of being mounted on a broomstick herself. The cucumbers were from the little patch she made me tend each summer on the pretext that farming was boy's work; girls only grew flowers. And help-yourself sandwiches from an assortment of the less-lethal varieties of meats and such—cheeses offensively labeled LITE, ham, and a tuna salad with practically no mayo. Iced tea. No beer. I've come to look on it as terrific, even if it doesn't keep my weight down. (It's one of Harriet's frustrations; she says I'd probably gain weight even if she put me on a straight lettuce-and-hay diet.)

"Good," I said, with my mouth full. "What say I spring for dinner? It's seafood special night at the Inn."

"That'd be great. It's too warm to cook anyway. Now tell me what you found out at the school."

I told her. "Well, my hunch was right. Beasley had himself cast in the role of the long-suffering husband supporting his junky mate. Probably stopped strangers in the street to tell his story, like how she beat him with her pantyhose when he tried to straighten her out."

"The bastard. So he could get rid of her—"

"You mean kill her."

"—Kill her, make it look like she overdosed, and get together with his new lady friend."

"Yeah. But you left out collect on insurance. Listen, what did you find out there? Any old insurance policies laying around?"

"Well, that's sort of funny, Hugh. Florene's infuriating. She swore up and down that there wasn't anything in the house like that. I was all set to believe her. And then the police showed up again. Pinky was with them. Those records you turned over got them all in a tizzy and they decided to have another look around. The captain dressed them down for doing a sloppy job the first time."

"And?"

"And they found it. Taped to the underside of a drawer. They went all bureaucracy on me, even Pinky, and wouldn't let me see, but when the nitwits left Florene told me. It was a policy on her life."

"Why'd the girl keep it secret, for God's sake?" I picked up a half slice of cheese.

Harriet slapped my hand. "Honestly, Hugh, I wish you wouldn't. You've had enough." I shoved the goody in my mouth. "Just this one," I mumbled. "So what'd she say?"

"Oh, I don't know what goes through that one's mind. She said it was bad luck to let anybody know there's a policy on your life. She said she saw some movie on TV." Harriet threw her hands up. "Who the hell knows? I think she's got the idea that anybody who finds out something, anything, about her can claim a prize, as if they had shot a mechanical rabbit at the county fair. Who knows with Florene?" she repeated.

"You sure picked a client for me. What next, Daffy Duck?"

"Probably. But listen. It happened again. While I was out there, the phone rang and when Florene picked it up, they hung up on her. There's something going on. That's the third time when one of us has been there. It can't all be wrong numbers."

"No, it can't. And we'll find out. Sooner or later we'll find out. But right now, I'm going out to DeWitt Vineyards and see what I can see. You know anything about those people, the DeWitts?"

Harriet thought. Her trusty random-access memory kicked in, a couple of internal disk drives got into action, and my own sweet old talking memory bank came through again. "Let's see. He's old Dutch, Arthur DeWitt, and Michelle, that's the missus, was old Huguenot, born a Fevrier. When they got married, oh, maybe fifteen years ago, it was like the Hudson Valley equivalent of the joining of the Mississippi and the Missouri. The social event of the season. The Oostdyks, the Delavergnes, everybody was there."

"Were you there?"

"Not exactly. I didn't count as an everybody. I might have qualified for scrubbing potatoes in the kitchen, but it didn't occur to me to ask until too late."

"Okay, and since then, what've the young royals been up to?"

"He owned the land, and she owned the money and when they put them both together they were in the grape-growing, wine-making business. DeWitt Vineyards. Seyval blanc, chardonnay, anonymous blends of red that were supposed to be pretty good at one time. The usual for around here."

"And?"

Harriet's eyebrows went up. "And nothing. You know as much as I do. They were riding high when something went wrong one year and the business went as sour as the wine. That was when Beasley hopped off the bandwagon and went over to Clarendon. The word is that Michelle is teed off at Arthur, what with it being her money tied up in the operation. Far as I know nobody's claiming they're up to round sixty-seven in a fight to the finish, but they do seem to have perfected the art of glaring ice cubes."

"Like how?"

"Oh . . . like when Ellie Cunningham was out there for the cancer drive, she asked Arthur if he'd consider increasing DeWitt's contribution over last year. He said something that of course they'd be happy to do their part. Ellie says that Michelle didn't say a word, but she let out a great caw like a crow in a cornfield and then snorted exactly like that ancient steam engine that used to start up in Appleboro Junction after the apple crop was loaded."

"Really? I thought the old thing sounded like a gas attack."

"Did you, now! I wouldn't know about that. You could check Ellie, I guess, but watch out for her umbrella if you do."

"If it becomes important. Meanwhile, I'm headed out there. See you around dinner time."

The road to DeWitt Vineyards goes parallel to the Shawangunk Cliffs for a spell, and I feasted my eyes on those great white rocks. They're quiet, imperturbable, and on occasion as good as a sedative for making a body think that it might not be too unrealistic to dream of a calm and rational world some day. Some day soon. I spotted a moving object running parallel to the top of the cliff, almost a third of the way down—somebody's car, noiseless and smooth, gliding evenly along the road from the other side of the range. A young woman, maybe, with the window open, and the fresh breeze toying with her hair as she went. I sighed my approval.

Back to reality. I drew up at the DeWitt place. The house was Appleboro traditional, a white wooden structure that rambled asymetrically, each additional room or ell or wing reflecting some old farmer's need to house an extra child, an aging parent, or even, in the glory days of farming in the valley, a hired couple. It needed painting, but not too badly, striking the correct Appleboro medium between the uppity insolence of fresh paint and the shamelessness of paint that was peeling off the siding. A couple of red outbuildings, barns in earlier generations, had been adapted to the business of making and selling wine.

A window in the smaller of the red structures had a hand-lettered sign in the window facing the parking area: OFFICE. I headed that way, noting that the building was listing slightly off the perpendicular, like so many of the old wooden structures in the area. It looked more relaxed than decrepit, however. I knocked and opened the door in one movement.

There were two desks inside. DeWitt, more sober than the last time I had seen him, was writing in a ledger at the one nearer the door, and a woman was banging on a manual desk-model typewriter at the other, an ancient Underwood, battered, bloody, but unbowed. A counter bearing a stack of plastic glasses, a table that was probably used to hold bread and cheese for wine tastings, two unoccupied wooden chairs, and a few cartons shoved into a corner completed the furnishings. There were a couple of what appeared to be citations from some semiofficial source stuck up on the wall, and, for some reason most likely unrelated to anything meaningful, a large and colorful poster of a toreador facing a charging bull.

I approached the man. "Remember me, Mr. DeWitt? Hugh Morrison. We met at Carrie Nation's awhile back."

A soft round face looked up at me and peered through rimless glasses. "Sure," he said softly, after a quick and guilty look at the woman. He waved a soft, round hand at the seat next to his desk. "Grab a chair." Soft and round summed up Arthur DeWitt. Soft and round, mild and in his thirties.

"This is my wife, Michelle," he said, nodding toward the typewriter, which had stopped clacking. Michelle DeWitt looked up and favored me with a noncommittal nod. "How do," she said. She was a good-looking woman with a craggy face. Large nose of the variety that's generally supposed to indicate character, a long, firm chin, and long, bony hands. I knew for a certainty that when they both got old the usual aging process for the sexes would be reversed: she would be a gorgeous old thing with crisp, clean lines, while he would have the blurry look of someone who had managed to dissolve and get larger simultaneously.

"As you know, I'm representing Florene Beasley in this matter of her husband's death," I said. Arthur D. nodded slowly; Michelle D., much more efficient in her use of time, did it in two quick jerks—down, up, and let's keep going. "It's our belief that since Professor Beasley was a man who at the very least, let's say defied the conventions," (Michelle emitted one of those snorts Harriet had told me about.) "there might well be others besides Mrs. Beasley who would consider the world a better place without his presence."

"You can say that again," Michelle DeWitt said in a firm voice, "and you can count me among them."

"Michelle, please," her husband said.

"No sense pretending, Arthur. Doesn't mean we killed him. Doesn't even mean we're happy when another human being comes to a violent end." She turned to me. "As a matter of fact, we're not happy about it, but yes, the world is a better place without that... that slug."

Arthur gave up. He sagged in his chair and wordlessly shook his head from side to side. This family was big on nonverbal communication.

I didn't need a lifetime of training in police work to know that I'd get things done faster if I dealt with the wife, even though I was sitting next to the husband. "Could you tell me more about that, Mrs. DeWitt?"

She offered me a knowing smile. "Don't tell me you don't already know, Mr. Morrison. Everybody in Appleboro knows. That miserable worm ruined our wine, ruined our reputation, just about destroyed our business, and then nimbly hopped over to the competition."

"But why would he do that?"

"I'm sure for profit. I'm certain of it."

"But how could he profit from destroying your business?"

She looked at me hard, without speaking. Then she opened her mouth and snapped. "You tell me. You're the detective."

"Are you suggesting," I asked, "that the competition might have paid him to knock you out of the picture? Is that it?"

Arthur couldn't contain himself at this point. "Oh, no. We don't believe that for one minute. The Tuppers, Don and old Clarence are tough competitors, but they'd never stoop to that. We go back a long way together, the Tuppers and us."

Trying not to look as if I was ignoring Arthur DeWitt, I continued to look at his wife, the question still clearly imprinted on my face. She frowned and said, "I agree with my husband. Anything's possible, but I don't think the Tuppers would stoop that low. I'll say three things: Al Beasley deliberately ruined us, Al Beasley did it for his own advantage, probably monetary, and someone who wasn't the Tuppers paid him for it. That's it. You find out the rest. Period."

Period. End of Act One. I took the next step. "How was Beasley in a position to do all this? Isn't it pretty complicated?"

At this point, Arthur DeWitt took over. He stood. "Come with me and I'll show you." As we started out, Michelle DeWitt's typewriter resumed its racket. I think she was pounding on Beasley each time she slammed the carriage back at the end of a line.

The man led me into another building. There were a series of tanks and vats against the walls, and one more overhead. Just off the center of the room there was an arrangement of tables and gadgets. I learned later that these represented the last phase of the operation, when the finished product was poured into bottles and closed by a hand-operated corking machine.

"Okay, so on this wall," DeWitt explained, pointing at one row of tanks with his chin, "that's where you've got your wine in the making. The juice sets in there during fermentation. You got that?"

"Right. You taste it as it goes along?"

"Regularly."

"Then how come you didn't know things weren't working out right?"

"Hah!" Another helping of nonverbal communication from Michelle DeWitt. She had been unable to stay away from the action and had abandoned her typewriter to join her husband and me.

"I'll get to that," DeWitt said. "Lemme go on. After the wine is ready, all the tanks are emptied into this mixing vat here." He pointed to a large tublike container against a second wall. "From there it goes through a filtering operation and we pump it into the overhead tank. Then down these tubes into bottles and over to the corker. And that's it."

"Tell him about the case we took right up to the house," Michelle advised. "That's important."

"I don't see—" DeWitt started to say.

"Tell him anyway."

"All right, all right. We take a case up to the house first thing and celebrate that night. And the wine was terrific. Best we ever had. What the hell, a breakthrough for us," he said to me. To her he added, "Satisfied?"

She clucked and looked annoyed. I wondered if the lady also had drums and smoke signals in her repertory. "Look, Art, I'm not blaming you. You couldn't have known."

True, her words weren't blaming him for whatever it was, but the way she wielded them was something else again. I didn't want to get into the middle of a family fight; these days, if you watch the news on TV, it's the innocent bystanders who get clobbered. "Maybe if you could tell me what the problem is, I could get out of your way," I said. "Let you get back to your work?"

The DeWitts looked at each other. She gave the nod and he recommenced. "Ordinarily, we taste the wines regularly, especially when it's getting near time for bottling. Half a dozen vats down that wall, and I generally go down the line, right to left. Likely as not, Al Beasley would be here, tasting along with me. He was always so damned enthusiastic about our wines, and it never would have occurred to me—"

"Enthusiastic, my foot," Michelle put in. "What he was enthusiastic about was tanking up for free. He was always hanging around if he wasn't at the school, never wanted to go home, not that I can blame him much for that. Once I walked in here and the miserable pig was filling up a thermos bottle. He didn't even have the good grace to blush. Just said he had to let a couple of the local liquor stores have a taste, the miserable liar, and when I—"

"We're getting off the point, dear," DeWitt said.

I thought maybe we were finally getting on the point, now that the lady was beginning to use real words strung into sentences in place of meaningful grunts and clicks. But I let things take their own course.

"Anyway, about three weeks before the wine was ready," DeWitt went on, "I was in bad shape. That year had to be good or we were going to have trouble with the bank. And I had a recurrence of an old trouble. Incipient ulcers. The doctors said no alcohol. None. No tasting."

He shook his head. "And Michelle stays out of the day-to-day operations."

"Hate it," Michelle said, by way of no explanation.

"Al Beasley said he'd help out." (Snorts from the distaff side.) "I couldn't let him do it all. I had to know for myself, ulcers or not. So I worked from the right, tasting a few of the vats, and he came in from the left, doing the same thing. I let him do most of it. I mean, I already knew how good the wine was, and I thought I could afford to slack off, watch the ulcers."

Michelle, as I could have predicted, jumped in to take over the climax of the story. "That's when he did it, poured a gallon of vinegar with live mother in it into one of the tanks a few weeks in advance. A tank on the left, where he knew he'd be doing the tasting."

"The mother?" I asked. "What'zat?"

"It's an active ingredient that goes to turn wine or cider or anything else into vinegar. Anybody can buy it at a supply store. Some people make their own wine vinegar at home that way." She folded her arms across her chest and a grim expression settled over her craggy face. "To go on, everything went into the mixing vat, through the filter, into the overhead tank, into the bottles, and DeWitt Vineyards was up the creek with the best damned wine vinegar this side of Bordeaux, and may the man rot in hell."

"But couldn't you tell then? Didn't you say you took a case up to the house and celebrated that night?"

"Nobody ever said Beasley was stupid," Michelle said. She banged her hand against one of the vats, and I think I heard some sloshing. "Sure, it would have been easy, or at least easier, to figure out if we knew right away. But what we had at the house was good."

DeWitt corrected her. "It was great."

She ignored that. "We didn't know anything was wrong for six, eight weeks, when the complaints started rolling in. And then we couldn't figure what had happened. Not for months. By then it was too late."

"Too late for us to save the vineyard's reputation, too late to prove anything about Beasley," DeWitt added.

"How'd he segregate a case of unspoiled wine to get to you in your house?"

DeWitt smiled sadly. "That was the big one, especially when we had no reason to suspect the man. We saw a smear and a bit of paper on a bottle at dinner one night. I thought the men—the temporary help we have in at bottling time—had done a sloppy job labeling, maybe slapped it on crooked, and had scraped it off to put a new one on. I meant to speak to them about that, but I never got to it."

"You never do," the lady muttered.

"And even after the trouble started it took us time to work it out."

"Took *me* time," she corrected.

"Right. Beasley had to have gotten a case from the year before, taken off the '91 labels and slapped on new '92 labels. Then he had it taken up to the house."

Michelle said, "We should've realized, but Arthur kept saying how great the stuff was, never cottoning on to the truth that it was a different vintage." She seemed to have left all the blame for Arthur, without actually saying so. Clearly, when Michelle DeWitt did use words, she could use them like a butcher's cleaver if that took her fancy.

"Did you do anything about it?"

"What could we do?" DeWitt asked. "Who could we accuse by that time? How could we prove anything? People would only say we were irresponsible for not tasting our own product and trying to palm off garbage on people who thought they were paying good money for good wine."

Michelle added, "And Beasley was off with the competition by then, anyway. We would have looked as if we were simply vindictive, trying to excuse ourselves and lay the blame on somebody else."

There was a long silence. I sensed a sort of symbolic smoke coming out of the ruins of DeWitt Vineyards. "Maybe I should have killed him," DeWitt said sadly. "I felt like it, the bastard."

Michelle humphed her disbelief; she didn't say her old man couldn't have killed a crippled mouse with a hydrogen bomb, but she humphed it very clearly.

I left. "Incidentally," I said as I opened the door, "when did you last see Al Beasley?"

"Not in over a year," DeWitt said.

"Why?" the missus asked.

"No particular reason. It's only that the young man down the road, Timmy Young, told me he saw you drive by a few weeks ago, headed for Swamp Bottom."

"Supposing we did," Michelle snapped. "Beasley's not the only one down that road, you know."

DeWitt took courage from his wife's irritation and did a little snapping on his own. "That's right, and, oh, yeah, if you want to be technical, I did see Beasley a couple of weeks ago, but he didn't see me. He was too busy yelling instructions on how to dig a pond to look at me at the Parkers. I suppose he was a civil engineer too, the way he was a wine expert. Anyway, I was next door. The Parkers are old friends. He used to work for us."

"That's right," Michelle agreed. "When we had work for someone to do. Before Beasley took care of that."

"Just thought I'd ask," I said. "Thanks." It could have been true, he could have been visiting the Parkers. But it never hurts to ask, unless you don't enjoy getting people riled up. Like me.

TWENTY-NINE

WE WERE AT THE INN, seated at our favorite table, the one equidistant from the door, the kitchen, and the men's room, thus avoiding drafts from outside, cooking odors, and the heady perfume of scented camphor balls. That's the Shawangunk Inn, pronounced Shongum, though for no other reason than to confound the tourists and provide a couple of one-upmanship points for us local yokels. (Shawangunk is Indian for something or other, depending on which one of us a tourist is hapless enough to ask.)

The Inn is normally a steak house, but there are seafood special nights, when Harriet deigns to let me attend. This evening I went around left end, cleverly avoiding her defensive line, and ordered a steak and seafood combination. I don't really have too much of a cholesterol problem, but Harriet likes to pretend I do in order to gain the upper hand. And I like to pretend to chafe under the restraints she lays on me. Games people play, I suppose, but at least this one did no harm, may have done some good, and certainly gave both of us pleasure.

I was on my second Scotch and water, and she was digging the olive out of her second vodka martini with a forefinger. "You sure that's not unsanitary?" I asked.

"I'm not at all sure," she said. "And I don't much care. You should have asked me after the first one."

"I like a woman not afraid to take a chance," I said. "A spirited filly."

"I'll filly you, you sexist gumshoe. And speaking of which, how'd it go today?"

I tore off a piece of warm bread and put a dab of butter on it. "Not bad. I've already told you that Beasley was damn near stopping people on the street to let them know what a problem his dear wife was, sniffing cocaine, popping pills, whatever."

"Then you're almost certainly right. He would have arranged something to look like Florene overdosed, collect on her insurance, and then gone off with this woman from Middletown."

"Or not gone off with her. We don't know that he had any serious plans about marrying again, just her word for it."

The waiter arrived with the entrees, the steak and shrimp for me, and Harriet's broiled salmon. "You folks want sour cream and chives for your baked potato?" he asked.

I opened my mouth to reply, but Harriet got there first. "Thank you, no. The butter is all we need." I made a face.

"Okay, folks," he said. "Enjoy."

"Insofar as I can," I said, to no one in particular. Back to the subject, I said, "So theoretically, I think we can add the lady to the list of suspects, though I doubt there's much in it. He might even have planned on marrying her, and if he didn't he wouldn't have told her that before Florene was out of the picture and he had to jump one way or the other."

Harriet shook her head. "If I had known about this creep, you'd have had to add me to the suspect list. Why, he's loathsome!"

"You sound surprised."

"I suppose I am. You never think people you see around you from day to day can be so monumentally miserable. At least I never do."

"Nobody does. Your everyday villain isn't likely to be a fascinating standout, just stupid and boring."

"In a way that's a consolation."

With that, we ate quietly for a bit, tugging on a half bottle of Brimstone Hill Vin Rouge, a local quaff heavy enough for my steak, light enough for Harriet's fish, and yummy enough to give us pleasure. "The local wines get better every year," Harriet said. I nodded a silent agreement, my mouth being in overload at the moment.

"Where do things stand now, Hugh? Is it getting any clearer?"

"Nope," I said, "not really. Florene's still a suspect in my book. The girl's a dummy, but not in a class with Timmy

Young. She could've decided, in her whacky way, that with a husband like hers it was either kill or be killed.''

"At least that'd make a good defense for her."

"Right." The little candle on our table sputtered and went out. I got out and filched another from an empty table. The lighting is dim in the Shawangunk Inn and you need all the help you can get, especially if you're not in the courting years, which Harriet and I clearly were not. "The Wellers, at least Florene's old man, are still reasonable suspects. So help me, he honestly thinks that Beasley transformed that girl from Miss America with a Ph.D. from Harvard into what she is today, and with every day that passes, he's even more convinced.

"I think Cribbs is out. He certainly must have hated Beasley, but he was dependent on him. A professor with a drug habit is better off getting what he needs from a colleague, somebody who'd be less likely to get him in trouble by talking because he'd get himself in trouble at the same time. Not like some kid who'd start gossiping. 'Hey, ya know what? Old Cribbs keeps hassling me for crack, ya know? Jeez!''' I drained the last of my wine. "But Blackman is in."

"I thought you liked that boy."

"I do. Some of my best friends are assassins. But think what Beasley was doing to him. Stealing his stuff, running him down professionally. Think what that means in the academic world when you're just starting out. Blackman's low man on the academic totem pole, and if he's ambitious—which he is—he's got to make time now, while he's young. He's got the brain and the energy to climb to the top unless some bastard like Beasley knocks him out. So Blackman's in. You want dessert?''

She shook her head. "Thanks, no. And neither do you."

"If you say so. How about coffee?"

"Decaffeinated. Thanks."

I ordered two decafs. "The Parkers were on my list. Beasley was driving them nuts with his pond and the fun house he lived in. And they were flashing signals to each other when I told them Florene was worried about her husband. You know, I still have the feeling something was going on with them, and maybe by tomorrow I could have a little word with Cynthia Parker."

Harriet looked unhappy. "Don't worry. Nothing to upset the girl; I'm not that much of a heel."

"Well, okay, if you must, you must, so long as you take it easy with her. But what about the DeWitts and Don Tupper?"

"You know, on the face of it, the DeWitts ought to be on the top of the list. Beasley ruined them."

I explained the drill Beasley had almost certainly gone through to change wine into vinegar. "They're strong candidates, all right, and I don't think Michelle is the type to brood about it for a couple of years. If she'd had a mind to kill anybody, that woman would've marched over with a cannon under her arm and done it right off. She's tough enough. Art DeWitt would have needed a year or so to brood about it, and besides I think he's too mousey for murder under any conditions."

"But suppose Beasley had thumbed his nose at the man in some way. Maybe said something nasty about his wines. Timid people can flare up, given enough provocation, can't they?"

"Oh, yes. Arthur's definitely still a possibility. He's not my favorite, but the odds are still good enough for him to be a winner."

"Sounds like a horse race."

"Yeah, it does. But in this case it's winner lose all. And listen, let's not rule out Don Tupper. Middle-aged man with a young wife. No matter how relaxed he let me know he was about her hanging out at Beasley's brawls, you can't tell me that it didn't get to the man somehow. He had to be wondering about it."

"But you know she didn't play games out there. Even Mittleman said so."

"Uh huh. I know, and you know. Or do we? But tell that to the middle-aged husband. And if that's not enough, it looked to me like the upkeep on Betty Ann might run kind of high. Sexy dresses, jewelry, just to sit around a shack on a work day in the country? What the hell. At best, the girl's a tease. And don't forget that Timmy saw the man drive by at what could have been the right time."

"So where does that leave us?"

"It leaves us with how I want to talk to Cynthia Parker, plus the Middletown tootsie, and the Johnnie with the orange hair, spike division. There's that drug angle and we don't know enough about it yet. After that we can start the guessing games again."

I signaled the waiter for the check. "Let's get out of here before we think of somebody else who might have wanted Beasley dead."

"I'm surprised he had time for his classes," Harriet said, "such an enterprising individual."

"Hey, maybe you've got something. Maybe he was a no-show once too often. Maybe a student did it."

"Maybe a bunch of students got together."

We both laughed, though not happily. "And of course," I concluded, "let's not forget Florene. She's still the logical candidate, unless she's dumber than I think she is, which would be difficult."

THIRTY

I WASN'T AT ALL SURE Cynthia Parker was going to let me in the front door. There was little doubt but that her husband was dead because someone had the idea he was about to talk to me, even though, just possibly at her insistence, he had backed out. There was no point in phoning to ask if I could see her. It called for a sneakier approach, much as I disliked the idea.

It was Friday, the local housewives' favorite shopping day, and I took a chance that Florene might be normal enough to be out at the market midmorning if I knocked on her door. Happily, she was. I walked over to the Parker house.

A heavyset woman in her fifties whose reddened eyes told me she had completed her exercise that day through a heavy crying drill opened the front door. She looked familiar, but I couldn't place her. Obviously exhausted, she waited mutely for me to say something.

I introduced myself, and said, "I had an appointment with Mrs. Beasley next door and she isn't home. I thought I'd come over and pay my respects to Mrs. Parker, if she's up to seeing anybody."

The lady nodded. "Come in," she said. "I'm Cynthia's aunt. I came down from Rosendale yesterday to stay with the poor girl." She led the way into the living room. "You set there and I'll go see. She may be asleep. Lord knows she got precious little sleep last night." Shaking her head sadly, she left me and lumbered down the hall.

Three minutes later, she was back with her niece. The young woman was equally red eyed as her aunt; tears were the only recourse when neither the mind nor the emotions can come up with any more productive suggestions. Cynthia stared at me, but spoke to her aunt. "Please," she said, "see how the baby is doing. I'll stay here with Mr. Morrison."

When we were alone, and both of us seated, she continued to look at me, without talking. But even without words, she was sending a message. What did I want? What did I have to say? What *could* I say, when, however innocently, I was involved in her husband's death?

"I'm sorry, Mrs. Parker."

"Thank you."

"If there's anything I can do . . ."

"There's nothing anyone can do, is there? It's all been done."

"Can I do any shopping for you? Anything like that?"

"I don't think so. My aunt has taken care of things."

"Well, if you think of something, please don't hesitate . . . There's one thing I'd like to ask you, Mrs. Parker—"

Her head went violently from side to side, almost the first movement she had made since sitting and folding her hands in her lap. "No. No questions."

I had to keep going. "Mrs. Parker, there's a madman on the loose. Your husband knew something he wanted me to know. If you don't want to talk to me—and I can understand that— at least please talk to the police before somebody else, someone just as innocent, gets hurt. It may be painful for you, but at the risk of being presumptuous, I have to say to you to please tell someone what you know, for your husband's sake, if for no other reason."

"Mr. Morrison." There was a flash of anger in her voice. "Please don't tell me what to do for my husband's sake. I hold nothing against you—that would be stupid and useless—but I can't help wondering about your part in—what happened. I appreciate your coming. Thank you. If you want to do something for me, you can take my aunt to the bus station in town. She's already taken over a day off from her own business and she should be catching the late morning bus to Rosendale. You'll save me a trip if you'll do that." She stood, indicating that my condolence call was over.

"Gladly," I said, and a few minutes later the aunt and I were headed out. "Thank you kindly," she said, wiggling herself into a comfortable position in the car seat.

"Not at all," I said.

We clucked a few sad regrets over Elroy Parker and when the required formalities had been sufficiently observed, I said, "Cynthia says you've got a business to get back to in Rosendale?"

The lady smiled. "Oh, that's putting it too strong. I took early retirement from my job last year, and to keep from going stale, I turned myself into a little old-fashioned seamstress. You know, alterations, putting in hems, letting out hems, simple jobs." She looked at me critically. "You look like a man who has to have the waist let out in his trousers from time to time. If you need anybody to do a good job, look me up."

"I guess it shows, huh?" I said ruefully. "I'll tell you what, next time a seam gives way I'll get in touch."

"Half a sec," she said, burrowing through the cavernous depths of her purse. "Here it is." She drew out a card and lifted it for me to see. "My card. Give me a call when you need to."

"Thanks," I said. I took the card, put it in my shirt pocket, and promptly forgot about it.

I dropped her at the bus station and watched her comfortably padded body roll inside to buy herself a ticket. I still wondered where I knew her from, but not with any particular urgency.

Back home, I fixed myself a light lunch. Actually light, nothing Harriet would beat up on me for. Vegetable juice, lettuce and tomato on whole wheat with mustard instead of mayo, a couple of peaches, and a glass of skim-milk buttermilk. I reminded myself to tell Harriet what a good boy I had been.

There were no messages on the machine, and since I needed some time for myself—to think, to relax, and to tidy up my life—I took the rest of the afternoon off. Wagging a load of laundry down into Harriet's basement, I squeezed all the pockets to make sure there were no coins, tissues, keys, or whatnot in them, and loaded the washing machine. The two quarters and three pennies I had retrieved I placed on the ironing board, together with the card Cynthia Parker's aunt had given me.

When all was washed and dried, I flopped into the car and did my grocery shopping. A soothing, domestic day. Just what I had wanted, though despite the time I had given myself to think, I experienced no particularly blinding insights. After dinner—four ounces (damnit) of beef, a baked potato with no-fat yogurt (damnit), a big fat tomato with oil (nobody's perfect) and vinegar, and some more fruit for dessert, I settled down with a mystery book of all things. There were no insights in it, either. As a matter of fact, I fell asleep over it, woke some time later, and turned in early.

THIRTY-ONE

ED WELLER WAS ON DUTY at the school when I contacted him early the next morning. He wasn't wearing his security-guard uniform, and he looked gloomy enough to have pounded anyone in the snout if they had commented on his being improperly dressed. He was sporting his uniform cap, however, and that was sufficient to identify him as he walked around the campus, me at his side, unlocking some building doors and testing the locks on others. Also, he looked like a large, discontented bullfrog, which in itself tagged him as an *apparatchik* in the security detail.

I brought him up to date on the investigation, which didn't improve his expression. "All I want to know is, is my little girl going to be okay," he said.

It made me feel sad. Anybody who could refer to Florene as a little girl and still keep a straight face was truly a loving parent. "Yes," I promised, with a sincerity I didn't entirely feel, "she's going to be okay. But I still have to keep looking, and I need your help."

"You got it." He inserted a key in an electronic timer that would indicate when he had arrived at that particular spot in his rounds. "What can I do?" I followed along as he set off toward his next checkpoint.

"There's a kid on campus who deals drugs, and I want to talk to him. I don't know his name, only that his hair is dyed orange and he's got it trained to stand up in spikes."

"That little sleaze. Sure. Danny Leonard. His old man's a lawyer, owns half the state. Danny Leonard. What do you want with that one?"

"It's complicated, but I can tell you that there could be a drug angle in Beasley's murder, nothing to do with Florene. But let me ask you something. How come you people haven't cracked down on this Leonard kid yourselves?"

"Man, would I love to. But we got orders."

"What orders? Who from?"

"Don't ask me, Morrison. I just work here. From the school administration, the governor, what the hell, the President of the United States for all I know. But I'll tell you, in a screwed-up way it makes sense. This kid'll be gone in two more years. Meanwhile, he only deals in pot. No heroin, crack, nothing like that. We know who he is, what he does. We bust him, God knows what'll move in next, but sure as shit, something will. Marijuana we don't have to like, but we can live with it."

"The cops know about this?"

He laughed. "The cops? For chrissake, of course they know! How do you think they keep things from blowing up? It's like you let the little darlings play with water pistols so they won't go for semiautomatics. It's like somebody says, get real, this is what it's all about, so grin and bend over. You ought to know that yourself, you an ex-cop."

I knew. The great moral majority passes laws against human nature and expects the police to enforce them. And the police can't. All they can do is turn people in the least bad direction and hope that'll hold the world together. Drugs are illegal, but they're here, and here they are. A cop can't change the world, so somebody, maybe even sadly, decided that if young Leonard confined his illegal operations to marijuana, the smartest move would be to keep an eye on him but let him alone. (Don't tell your congressman I said so; it might overheat his moral indignation gland, not to mention his family values.)

"I know," I said, "but I hadda ask."

We stopped at another building. The plaque by the door identified it as the Moore Ceramics Studio. I could see a lopsided tea set in the window, probably a student's senior project. It looked as if your wrist would snap if you picked up a cup, with or without tea in it. Weller unlocked the door, stuck his hand in and flipped on the hall lights. "That all?" he asked. "Anything else you want?"

"Where's this Danny Leonard live? You know his address?"

"We all know his address. I told you we keep an eye on him. Eighty-seven East Chestnut. We made it clear we'd crack down if he lived on campus. Keeps him further away from the new kids, makes it harder for him to deal without our knowing what he's up to. Anyway, that's what they say, but if you ask me, all that's only pissing into the wind. It don't hurt, I guess, but it don't do much good either."

I thanked him and left. He called after me. "Keep in touch, hey? Leona and me worry about our girl."

I promised.

I hurried over to East Chestnut. If Danny Leonard had two years to go he was in his junior year. In his junior year, he'd be taking a number of electives, and nobody, particularly an orange-spiked pusher who has his choice of electives ever signs up for a course that begins before ten in the morning. I remember a kid when I was in school who decided on a class in Italian literature since the Council of Trent. He told me confidentially over a couple of beers he never found out what or when the Council of Trent was, but it got him out early on a Friday afternoon for a good headstart on the weekend.

Eighty-seven East Chestnut was a weary wooden house built before people worried about whether their homes should look like Louisiana before the Civil War or Massachusetts before the Revolutionary War. It had been somebody's home before the street had turned into a main road to Kingston, and now it was a rooming house for students. Its neighbors had metamorphosed into storefronts, lawyers' and chiropractors' offices, plus assorted commercial or nonprofit enterprises of no distinction.

The front door was open. I went in and found a list of names and room numbers tacked to a bulletin board in the hall. Leonard was on the second floor, front left. I labored up the staircase, catching my shoe on a rubber tread that had worked its way off the nails that were supposed to hold it in place. I turned down the hall toward the front. The left-hand door had a notice on it: KNOCK HARD AND GO AWAY. The boy may have been a junior, but the humor came from a year earlier. I knocked hard and stayed.

"Come," a sleepy voice called. I went in and saw a kid in pajamas, clearly just out of bed, scratching himself luxuriously, and yawning. The orange-spiked hair was standing up as triumphantly as the Statue of Liberty's tiara, and for one mad moment I wondered if he wore a catcher's mask on top of his head to protect it at night.

The windows were shut and the air was stale. The room was an archetypal student room—clothing and papers and books on desks, chairs, and floor, the kind of disorder that would be easy for the occupant to thread his way through but that would stymie anyone else. "Who're you?" he asked. "Whatcha want? What time is it?"

"Hugh Morrison," I said. "Some information. Three minutes after nine—morning, not evening."

"Funnee," he said. "Look, what the heck do you want, busting in on me like this. You got five minutes."

"Fair-enough question. But it's going to take more than five minutes, so let's relax. A couple of small points of information is all, and I'll be out of here. And just for the record, I didn't bust in. I was invited."

He started to get dressed. "This is crazy. Go ahead. Maybe I'll answer. But I want to know what this is all about." He stopped and stared at me. "You get wise with me, mister, you'll be sorry."

I nodded. "Sure, kid, you got rights. I'm not out to make waves. All I want to know is what kind of dealings you had with Professor Beasley."

"The one who got killed? None. I didn't take his courses. Why? And who wants to know?"

I sighed. "Ah, come on. Look. I know and you know and the campus cops and the town cops know you deal drugs. You took deliveries. I figure you passed the real bad-boy stuff over to Beasley for further distribution, and only kept some pot to deal yourself. I don't give a damn about that or about you. Neither do the cops so long as you stick to marijuana. And by the way, I'd guess the local gendarmerie doesn't know about the heavy stuff—yet. I'm working for Mrs. Beasley because the police think she killed her husband and I think she didn't. Got that so far? Good."

"No," he said. "Not good. I still don't know what you're after, and whatever it is you're not getting it from me. What happened to Beasley's no skin off my ass. Nothing to do with me."

"That's fine," I said. "I'm glad to hear it. Delighted." The boy looked puzzled, which was reasonable. "The thing is, I've got this idea that Beasley was behind in his payments to someone, and I want to speak to that someone. You can help, if you will."

"No, I can't."

"You mean, no, you won't. That right?"

A nineteen-year-old's version of bored sophistication settled on his face. It was unconvincing. "If you like. However you want to slice it. But that's it. Now get the fuck outa here, huh?"

"Oh," I said, an octogenarian's version of shock flickering across my features, "that's no way to talk to an old gentleman. I'll put it to you straight. You get me together with Beasley's supplier and there's no trouble for anybody. Not for you, not for him, unless he's responsible for what happened out at Swamp Bottom, which I don't think he is. I'm not police. But don't help me and I'm an indignant private citizen. I'll make noise about drugs. Letters to the editor. Shouting at the next town meeting. The cops'll have no alternative; they'll have to shut you down. Is that clear?"

The kid segued into a tough-guy slouch, chest in, pelvis out, lips in a sneer. It might only have been an impressive pose for a bona fide hood, but it was only kind of sweet for a rich lawyer's baby boy. "Yeah, that's clear," he said. "How about this? This clear?" He started toward me, arms crooked, fists clenched.

I'm not very fast anymore, but at least I'm experienced, which the boy wasn't. He moved on me with as much advance notice as an old-fashioned locomotive getting up a head of steam, whoo-whooing its whistle, and chugging down the track.

That was his first mistake, and his last one as well. He came at me, and if I had let us meet head on, nineteen years of young muscle could have floored this droopy old frame in a flash. But the police academy had been thoughtful enough to instruct us dodderers in the un-American techniques of Oriental self-defense. I sidestepped, grabbed his fist, and pulled it along. At the same time my other foot, daintily extended, helped the laddy stumble as he charged forward. A tug and a twist on his arm and he was flat on the floor, facedown, my full weight squatting on his back. (How fortunate that Harriet had had only limited success in trimming me to the proportions of a Greek god!)

Slow and unsteady won the race, just the way I like it these days.

"Now look, son, I'll give it to you straight. And for the last time, I don't give a damn about you or your connection, and neither, for the moment, do the cops. Matter of fact, I told you already I'm not even sure they know about more than your marijuana business, like crack or heroin or whatever it is. But if your little forays into private enterprise get too much publicity, they'll do something. Who knows, maybe they'll suddenly discover you're feeding will-destroying drugs to thirteen-year-old girls, forcing boys to hustle Forty-second Street, something, anything. You'll be in trouble with them, and even worse, with your sources. The nicest thing they'll do is discontinue your services and tell you to shut up. The worst they could do I wouldn't want to hear on an empty stomach. Now," I concluded, "you wanna play nice, or do I have to play rough?"

He made a half-hearted effort to break free and I twisted his arm up farther until he sagged. "For the last time," I said, "I think you're a little shit, but I don't give a damn what you do unless you force me to think about it. Got it?"

There was no answer. I put a dab more force on his arm. "I said, Got it?"

There was a muffled grunt, which I accepted as agreement. "Good," I said. "You're a smart kid. Bet you get straight A's, deportment excepted. Now," I said more emphatically, "listen carefully. You tell your contact what the story is, and make sure they understand I'm not interested in them or their business. They don't make waves, I don't make waves. But I have to talk to them about Beasley. They've got a nice little operation going here, and I'm sure they'd like to keep it that way. You hearing me good?"

Another affirmative snarl came out of those healthy young lips. I let him up. "Think you're smart, don't you?" he said.

"No," I said. "Smart would have tossed you through a window and then got you kicked out of school. But I think you're smart, at least smart enough to keep cool and play along. I want you to set it up so I talk to your man, and I want him to meet me in the student cafeteria on campus. He can pick the day and time. But soon."

I went home feeling good; at least I could still frighten small boys.

THAT EVENING, Harriet asked me if that was wise. "Honestly, Hugh, you don't really know these men didn't kill Beasley, and if they did— Oh, Hugh!"

"Nah. Don't worry. You see too many movies. First place, with most of these guys, killing is a last resort. Not that they have anything against it—perish the thought! But if Beasley was behind in his payments, they'd try a couple of other things first. Put pressure on him. A murder could foul up their local operation, and as sensible businessmen, they'd just as soon not have that happen. Killing is only a marketing tool. They don't use it when something simpler will do the job as well."

"Something simpler? Like what?" Harriet put her hand on her throat, as if warding off blows.

"Oh, maybe they'd've busted his arm. Beat up one of the kids or Florene." I shrugged. "I don't know, any kind of a gentle reminder that they don't extend credit. You know, 'In God we trust, all others pay cash.'"

"Breaking an arm, hurting kids, is a simple warning?"

"Bones knit, bruises heal. And if the chump takes the hint, business can go on as usual. But since none of that happened, I figure they didn't have to resort to any special pressure to convince the man to pay up. They got paid without it. Or else, my dear, the whole idea is wrong and Beasley wasn't behind in payments in the first place."

"You're still taking a chance, Hugh."

"Sure I am, but we've got to play the odds, and I say they're with us. Just keep remembering that with these guys, drugs is a business like IBM or McDonald's. They may keep a stable of hoods to shoot up the competition, but once the distribution system is in place, the day-to-day routine is about as exciting as a convention of certified public accountants. Law-abiding crooks, that's what they aim to be. They dream about the day they'll be able to send out cutesy notices like department stores. You know—'Please do forgive us for our impertinence, but we'd like to remind you that you're two months behind in your payments, you naughty puss,' and so forth."

"All right, Hugh," Harriet said, shaking her head slowly, "that's enough. Don't joke. And please be careful."

"Don't you worry," I told her. "I'll be careful. This time of year, when you begin to think about the cold coming back to this frozen tundra you and I are camped on, I sit down and plot and plan about being careful. I've always got in mind lasting through one more winter so I can feel the sun again, walk down Main Street with you, guzzling something alcoholic and iced."

THIRTY-TWO

BUT MAYBE I hadn't been careful enough. That night there was a cold rain, and the wind was sufficiently strong enough to moan through trees and rattle windowpanes. I lay in bed and listened. Fall was still officially a couple of days off, but I knew that when daylight broke I'd see the first swirls of fallen leaves tracing cyclones across lawns, piling up against buildings, and scratching paths along concrete walks and flagstone terraces and whatever other hard surfaces Appleboro could offer for their fun and games.

The thought of the gray world that would be waiting to pounce at dawn was depressing. I decided not to get up until the morning light was strong. But the phone rang. It wasn't quite five-thirty and the steely glimmer of dawn that made it through the clouds looked like a photograph of the North Atlantic taken underwater in February, just off Iceland.

"Yeah?" I said in a voice intended to discourage.

"It's me." It was Harriet, but it wasn't Harriet's voice. There was an uncertain tone, a quaver to the words that I would never in the world have associated with her. "I think you'd better come over. Something's happened."

I grabbed the clothes that were piled up on the chair next to my bed, including yesterday's socks, rinsed my mouth with something advertised and green, and ran out.

She met me at the back door. "Look, Hugh, look in the living room." She was shivering inside her robe and she rubbed her hands together nervously, unconsciously twisting her wedding ring. It was as if she were trying to summon up some protective genie. She stayed behind me as I went inside.

"When did this happen?" I asked. "Last night?" If mild violence is a legitimate expression, this was an example of it. Her family photos, three of them, had been taken from their frames and shredded; a throw pillow had been ripped open and its foam-rubber contents shaken out on the couch; and, of all things, a bag of cow manure, the sanitized kind that garden centers sell, had been dumped on the floor. Enough to scare, but nothing—except for the photographs and the pillow—that couldn't easily be set to rights again.

She nodded. "Last night sometime. I didn't hear a thing." Her eyes met mine. "I didn't have the back door locked. I'm sorry." She looked away. "And there was this note." She took a paper from the pocket of her robe and handed it to me.

It read: "Tell your boyfriend to mind his own business or else." That was all.

"What does it mean, Hugh?" she asked. "I'm scared silly."

"Of course you are, and you've got a right to be," I said. "But honestly, kid, from the looks of this, I'm not so sure the guy who did it really wants trouble. I think he's as scared as you are."

"That's pretty darn scared, I'll tell you."

"Look at it this way. No major damage. Nothing to get an insurance company upset or start the police to working overtime. Kids on a rampage would've done worse. And do you think someone bent on real trouble would've gone to a garden center and bought a sack of cow manure, for God's sake? Hell, no!"

"But—"

"Let me finish. The way I see it, this is some kook as worried as you and I are. A real pro wouldn't have stopped with a couple of pictures and a cushion, Harriet. He would have ripped up the couch with a knife, taken that mirror down, put it under a cushion to kill the noise, and smashed it. The lamps, the pictures, everything. And let me tell you, there might've been manure in the place, but it wouldn't have come from a cow."

"Oh, Hugh! What's it about then? Why? Who?"

"'Why' is easy. To get at me through you. To get me off the Beasley case. 'Who' is harder. Somebody who doesn't want trouble. Maybe our killer is an amateur, crazy enough to think he can still keep from getting in over his head. But if by some small chance there's a full-time criminal in this, like from the drug connection, he doesn't want to make any more waves than he has to. Just a gentle reminder, that's all. They want me out, Harriet, and they're giving us a little nudge. Listen, if you say the word, I'll drop the whole damn thing right now. We've got enough trouble staying in one piece at our age without adding more to the pile."

Harriet was quiet. And if you think what I told her was a lot of guff, you're right. It sounded pretty logical—I hope—but I wasn't all that certain that the warning wasn't more deadly than I made it out to be in order to reassure her.

"Hugh," she said slowly, "you've said they can't convict Florene on what they've got." I nodded. "Are you absolutely sure of that? I mean absolutely."

"Absolutely?" I shrugged. "Honestly—no. You can never be positive about a courtroom situation. Pretty sure, yes; absolutely sure, I'm afraid not."

"Then this is easy." She pulled together the lapels of her robe over her throat and smiled. "Go ahead. See these drug people. See what you can find out."

"I knew you'd say that." Then I added, but silently, talking to myself, "The only problem is that I don't know whether I'm glad or sad that you did."

THIRTY-THREE

A TALL WOMAN, quite thin, opened the door. "Miss Saddler?" I asked. "I'm Hugh Morrison." I had called Mildred Saddler and set up an appointment, explaining I was working for Florene Beasley.

"Come in, Mr. Morrison," she said in a light, thin voice, and she led the way into the living room.

She was the antithesis of Florene. Beasley's latest—and last—fiancée was a combination of pastels. She had light brown hair that seemed to possess a touch of gray, though you couldn't be sure, and face and hands that looked fleshless, with pale skin stretched over an angular frame. And as I trailed behind her, I considered the grim aspect of a bottom that was bony and unfeminine to the point of defiance. Her voice was cool and collected and gave the impression of being quieter than it actually was. A very un-Beasley lady.

But she was pleasant, in a removed sort of way. "Can I get you something?" she asked. "If you like beer, I used to keep it on hand for him. I don't touch it myself."

"If you're having something, then yes, I'd like a beer." I pegged her for dry sherry, unless it was tea with lemon.

"I'll join you. Usually I have tea this time of day, but a sherry would be nice." I didn't ask how she took her tea, but the sherry was too pale to be anything but dry.

Once we were settled, Mildred Saddler started the conversation. "I'd like to help you, Mr. Morrison, though more for the sake of that poor woman than because of what happened to Al. I know that that's the wrong attitude for a school teacher, but we should get that straight at the start." She sipped her sherry, cool and composed, and if a voice can be described as bloodless, then that was hers. "Now, what would you like to know?"

"Would you mind telling me how you met Beasley? Frankly, you don't precisely fit his, uh—"

"—his type? His M.O., as the police on television always put it? No, I don't suppose I do. But you have to remember that there was something chameleonlike about the man. I met him when he addressed our high school English teachers here in Middletown, and he was very much my type, as you put it."

"As *you* put it, Miss Saddler."

"I stand corrected. As I put it. He was amusing, witty, and intellectual enough to attract an almost middle-aged middle school teacher more than eager to think about settling down. Correction: who was tired of being settled down and was open to the possibilities of resettlement."

"I see."

"I'm not sure you do, and I don't mean that in any belligerent sense. My future here was only too certain, and certainly too lonely. Here was a man who had a great deal of charm, and he not only offered marriage, but offered it at a distance! I'd keep my job and my place in Middletown, and he'd stay in Appleboro with an easy commute to the university. I think I'd've been too old for a complete change of seven days a week adjusting to someone else's presence in my home, but a weekend marriage," she said, shaking her head, "seemed ideal."

She smoothed her skirt gently, wiping out an imaginary wrinkle. The skirt was gray, too, the same soft gray young men used to wear in the gray flannel suit generation, and I was one of them.

"He told you about his wife. Were you at all concerned about that?"

"Not particularly. My God, do I really seem that Victorian? After all, I've been around and alive in this world we're in, but when you get to be my age you're either gently or roughly informed, somehow, that younger people aren't interested in your presence on their merry-go-round any longer. Unless, of course, you're especially brilliant or beautiful, neither of which I am. And he was honest about his family and—" She stopped short. "That's a laugh, isn't it? Al Beasley honest! After I went over to Appleboro to find out why I hadn't heard from him in weeks, I found out just how honest he had been, didn't I?"

"Speaking of that," I said, "I know he told you his wife had a major drug habit. Did he ever say anything about needing money?"

One of her eyebrows went up. "You mean did he ever try to put the touch on this potential old patsy for money? You'll have to try again, Mr. Morrison. Again, I have to remind you that I'm part of this world, not precisely a nineteenth-century maiden. He didn't try conning me out of my old-age nest egg, since that seems to be what you're hinting at. And if he had, he wouldn't have succeeded."

She was right. I was trying to be too clever. "I apologize. Let's try it this way: Did he ever let you know he had trouble paying for his wife's habit, even without asking you to help him out?"

"Yes, to be truthful, he did. But not in the context of his needing more money than he had. More as an explanation of why he was ending his marriage and why I shouldn't feel that I was in any way responsible for the break-up. As a matter of fact, that was one of the most charming things about him, his fretting about any guilt I might be feeling." She laughed. "And one of the most convincing things about him as well."

"You don't seem too upset by what's happened. I'm glad you can look at it that way."

"Oh, I'm upset, all right. Believe me. But I'm not the type to lose control. That may be my problem, as a matter of fact. I can just hear the boys twenty years ago saying 'C'mon, Millie, loosen up, willya!' But that's not me. You might even say that marrying Al Beasley would have been my try at a little loosening up, but that's all past now, isn't it? Another beer?"

The offer of another beer meant the interview was shortly to be concluded. I was willing to take the suggestion. "No thanks, Miss Saddler. I'll be on my way soon. I appreciate your taking the time to see me."

"Not at all. My pleasure." She stopped short. "God, that's a silly thing to say, isn't it! But before you go, you tell me something. Is that poor woman going to be all right?"

"I think so. I don't think she's the guilty party. She'll get the insurance money, and in all honesty, she's relieved to be free of the man. In a way, you're a lucky woman, Miss Saddler."

"Lucky that I got out of the fire and back into the comfortable old frying pan? Is that it?"

"I wouldn't put it quite that way."

"I would, I'm afraid. In any event, I can't say I hope you catch the killer, because in the immortal words beloved of all students of the classics, 'Frankly, my dear, I don't give a damn.'"

As I drove home I thought it over. I couldn't believe she didn't give a damn about Beasley. As to her not hoping the killer was caught, I believed that too, but I wasn't sure why she felt that way. Was it only because of her contempt for the way the man had led her on? Or was it because underneath that cool gray front something more lethal had stirred a few weeks ago and she, of all of us, knew precisely who the killer was? Maybe the visit to Appleboro only to find Florene was a ruse, a way to demonstrate that she knew nothing about the games Beasley was playing until long after his death. The lady was low on my list, but she was on it. Cool and gray may signify calm, but they tell me the top of Mount Etna is like that too, a light gray cloud of smoke nesting gently on the snow while down inside there's—what do you think—a raging volcano?

BACK HOME I found a message waiting for me on the machine from Clarence Tupper. Urgent, it said. I called and identified myself.

"Sorry to bother you, Morrison," Tupper said, "but I just heard the news about the Parker boy. You figure it's the same one as killed Beasley?"

"Seems reasonable," I said, "but, hell, there's no way for me to know."

"Well, anyway, if it was, I guess that takes Donnie off the hook."

"It does?" He wanted to tease me into asking how that did anything for Donnie, but I wasn't playing. If he wanted to tell me something bad enough, he'd tell me.

He told me. "Sure does. My boy's been away. California. Got two of our wines in a wine tasting out there. There's no way he could've been up to anything back here, right?"

"If you say so, Tupper, if you say so. Thanks for letting me know."

Maybe it was mean of me not to bubble with the enthusiasm that was expected of me, but the man annoyed me. Why didn't he stop hovering over his elderly teenaged boy? It was a wonder son Don wasn't as nutty as the old man liked to think he was, what with all the fussing and hovering and protecting— yes, and bossing around—the old man was tossing his way. I felt sorry for both father and son. Smother love, I'd call it.

I suppose, though, I should have been grateful; at least one potential murderer had been lifted from my list.

THIRTY-FOUR

EVERY ONCE IN A WHILE I have Harriet over for cocktails, especially when the weather is cool enough for me to let those ancient air-conditioners sit back and lick their wounds. This was one of those afternoons, and I had picked up some extra-fancy goodies at the expensive deli to make up for the five times to one that I'm over at her place. I had just finished putting out the smoked buffalo mozzarella, stuffed eggplant, smoked trout, and fancy crackers when she walked in and threw herself into a chair.

"Looks good," she said. "I do enjoy a good party."

"Good. This time, for heaven's sake, don't get loaded. If I have to carry you home tomorrow morning, the neighbors'll be scandalized."

"Don't worry. I'll tell the reporters I was drugged." She paused for a nibble. "Hey, this mozzarella is wonderful. How can you afford it, the way you throw money all over the place, is beyond me."

"Come again?"

"Here," she said, dropping a couple of quarters and pennies on the table. "You left this on the basement worktable." I looked blank. "When you did your laundry, dummy. And this." She added a printed card to the coins.

"What's this?" I asked and picked it up. "Oh, I remember. It's the Parker girl's aunt's— Oh, my Lord! Phoebe Cribbs. Cribbs! No wonder she looked familiar."

"What is it, Hugh?"

"Cynthia Parker's aunt is Fabian Cribbs's sister! I'm dead certain. She even has the same black hair, without the lard. And that means—"

"—that Cynthia Parker is either Fabian's daughter, or if there's another one of the older Cribbs, Fabian's niece."

We looked at each other, dawn breaking in our heads.

"Do you realize what this means?" I asked. "Especially if the old guy's her father? It means she was living next door to the man who almost certainly got her daddy hooked on drugs."

"And maybe that's why she stopped her husband from talking to you. He might have said something that would involve her father in Beasley's death." Harriet looked at me, her hand over her mouth as if to tuck the awful words back in.

"Involve, my eye. Incriminate, you mean." We let this sink in our respective skulls, and then I added, "Harriet, I'm going out there right now. I've got to speak to her. You can come if you want."

"I'll come. Meet you out front. I need to get my bag."

TWENTY MINUTES LATER we were on the Parker front steps, explaining our visit to Cynthia. I said there was something important I had to talk to her about, concerning her husband. Harriet added that she was here to offer help with the house or to take care of the child while we talked. None of this made much sense, but it got us in the door.

"Mrs. Parker," I said, after a few feeble warm-up words, "Fabian Cribbs is your father, isn't he." It wasn't a question.

She nodded. "Why?" she asked.

"Because as we both know, your neighbor got your father dependent on drugs and made his life miserable. Isn't that so?"

"Please leave my father out of this. His life has been hell since Beasley lied to him, tricked him. My father's an innocent about these things. If it isn't in Shakespeare, he doesn't—" She started to cry. "He's had his nose in old books for half a century and he doesn't realize how people can be so, so corrupt."

Harriet moved in with the ritual all-purpose women's comforter, a couple of sheets of facial tissue. It must provide something lacking in the female diet, because it calmed the young woman down almost immediately, the way it always does.

I hated this, but I had to say it. "Mrs. Parker, you stopped your husband from telling me about this, didn't you? You were afraid I might conclude that your father had killed Alfred Beasley, isn't that it?"

"But he didn't! He couldn't have!"

"Now, now," Harriet said, "nobody said he did. But it might have looked that way to some. Isn't that it?"

She nodded.

It wasn't for me to agree or disagree. "Tell me frankly," I said, "did your father ever threaten Beasley?" The answer was another nod. "In front of witnesses?"

"The people at those parties," she replied faintly. "And he told me once that he lost control of himself on campus and was screaming at the man in the hall of the humanities building. The students were there. Probably faculty, too. But he was desperate; it didn't mean anything. I wanted him to get help, but he was afraid. His position—the University—" Her hand fluttered.

"All right. I believe you. But there's one thing you've got to do. You've got to tell the police about this. If you don't, I'll have to, whether I want to or not. That's the law. They'll have to investigate any possible connection with Beasley. And then there's the matter of your husband, who somebody thought was going to tell me something important. It'd be better if you go to them than if they find out some other way."

She looked ready to break down again, and Harriet said, "Please, dear. Nobody could possibly imagine a man of your father's age and with his background able to shoot a gun into a moving car. It'll be all right, I promise you."

The woman looked at Harriet, pleading with her eyes. "Daddy had a marksman's medal from when he was in the army. In World War II. He was a sharpshooter."

We left.

THIRTY-FIVE

EVEN WITHOUT DIRECT PROOF, it seemed logical to assume that both killings in Swamp Bottom were the work of one demented citizen. Florene could have been guilty of dispatching her old man, but she'd never have been able to wing anybody in a moving vehicle. Fabian Cribbs was more likely, despite that thin-blooded, overcivilized, gentility; drugs, or the lack of them, for an addict are a remarkable source of energy for irresponsible madness. And he could have, I suppose, staged that feeble stab at vandalism at Harriet's place. It was the sort of poorly thought-out action a solid citizen turned addict might resort to. But that left the attempt on me, and no matter how inspired Fabian Cribbs might have been by hysteria and fear, I couldn't see him as capable of tying his own shoelaces, much less of either hiring someone to construct and place a bomb or managing it all by himself.

Was the drug connection the answer? Should I try to find out or should I quit now, since Florene was almost certainly in the clear to any reasonable observer. There's the rub; the key word was *reasonable,* and no insurance company is reasonable when large sums are at stake. It'd almost certainly hold back the girl's money for as near to forever as it could manage, wanting final proof, raising the possibility that if she couldn't do it all herself, then perhaps she had taken on a hired hand to do the dirty work for her.

So I was still in, and this was true even two days later, when buckets of blood began to flow once more in Appleboro, even though buckets of blood have never been my cup of tea, not when I was on the force and not these days either. This time I was one of the last to know, not being in the gossip loop as securely as Harriet. In fact, by the time I was cued in, everything was in hand: Timmy was in bed in the hospital, Florene was in trauma back home, Harriet was in tears all over the place, and

Pinky and the rest of the force were in a state of Keystone Kop Konfusion.

Harriet was the first to relay the details. Somebody had winged poor Timmy, out in the swamp behind his home. The bullet wound hadn't in itself been life threatening, but he had been lying in the muck for at least a day, and an infection had set in. Matters weren't helped by his loss of blood, and as if that weren't enough, Florene had found him and carried him out, which started the blood flowing all over again.

"What the hell were those two loonies doing out in the swamp anyway?" I bellowed at Harriet.

"Don't shout, dear," she said. "You know Timmy always wanders around back there, and Florene was looking for mushrooms."

"Mushrooms?"

"That's what I said, I think. The chanterelles are in season now, and so are the puffballs. And she knows her way around the woods."

I still wanted to complain, so I said, quite unreasonably, "Uh huh, well it's a good thing Beasley wasn't dispatched by poisoned mushrooms. That girl ought to stay home. Timmy's place is at least five miles from hers. I'm surprised she could find her way back without a seeing eye dog. Damn fool woman."

"Don't be childish, Hugh," Harriet suggested, putting her finger, as ever, on the heart of the problem. "Have you been drinking? This early? Before five?"

I started to laugh. "Yes, I have. A thimbleful of warm beer. Not a premium brand, either. But you're right; tell me slowly what happened."

"There's very little else to say. Florene found the boy near his house and she carried him back. She stripped off his shirt and washed his shoulder, which was where the poor child was hurt, put him under some covers, and hiked back to her own place. Then she called the police."

"Wait a minute now. Two questions. First, why didn't she call from Timmy's, for God's sake?"

"That's a funny thing. She says he doesn't have a phone, which he certainly did have the last time you and I were out there. And I've been thinking about that...."

"And?"

"Ask me your other question first."

"Do you know if she said to the police that Timmy had been shot?"

"You're a shrewdie, Hugh Morrison. I don't really know. You'll have to ask them yourself. You know they won't tell me anything, but it's my understanding that she said he was hurt bad and she didn't know what was wrong. Look, I'm going out tonight with some of the girls to see if we can find a candidate for town council this November who's at least female and toilet trained, neither of which qualifications describes any of the current councilmen."

"Councilpersons," I corrected.

"You're right, and don't be so funny. The women couldn't do a worse job than what we've got now, and it's my opinion that any one of them might do a helluva lot better."

"That right?" I countered. "Florene, too?"

"Don't get me started," she warned. "What I'm getting at is that I can't stand these long phone talks, so if you want to get the rest of the story, why don't you lumber over right now so I can tell you what I know and still make my meeting. I've got a hunch about something."

"I'm on my way."

Before I could hang up, she said, "By the way, now that you mention it, yes, Florene, too."

Thirty seconds later I was in Harriet's kitchen, huddled over a cup of black coffee. She told me the story again, from the beginning. I asked, "Do they know what he was shot with?"

"Pinky told me—I forget exactly, but whatever it was Pinky said it was probably something every deer hunter in the county has stashed in a closet. A thirty-thirty? Could that be right?"

"It could. Which means that it'd be next to impossible to locate the weapon, even if they had the shell and could examine it for markings."

"Don't get your hopes up, and that's your last cookie, Hugh. You're putting on weight again. Florene's so upset she isn't sure where she found Timmy, though they'll try to find out again after she's calmed down. But even if they do—''

"Even if they do know the spot," I finished the sentence for Harriet, "they haven't got half a chance of finding the shell."

"Precisely."

We sat quietly for a moment, contemplating blank walls and dead ends. "What's your hunch, Harriet? What do you want to tell me?"

"It's about Timmy's phone. I've been fretting about that phone for weeks now. It never seemed quite right to me, and then I remembered. Hugh, that boy had a phone a few years ago, and they had to take it out."

"'They'?"

"His guardian. The poor child would be watching TV and he'd see all those commercials telling him to call nine hundred numbers, and like an obedient lamb he'd do just that. And before anybody knew it he'd have these charges on his bill for ten dollars here, fifteen dollars there, for obscene phone calls, Las Vegas lucky-number prize awards, and I don't know what all. That's when they cut off the service; Timmy simply couldn't deal with all the con games he was exposed to."

"And now you're wondering how come he's got a phone again. Or had one until now."

"Yes, but there's more to it than that. Think about this, Hugh. You and I have been out to Florene's and we've both heard her phone ring. But when she answers whoever is on the line hangs up."

"So? That happens to all of us, doesn't it?"

"Yes, but think about what happened after that."

"Nothing happened. Did it?"

"It certainly did. Every time one of those calls came in, a few minutes later the police would show up. Every time. Now, anybody who goes out to Swamp Bottom has to go past Timmy's. His place is right where the road cuts off from the highway, right?"

"Right."

"And Timmy practically makes a religion out of knowing who heads out that way, right?"

"Right again."

"Well then, I think that somebody gave Timmy the phone and paid the bills, and in return, Timmy took on the job of phoning Beasley anytime a police car headed down that road. And that would explain why they were never able to find any drugs when they broke up the parties out there. You know that's what Pinky said, and the Parkers told you nothing ever came of those raids."

"It keeps coming back to drugs, doesn't it," I said. "Beasley could have bought cheap protection for himself by putting in a phone for the boy."

"And I've been thinking that whoever killed the man might have realized that Timmy was keeping an eye on things, and they could have panicked and gone over to silence that poor child. The drug people probably knew; they'd want to be assured that Beasley's wild parties weren't going to put too much of a spotlight on their dealings in Appleboro, and having Timmy stand guard would have been a way of keeping them happy."

I clapped my forehead. "Oh, no!" I moaned. "You're probably on to something, Harriet, but I just realized!"

"Realized what?"

"That I've told half the town that Timmy knows everybody who goes down the Swamp Bottom road. Both DeWitts, Tupper and his wife and father, even John Mittleman."

"Oh, dear," Harriet said. "That doesn't make things any simpler, does it."

"You might say that," I replied glumly. "You just might. Well, we'll just carry on from here. I've got a hunch things are coming to a head. Somebody's scared."

"Somebody besides me?"

"We can but hope."

THIRTY-SIX

HALF AN HOUR LATER, back in my roost over Harriet's garage, the phone rang. It was old spikey-hair. "They're not going to meet an ancient piece of fuzz like you in any cafeteria," he crowed. "You still want to see them, you go to them. They don't go to you."

I sighed. Let junior have his little triumph. "Okay, small fry, what's the deal?"

"I'll say this once. Take it or leave it. You get yourself down to New York tomorrow morning. Eleven o'clock you be on Canal Street at the Bowery, southwest corner. Look for a Lincoln limo. It'll stop. You get in. Take it or leave it. You got that?"

"Yeah, but how will they know—"

"I described you." He laughed.

That laugh told me the description was nearer to Oliver Hardy than to Clark Gable, but I swallowed hard and let it go. "I'll be there," I said, and I hung up fast, before the little toad had a chance to laugh again.

I wrote a letter to Harriet, telling her what I was about to do and where I was about to do it. At the close, I wrote, "If I get a chance I'll jot down the license number of the limo on an envelope and pop it in a mailbox, just in case. If you don't hear from me by the time you get this letter, get in touch with Pinky." I hesitated for a moment before signing off, and then figured what the hell and I penned in, "Love, Hugh."

Ten to eleven the next morning I was at the rendezvous. It was the usual mob scene. Chinatown had displaced Little Italy on Canal Street, and it was as if two tectonic plates had collided and set off earthquakes. Chinese and Italian both filled the air, and contrapuntal dins of Yiddish and Spanish and even English made their additional contributions. Crowds pushed past each other or bumped each other and no one paid the slightest attention; this was normal life on Canal. Strange and spicy smells wafted by me; I wondered if I could order a chow-mein pizza for lunch, if I lived that long.

Cars can't move very fast on Canal Street, not only because of the automobile traffic, but at least as much because of the pedestrians who surge out into the gutters at will, the traffic lights being considered not much more than a festive decoration for a permanent street fair. I saw a Lincoln limo crawling down toward me at eleven. There was plenty of time for me to write the license number on the envelope addressed to Harriet. All I had to do was walk fifteen feet from the corner, get a look at the plate, make a note of it, and pop it into a mailbox. And then get myself back to the corner.

The car stopped and a door to the back opened. I got in.

And I got a big surprise. Seated next to me was a lovely young woman in her upper twenties. I drank in this clear-skinned beauty with fashionably frizzed hair, light-gray eyes, no makeup that I could discern, and crisp features above an elegant frame in a loose wool sweater and slacks. The difference between her and most of the college kids back at the school was that the kids' sweaters were always large enough to accommodate a litter of mastiffs, and in addition looked as if they had previously done time as pizza wrappers.

"Mr. Morrison?" she asked. I nodded. She turned to the chauffeur. "All right, Felix," she said, "let's proceed." She turned back to me. "Is something wrong? You look surprised."

"I am. In my day, you would have been wearing a cashmere sweater with the sleeves pushed up, plus a gray-flannel skirt with pleats. And gone to Vassar."

Someone else might have smiled. She twitched a lip, and it didn't look nice. "You're describing my mother. I went to Sarah Lawrence."

I twitched back. "I wish a lady friend of mine could see you."

"Oh?"

"Yes. She's forever telling me that women can do things as well as men, and that they're going to get their chance to prove it."

"I see. And you'd like her to know that that includes doing the wrong things as well as men."

"Something like that," I confessed.

She turned her patrician gaze to the front. "Felix," she said, "turn into Chinatown anywhere you can and park for a moment." Felix did as ordered, and stopped the car on Mulberry Street. Back to me, the lady said, "Don't be alarmed, but I'll have to ask you to get out for a moment. Felix has to make sure you're not wired for sound. I apologize."

I got out. Felix took me by the arm and led me into a doorway. He frisked me. Then he nodded, satisfied that I wasn't wearing a bug, and mutely motioned me back to the car. Felix wasn't much of a boy for conversation. Maybe he figured it'd be wasted on the likes of me.

Back in my seat, I said, "I apologize too. I put your license number on an envelope and mailed it just as you drove up."

"I'd have less respect for you if you hadn't," she replied. Then she smiled. "What if the car was stolen? But don't worry, we mean you no harm. Felix will drive us around and I suggest we get to the point as quickly as possible. You asked for this party, Hugh, so you start."

I hate it when strangers call me by my first name. I hate it even more when they're less than half my age. "Since we're on a first-name basis, what's yours?"

"Doesn't matter. Whatever you like."

I thought of a couple I liked. "Okay, how's about madam?" I asked.

"Is that a name or a professional designation?" Those gray lasers bored into my skull, and I could tell they hadn't landed on anything they liked. For a moment they looked as hard and lifeless as the quartz that makes up the Shawangunk Cliffs.

"Whichever. As they say, 'If the shoe fits . . .'"

She came near to showing something that in a real person might have passed for emotion. "Enough games. Let's get to the point," she ordered.

"Gladly. Our late friend Beasley—or should I say Al—wasn't a very solid citizen, as we both know. And careless about his finances."

"Was he? We both didn't know that. At least my friends and I didn't."

"I stand corrected. But can we at least agree that he was occasionally late in paying his bills?"

"Oh, yes. He was that. But if that was reason enough for violence most of the credit-card holders in the country would be dead, and the masters of American Express would be in jail."

"I take it, then, that you're not too upset by what happened to him?"

She frowned her disapproval. "Oh, no, Hugh, you take it wrong. Very wrong. Beasley was a useful nuisance. Stupid, but useful. Stupid, but smart enough to realize that he or members of his household might run into some inconveniences if his credit rating wasn't kept up." She shrugged elegantly as she spoke of inconveniences. "I can't emphasize enough that 'useful' is the key concept. It's hard breaking in new people, he had the proper credentials on campus, and as well as being stupid, he was sufficiently craven to keep to his place."

"Keep to his place?"

"Not get greedy. Not try to hit out on his own. Why do you think I agreed to see you today? If you'll pardon my saying so, why the devil should my people make time for a retired policeman who can't bother us much more than a gnat?" She answered her own question. "It's because we don't want even the small amount of difficulty you might cause us. I'm here to tell you that we don't want trouble, and we didn't make trouble. If we had, you would have seen some of these inconveniences to Beasley and his family. And then, only if that had failed would we have considered taking any—how shall I put it?—irrevocable action."

It was going the way I had predicted to Harriet: Beasley was late with his payments, blew money recklessly on parties, free drugs, and lady friends in Middletown, and supported his family after a fashion on the little that was left. But when he was threatened, the way madam said, he was smart enough to get the cash somehow to avoid madam's "inconveniences," those broken arms, fires, and most important, the possibility of violent death that hung over him as the ultimate penalty for nonpayment of bills. These people hadn't killed the man; someone else had extended that particular courtesy to him.

"Do you happen to know," I asked, "how he got the necessary to settle up with you people?"

She looked at me as if I were even stupider than Beasley. "We wouldn't have dreamt of asking. And if he had tried to tell us, we would have shut him up. He got it, that's all. Prying would have been impolite." Looking nearly happy at this evidence of my mental retardation, she added, "Do I happen to know... Christ, what a question!" She looked out the window.

We were driving west and we had reached the river. I saw the rotted piers, the grimy ruin of the abandoned elevated highway. The Hudson, the same river that washed the country around Appleboro in such splendor. I asked myself, was that a million miles from here? I answered yes, in the ways that mattered it was a million miles or even more from here.

Neither of us spoke for a moment. The lady broke the silence. "Hugh, I love chatting with you, but duty calls. You know where we stand, I hope. Is there anything else?"

"One last question. A lady friend of mine was given a scare the other day. Her living room met up with a bulldozer while it was sitting there minding its own business. We were wondering if that might have been a hint from your people for me to cool my investigation. Do you think you could tell me about that?"

She shook her head. "That's the Latin American peasant approach, not ours. Give us a little credit. We don't spook lady friends over a piddling operation like this. Especially when we've got no reason to. And incidentally, you can be grateful you're not dealing with the Colombians, and if you ever do—don't, dear Hugh, don't."

"Thanks for the advice, dear madam. I won't. And thanks for your help."

"My pleasure. Now, where can we drop you? We're at the river."

"Not in it, if possible."

She smiled. "Don't give me any ideas, Hugh. And a word of advice. Don't mistake my talking with you as a sign of weakness. We may prefer to settle problems peacefully, but when necessary—some of our best friends come from South America. Colombia, in particular. Try to remember that.''

"I couldn't possibly forget," I replied, and it was nothing less than the truth.

We settled on Thirty-fourth Street and Sixth Avenue, at Macy's. I figured a store that big would have something I could buy for Harriet, and maybe a little present for myself as well. (I got Harriet half a pound of smoked salmon, and for me I chose a box of Perugina chocolates, the ones with hazelnuts. I ate half of it while I walked uptown to the bus terminal.)

As I walked, I thought about the day. There was a strange, unsettled feeling in my stomach, and it had nothing to do with the chocolates. It was a feeling I hadn't known in years and I sought to recollect it. It came to me. In younger days, when I was married, we lived in the city. Everybody there seemed covered by an invisible force field, the science fiction variety, to fend off all but the most impersonal human contact. In contact lies danger. And that's how it had been with the beautiful young woman I had met. She was a humanoid, a robot, a computerized projection of virtual reality.

I suppose it's the same in all big cities, but New York is the biggest, and it's more so there. I used to say hello to people in the elevator each day, and we'd trade smiles. Then one day they wouldn't be there any longer, or else we'd be the ones to move away, and none of us knew the slightest thing about the others, not even names, but only whether the teeth in the smiles were white, yellow, or absent.

The city left me feeling like the latest murder victim on the TV news, existing only as a splash of red blood on the sidewalk that the camera would zoom in on, and knowing that even that pathetic proof of existence would be flushed away by a Department of Sanitation water truck in the morning.

That's how she had affected me. There she had been, young, handsome, intelligent, educated, and her invisible force field was made of ice at absolute zero, rendering her unapproachable, and terminally unknowable. I was wrong in calling her madam. In that profession she would have been a failure. She would have frightened off the clients. I shuddered; God save the republic.

THIRTY-SEVEN

A DAY LATER I entered Timmy Young's hospital room. A young woman was sitting with him. I looked at him and then at her. Then I did a quick double take on both of them, which I suppose adds up to a quadruple take, but under the circumstances I can't criticize myself. It wasn't only that the woman was feeding Timmy something moist and dark gray and that he was snapping at it eagerly, and it wasn't only that the woman was Florene.

But her hair was combed and looked clean, and if she wasn't tucked into a chic little black outfit by Chanel topped by a single strand of pearls, she at last had managed to avoid her normal appearance of having recently been disgorged by a threshing machine. For a fleeting moment of madness I entertained the hopeful thought that she had drowned her kids and gone to modeling school.

"Hi," I said. "How are you feeling, Timmy?"

"I feel real good. Tomorrow I get out of here. Mrs. Beasley is helping me eat only because I can't use my right hand so good, but I'm fine otherwise."

"What's that you've got there?" I asked.

"Mushroom stew," Florene said. "I picked them myself. You wanna taste?"

My first thought was that if Florene had dragged the goodies out of the woods I was too young to die. My second thought was that this stuff would probably cost seven bucks a bowl in a restaurant. "Yeah," I said, greed conquering caution. "I would like to taste, if you've got a little extra."

She extracted a second plastic spoon from her bag and handed it to me along with the plastic container the mushrooms were in. I took a timid nibble, and it was marvelous. "Hey, this is great! What's in here, anyway?"

Florene dismissed the question. "Things I get. I don't know, one time to the next. Just things. You can't have no more this time. It's for Timmy."

I looked at her again and this time saw that her skin was clear and that she had managed to shed—what, ten pounds, maybe? She was still no beauty queen, but she was getting near to looking like an ordinary housewife, which isn't a bad thing to be getting near to for a hard-luck muddlehead like Florene. I was pleased, strangely enough, that the girl was shedding the ugly-duckling role and turning into—what, the merely slightly dumpy duckling?

"Where are your kids today?" I asked.

"The big one's in school, and the two little ones are at your place."

"My place?"

"Yeah. I couldn't take them to the hospital so I asked Mrs. Lorimer could she take them for a while. She said how you were like working for me, so she'd put them in your office till I got back. I gave them some peanut butter and jelly. They'll be all right."

There was no point in expressing annoyance; I'd save that for Harriet. A more practical approach was to get them out of the place before the walls were festooned with peanut butter and jelly trim. I wondered idly if there were seeds in the jelly, if it was raspberry, maybe.

"Okay," I said, "I've got a few questions for Timmy. Then we can both get out of here, let him rest."

"He can rest while I'm here," Florene objected.

"I don't need rest," Timmy said. "I'm tired of rest."

"People in hospitals need rest," I countered. "That's why they're in bed."

"The doctor said I should get up lots and walk around," Timmy said.

I ignored the boy. "Timmy," I said, "I have to know how you got that telephone of yours."

"I just got it," he said. "They put it in."

"I know they put it in. It didn't just grow there. Somebody paid for it. Who, Timmy?"

His eyes were wide with simulated innocence. "I don't know. How should I know?"

"Now look, son. Florene's husband was killed and some people say that Florene did it. You have to help me find the truth so Florene will be all right, and right now I need to know about that telephone."

He looked at her. She nodded. "That's right. Far as I can see, I'm not getting much for my money from Mr. Morrison, but maybe if we help him, we'll get somewhere."

I had the horrible feeling that Florene was going to deduct $4.98 from my fee for advice and assistance provided by outside sources.

"Well," Timmy said, reluctantly, "Mr. Beasley, he said he'd put a phone in my house if I did something for him. He said whenever I was home I should watch for all the cars that went down the road. He said I was home most all the time—I am, too, 'cept when I go shopping—and then he said I should call him right away and tell him when certain cars were on the way."

"What certain cars?"

Timmy stuck out his lower lip. He looked at Florene. "Do I have to?" She nodded.

"But I promised not to."

"You promised Mr. Beasley," I explained. "But he's dead now, so you can tell me."

Florene frowned. "I don't know about that, Mr. Morrison. I promised my grandma things and she's dead and I still have to keep my promises to her."

I wondered who the hell's side she was on. I wanted to say, "Screw your grandma," but I settled for, "that's different," and then went on before she could ask me how it was different, which was something I didn't know. "Come on, Timmy, out with it."

"He said—he said, if it was a police car I should call him." Once Timmy opened up his mouth, the rest spilled out more easily. "He said I should always be home on Saturdays and Sundays in the afternoon and evening and if I wasn't, he'd take the phone away."

That, of course, covered the times Beasley would be most likely to be staging his little parties.

"And he said I should practice other times so's I wouldn't forget and just keep track of everybody I saw even when it wasn't Saturday or Sunday."

"Awhile back you told me about the people you saw going down the road about the time Mr. Beasley was killed. Do you remember?"

"Sure I do." He frowned. "Uh, Mr. Tupper. Mr. DeWitt. Mrs. DeWitt. Florene's dad." He stopped. "Gosh, it's so long ago. Mr., uh, Tupper."

"You already said Mr. Tupper. Who else?"

"Mr. Mittleman, I think. Maybe the telephone-company man. Oh, yeah, and that man with the funny hair." He looked up at me, his eyes bright with anxiety. "I'm sorry, Mr. Morrison. I can't remember. It's too long ago."

"You did just fine, Timmy," I said. "I think you told me what I wanted to hear." I didn't explain any further, not with Florene right there. No point in giving the girl any ideas. But Timmy had given me an idea.

THIRTY-EIGHT

"HARRIET, HONEY, how'd you like to get your gossip gland revved up into action and give me a hand?"

"Hugh, dear, how'd you like a fat lip, talking to me that way? Why do you men always assume that women naturally have some special talent for gossip? What do you want, and never mind the insults."

I should have watered her martinis before dinner; somehow Harriet always gets extra sensitive to what she calls my sexist attitudes when there's alcohol chugging through her veins. "Sorry. Just kidding. I need your help in spreading a couple of rumors around town, and making sure they get to the right people."

"All right, then say it that way, and never mind about gossip glands." She put a hand out and rumpled my hair. "What is it, Hugh? What can I do?"

"I've got an idea that I can flush out our killer. I'd rather not say who I think it is yet, but this may do it."

"You can tell me who you think it is. That is, if you want my help. Or are you afraid my gossip gland might be overstimulated by it all?"

She had me, so I told her who I thought, and why. "Oh, that couldn't be!" she objected.

"Maybe not, but this'll be a way to find out without getting anybody so worked up they might think of a libel suit, in case I'm wrong."

She nibbled on that and then agreed. "Okay, let's go. What do I do?"

"Two little things. First, you're pretty chummy with the gal who covers Appleboro for *The Clarion,* aren't you? (*The Clarion* is the weekly paper for four or five of the towns in the valley.)

"Yes, I'm pretty chummy with the *woman* who covers Appleboro if that's who you mean."

"I stand corrected." I made a mental note to make the martinis one part vodka to three parts water next time, and to slow down the absorption rate of the alcohol by laying on some serious hors d'oeuvres—if I could coax her off her diet.

"Okay. Try to remember. That's Pauline Beckman. What about her?"

"You think you could feed her a tidbit about how you heard the police found the shell that hit Timmy Young? Tell her it came from a thirty-thirty, a Winchester, the rifle of choice for deer hunters around here? And that they're planning to check everybody who's got a hunting license in the area, then see if anybody's gun puts out the same markings as on the shell?"

"I could, but Pauline's a pro. She'll doublecheck with the police and find out it's not so. What good'll that do you?"

"Don't you worry. The police will, in the classic phrase, neither confirm nor deny. 'No comment' will be the only response the gal—woman—will get out of them."

"Watch it, buster."

"Sorry."

"I hope so. What's the second little thing?"

"If you could pass along the same story to everybody you know, it'd be a great help. Everybody. Friends, enemies, clerks in the stores. Whatever. Whoever."

"One condition," Harriet said. "You get your male gossip gland revved up and do the same with friends, enemies, pool halls, barber shops. And if there's a whorehouse in town you can include that as well."

"Condition accepted. And, FYI, there are seven whorehouses in town, plus the freelancers who cruise town hall on town-meeting nights. It's a big condition, but I'm game."

"And then what happens?"

"And then I'm going to see if my candidate has a hunting license, but says he doesn't hunt or even have a gun, loves animals too much to shoot at one. Had a pet deer named Irving when he was a boy."

Harriet thought. Then her head bobbed. "You're on. I'll start right off with the paper. They're bound to carry the story about the attack on Timmy this Thursday. Pauline ought to jump at an item about the police having a lead on the assailant.''

And so Pauline did. *The Clarion*'s front page had a headline on local man shot, police may have a lead, see Appleboro news, page seven. Page seven revealed that Timmy was wounded but recovering. It further detailed that there was a persistent but unconfirmed rumor that the police were working on tracing the weapon through the markings on the bullet they had recovered. Finally, since the weapon was a thirty-thirty, popular among deer hunters, the assailant was likely to be a local person; hunters from other areas would not normally be in the vicinity until the season opened some weeks hence. So far as I was concerned, Pauline Beckman rated enshrinement with Walter Cronkite, Edward R. Murrow, and Ernie Pyle as one of America's great and fearless journalists.

There was another item on the Appleboro pages that made me even more certain that my hunch was a good one. It was about Clarendon wines. They had chalked up three gold medals and a silver in the Empire State competitions up in Albany, beating out some of the hottest competition from California. There was a picture of Don Tupper grinning like a fool and the caption read, ''Why is this man smiling?''

I could hardly wait to learn the answer, which was that not only had he knocked off those medals, but in addition, liquor stores in New York, Boston, and Albany had inquired about placing orders. And this was in contrast to the near bankrupt condition the vineyard was in only a few years ago. The article segued into a love song to the local bank (a miserable, penny-pinching bunch of villains, if you were to ask me) for displaying patience and faith in a local businessman, and to Don Tupper himself for his enterprise and perseverance. My stomach lurched from an overdose of schmaltz; I stopped reading at that point.

There was nothing to do now but wait. Wait and hope that if the proper party had failed to see the article about the bullet that had nailed Timmy, he had at least been reached by the rumors to that effect that we had started bouncing over back fences across the town.

There was, of course, the tiresome possibility that Appleboro's crime wave might be completely propelled by an out-of-town connection. In that case, all the derring-do with planted articles in *The Clarion* would be just dandy for eliminating our local suspects, but wouldn't do much toward finding us a killer. I tried not to think of it. *Think positive,* I told myself, though with little conviction.

THIRTY-NINE

IT OCCURRED TO ME that a planted story in *The Clarion* about police activities might not set very well with the authorities. If I wanted to get information about Fabian Cribbs from them, I'd better call while they were still in a cooperative mood. I got Pinky and asked him what was going on.

"Cribbs?" he said. "He's a nut-case. Comes in with his daughter to confess that he didn't kill anybody no matter what anybody says. It looks to us like he and Beasley were just a couple of hyenas running in circles so's they could bite each other on the can. That's what those damn people at the school are like."

"Did his daughter say anything about his problem?"

"You mean the drugs. Yeah, she let us in on it, and we'll be looking into it. You can't tell what a druggie'll get up to when he's on the outs with his connection and goes off his nut."

"But you think he's in the clear?"

"I didn't say that. He might not be likely, but he's right in there for now with Florene, and I don't know which one is harder to talk to. Jesus, what a pair! I shoulda been a concert violinist. And so long as you're interested, let me— Hold on a sec, willya?"

I held on. I heard a few background curses. Then some shouting. Then Pinky again: "Hugh, *The Clarion* just came into the station. One of the boys showed me this article. All about thirty-thirty's and markings on the shell and us hot on the trail. It's gotta be you. It sounds like you. What the hell are you up to?"

"Who, me?"

There were more loud background sounds. "Now I hear the front desk has been saying 'No comment' fourteen times in the last half hour. You know what that'll come to by tonight?"

"Should I multiply it out?"

"Don't be funny," he suggested. "What're you up to, Hugh? You on to something, I want to know."

I explained what I was up to. "I know it puts you in a spot, Pinky, but you guys couldn't do this. Me, I'm a private citizen; I can get away with it."

"Balls. You should've got in touch first."

"What the hell, boy, if I was in touch with you, you would have called the paper and stepped on it. You'd have had to, no?" I didn't wait for an answer. "Look, Pinky, it's done, and if you can help me a little further, maybe we can get somewhere. I think our man is going to deep-six a Winchester thirty-thirty and claim he doesn't hunt. I mean, you don't have to register rifles. There's no gun control on thirty-thirty's so we'd never be able to prove he had one once he got rid of it."

"You're a nut-case, Morrison. *If* it was somebody Timmy saw that day. *If* the shot was from a Winchester. *If* the guy's got a hunting license. *If* he's dumb enough to dump the rifle. And *if* Timmy Young got plugged because somebody thought he knew who killed Beasley, even without realizing it." He paused. "I leave out anything?"

There was nothing he had left out, so I did the only thing I could have done. I ignored him and went on. "And if you can get me the poop from the state records on hunting licenses for half a dozen people for maybe the last three years maybe we'll find somebody who says he gets hunting licenses all the time because they look so sporty framed on the wall of the den, but he thinks real hunters ought to be shot. What do you say?"

He grumbled, groused, and finally agreed, adding, "But if this kind of half-assed idea works, you let us take it from there, you get me!"

"Gladly."

I gave him the names of the men—and women—Timmy had seen going down the Swamp Bottom road. For good measure I threw in Beasley's office mate, just for the hell of it. It turned out that everybody on the list, including the DeWitt and Parker ladies, had hunting licenses. Even John Mittleman, which kind of surprised me; I had had him pegged for one of these pious types who was against killing any creature fashioned by the Lord unless, of course, it came into view medium rare with a bottle of ketchup and a portion of fries on the side, which would have made it food, not something out of God's hobby kit. Only one of the academics, Cribbs, had a license. So far, so good.

Most people around here who own a lot of acreage put up signs restricting hunting on their land to one or the other of the two local hunt clubs. This isn't necessarily because they love the hunt club, but because they know that hunters are going to trespass on their property no matter how many NO HUNTING signs they might tack up. It's a move to discourage macho types from outside the area from wandering in. Every once in a while a taxicab full of drunks will show up, generally from one of the bigger towns in the area, sometimes even from New York, and start popping at everything that twitches. You'd think they'd realize that a moving target that's more vertical than horizontal couldn't be a deer doing a tango on its hind legs, but it doesn't always work that way.

Harriet figured out how to find out who belonged to which hunt club and who didn't. She used to help out with the local amateur theater group, sewing costumes, selling tickets, and manning its phone from time to time, and she decided we would stage a public-opinion survey. Everybody knows about public-opinion surveys and will spend twenty minutes on the phone answering idiotic questions. Like which car, a Mercury or a Dodge or a Toyota, do you think a grandmother would be most likely to buy? A black rock guitarist? A serial killer? A bank president? A different kind of crook? People complain about all the questions they get asked and how much time it takes, but the truth is that they're kind of flattered too, and they go along with the interview so they can keep complaining.

Harriet got us a young actress with an irresistibly friendly voice to help out and then keep quiet about it until the affair had worked its way to some kind of conclusion. We wrote up a questionnaire. First, our coconspirator called the head honcho of each hunt club and identified herself as working for the New York Society for Public-Opinion Research, doing a survey among community leaders about game hunting in New York. "Since there have been a number of hunting accidents lately, some people feel gun control should be made stricter while others feel that local hunt clubs should set the standards for their communities. What are your feelings about this?'' Naturally, the feeling was that the state should mind its own damned business and stop wasting taxpayer money on the bureaucracy.

After a few sympathetic noises our interviewer asked if she could get a list of club members to elicit their opinions as well. ''We feel the survey sponsors will be very impressed if the others in your group feel as strongly about this as you do, sir.''

I think maybe this was illegal and that Harriet and I had committed something punishable by two days on the ducking stool, but it was in a good cause. Our interviewer got permission to copy names from the membership lists of both clubs. She visited the clubhouses and explained that she only needed a sample of names and that she would copy them down. Then, left alone to make notes, she looked for only the names we were interested in, and after writing down two dozen more to make it look good, thanked her benefactor, promised to provide a copy of the survey results, and drove off into the blue, forever, we hoped.

Everybody we were interested in belonged to one or another of the hunt clubs except for Michelle DeWitt. ''Maybe,'' I suggested to Harriet, ''she doesn't need to hunt for deer. Maybe when she sees them on the road she stops the car and orders them to drop dead.'' Even John Mittleman was a member, which came as a surprise, what with him being a self-appointed advance man for a real estate development in heaven.

''Well, sweetheart,'' I said to Harriet, ''now we go to work. See who says he doesn't have a rifle, doesn't hunt. It's a long shot, but maybe it'll work.''

''Who you starting with?'' Harriet asked.

''I don't know. What I do know is that we're staying away from the good Dr. Cribbs. The cops are working that angle since Cynthia Parker spoke to them, and we'd better stay away.'' I didn't mention that they were also somewhat sensitive on the subject of Cribbs and me.

''But I think I'll end with Don Tupper. He's my candidate. Bribed Beasley, which was undoubtedly very easy, to foul up DeWitt's wines, and then when Beasley wanted more money and laid on a little blackmail, helped him find eternal rest in the dam behind the house. And if that's not enough for you, there's always Beasley's greasy thumbprints on Betty Ann Tupper to provide an extra incentive.''

"I don't agree."

"You don't agree?"

"Didn't Clarence Tupper say that Don was in California when Timmy was shot? Doesn't that take him out of the running?"

"Not necessarily. Nobody can pinpoint exactly when Timmy was winged. It'd be easier if he'd been killed right off, but with him lying there in and out of consciousness for God knows how long, any guess about the timing is pretty iffy."

Harriet flipped a hand to dismiss my logic. "Shucks, how inconsiderate of the boy to linger on. But look, we're only playing games anyway, and it seems to me that Mittleman's just as good a possibility as Don Tupper. More so, even. Don's a level-headed, serious, responsible young man. The other one's in a permanent rage at anybody he fingers as a sinner. And we know he hated those parties down in Swamp Bottom. I can just hear Al Beasley making fun of him when he showed up there to go into his prophet of doom ballet. I think John Mittleman is as likely to be a suddenly boiling-over madman as anybody else I can think of in this whole miserable town."

"But why would he—"

"How should I know? You're the cop, not me. Arm of the Lord, rehearsal for Judgment Day. I figure it's as good a guess as yours."

"Okay. What you mean is that I'm only guessing so you can guess good too, huh?"

She dismissed that too. "If you say so."

"Well, this is America, sweetheart, so you're entitled to your opinion, even when you're wrong. I'll tell you what I'll do, though. I'll start with John Mittleman and finish with Don Tupper. Then we'll see where we stand."

I hesitated a moment and then added, "While we're up to this, Harriet, there's one big problem we've got to keep in mind."

"Only one?"

"Don't interrupt. If we're right about one crazy being be-hind everything that's happened, we've got to understand why he would have been after Beasley, Parker, Timmy, and even me; whether he was capable of each of these attempts; and whether he had the opportunity each time."

"Suppose it doesn't work out for any of them?"

"Then it's back to the starting gate."

"Right. Let's go. To horse, my masked avenger friend!" Harriet bellowed, "and let the devil take the hindmost!"

"Of the horse?"

FORTY

SUNDAY, and it didn't need a Sherlock Holmes to figure out where to find John Mittleman. True, I didn't know whether he'd be on display as a sacred relic or merely present as a congregant, possibly making sure the preacher didn't display too much ankle beneath his robe, but I knew he'd be in church. Even in the spring, when the local pastors can't fill two pews once the golf season starts, not without advertising a ten-minute *Reader's Digest* service, John could be counted on to show up, hymnal at the ready. John was sure his Maker would know he was sacrificing pleasure to religious duty, and if there had been any doubt, I'm sure John would have put Him straight.

All I had to do was to stroll down Maple Street when church let out and quite by accident run into him and Jenny. As I've said, we were once on casually good terms before the man found God and dropped the rest of his friends. "Hi there, you two," I chirped with false sincerity. "How're you this fine fall day?" I probably would have said that even if it had been raining, but fortunately it was one of those valley days when the air is so clear and crisp that the distant hills seem only two steps away, and the white-gold sun of fall is nearly as warm and friendly as its deep yellow brother of July, and twice as welcome.

The Mittlemans smiled. John agreed: "It's a fine fall day, all right. Yet every day has its purpose in this life, and every day is fine." Once again, inevitably, I was put in my place (on the bullet train to perdition, I guess).

Jenny Mittleman sighed. Or was it too loud to be only a sigh?

"Yeah," I said. "I guess you're right." I cleared my throat. "Listen, John, don't I remember that you used to do a bit of hunting, before, uh, you know, before?"

"That's right. But I've stopped all that nonsense."

"Really? Altogether? Get rid of your guns too? What'd you use, anyway? That's what I want to know about, for my cousin down in Jersey."

"A Winchester thirty-thirty. Dandy rifle it was. But I have no need for it now."

"Glad to get the damn thing out of the house," Jenny put in.

"The *blessed* thing," John admonished. "Man may use a weapon damnably, but nothing the Lord allows us to make is damned. Not in itself."

Jenny rose up as if she were about to ask if that went for nuclear bombs as well, but she closed her parted lips and sank back again. "Never heard you object to a table set with meat, John," she said. "Not even venison."

"You know the answer to that," Mittleman told her, and like a broken record, he continued. "The beasts of the field are provided for our sustenance. I'm no vegetarian. You put beef, venison, whatever, on the table, and you know how much I enjoy it. It's the hunters I object to. They kill for sport, not for food, and when I found I was doing the same, that's when I quit." He looked up toward the far horizon, possibly waiting for his halo to arrive via UFO, special delivery.

This was starting to sound like the music introducing an old family war dance, in which case the conversation would have gotten away from me completely. I tried to steer the troops in another direction. "You really quit cold, huh? Give up the hunt club, too?" I knew he hadn't quit the club. Maybe Harriet had something after all; why would someone who claimed to be without a rifle and who objected to hunters and hunting belong to a hunt club? Let's see if he lied.

"Oh, no. I get my license for deer every year. Religiously, you might say," he added, laughing mildly at his own bad joke. "And I keep up my membership in the Steven Haas Hunt Club out on Long Meadow Road."

"For heaven's sake, why?" I asked. After I said that I wished I hadn't; casual references to heaven might get me treated to a dissertation on blasphemy.

I was lucky. John was so pleased with himself that he let my dereliction go. "Because if I weren't a member they'd never let me in to distribute literature and talk to those boys, get them to see the light. Get them to understand that killing for the sake of killing is wrong, and that that's very different from killing for food." He warmed up to the topic, and spray came out of his mouth into the fresh air of Maple Street. "If I quit the club, they'd never let me in the door, but they wouldn't dare throw me out as long as my dues are paid on time. They read the paper. They know my pen is in the service of the Truth. And they'd be afraid." He nodded vigorously. "Religious freedom. They know."

Who wouldn't know, I wondered as long as John was around to tell them. Anyway, that was all I needed to find out. John Mittleman didn't have a gun and didn't hunt, he said. Yet he still had a license and a membership in the hunt club. That was my prescription for a liar and a murderer. But his explanation made sense, from his point of view. Maybe. And I was back where I started, for certain.

Score zero for the home team.

One way or another I spoke to the others on my brief list, except for Don Tupper, whom I was saving for the last. They all checked out, with no inconsistencies in their stories, no sudden aversions to hunting despite memberships in hunt clubs or the possession of hunting licenses. No claims to gunlessness either. No contradictions from either of the DeWitts. Florene's daddy, Ed Weller, even insisted on showing me his thirty-thirty and telling me what a fine instrument it was, gratuitously adding the names of a few people he'd like to have plugged, including the late Al Beasley.

These efforts only sharpened my appetite for Tupper, the last great hope before I had to admit I was sifting through the garbage in the wrong blind alley. I had to plan carefully. I had to talk over my approach with Harriet, whose talents for a roundabout and sideways shuffle toward a target could by contrast make me look like a small child simulating innocence with a mouth stuffed full of candy just before lunch.

"What do you think?" I asked. "If I blow this one, I'm back to square one."

"Don Tupper still your favorite suspect, is he?" Harriet asked doubtfully.

"Not just the favorite. The only one I've got left. If this doesn't pan out, it's back to the old drawing board with the whole damned kaboodle. I'm getting awful tired of this, Harriet. Once this is over, I hope I never have to gaze upon the widow Beasley's loveliness again, and the only cases I'm going to take are people snitching cans of tuna from the deli."

"Now, don't you worry." She reached over and patted my hand. "We'll work something out. Don may still be completely innocent, which is what I think, but we'll get this set up nice and natural so you can talk to him without looking sneaky. You'll see."

And we did see. Harriet phoned the vineyard and identified herself. "Oh, Don," she said, "I was just delighted to see that article about you in *The Clarion*. All those medals up in Albany!"

I could hear a couple of barks of laughter followed by a few words I couldn't make out.

"Oh, but it *is* something!" she said. "And I do hope this means Clarendon is going to sail up to the top where it belongs."

Harriet is not the kind of woman to go into gasps and gushes and aerobic seizures of mindless admiration, but she's a miracle at simulating the condition. In fact, she's quite capable of getting carried away by her own routine, and that's what was happening now. The exchange of Lorimer praise and Tupper protests of modesty went on and on, it seemed to me, until I parodied a great big yawn and lobbed it in my coconspirator's direction. She got the message and she shifted gears. "Listen, Don," she said in a hesitant tone, "I have a big favor to ask you. I'm having a group of women in the political club over to raise some money for our candidate for supervisor, and it occurred to me that maybe we could have a wine tasting to draw people in. You know?"

He knew.

"The thing is," she said, stumbling artfully over her words, the sly minx, "I thought that we'd get a bigger crowd, what with you getting all those medals, and also that—well, I wondered, since it'd be sort of like a local promotion for you—

maybe you could give us a good price? Would that be possible, do you think? It'd just be for maybe two cases?''

Tupper said something and Harriet replied with an uncharacteristic and unconvincing giggle. ''No, it's not going to be the Socialist Labor Party, I promise you. All the girls are rich, fat capitalists who'll be able to afford your vintage champagnes ... Oh, that's wonderful! In that case, can we make it three cases, sort of all your prize winners mixed? ... You're a dear. I'll get Hugh Morrison to come out with me and get them into the station wagon... Tomorrow about ten will be just fine. Thank you so much.'' They broke the connection.

She turned to me, a triumphant smile on her face. ''It worked just fine. And it isn't going to cost you very much, either. Probably under a hundred for three cases. Maybe a little more, but not much.''

''Me? A hundred bucks! What the hell, Harriet!''

''Oh,'' she said airily, ''put it on Florene's bill. It'll be worth it, even if she doesn't pay. When we go out there you can get into a casual talk with Don. Then we'll have him at the wine tasting to mingle with the girls and you can talk to him some more. That way there won't be any need to grill the poor boy all at once. Just natural conversation. And don't you think it's a good idea to get campaign money for the election at the same time? I thought it was pretty neat.''

''So you can elect a female town supervisor?''

She nodded. ''That's the idea, buster.''

''No,'' I said, just to be negative, ''I don't think it's a good idea.'' I had no real objection to a female supervisor, who couldn't turn out worse than the nonfemale bum we had stumbling around town hall, but the point was that I knew I'd never get that hundred bucks back. The take would all go into the campaign fund and what I'd get out of it would be glory—if she won. Damn all.

FORTY-ONE

At ten the next morning we were out at Clarendon. Tupper had three cases waiting for us in his office. "There they are," he said. "One each Chardonnay, Seyval Blanc, and Cabernet Franc. My three medal winners."

"That's wonderful, Don," Harriet said. "We'll get them right into the wagon and be out of the way. What do we owe you?"

He shrugged. "Oh, let's just make it a round hundred dollars. What the heck, my first local tasting."

I glared at Harriet, but held my tongue except to say, "Check all right?"

"Why, sure," he said, laughing, "but first I'll have to have some identification. Your driver's license and one major credit card will do."

Then we all three had a nice laugh, except, that is, for me. I filled out a check, and bent over to pick up the first case. But I wanted to delay us a moment so I could talk to the man. All I could think of saying with what I hoped wouldn't be too obvious a dollop of kittenish hypocrisy, was "Hey, for that kind of money, don't we get a taste first?"

"In the *morning?*" Harriet asked.

"Before *five?*" Tupper asked.

"Sure," I answered. "Like we always do at Harriet's place. Even on Sunday. Especially on Sunday, seems like."

For a second time all three of us laughed except, this time, Harriet, and Tupper got out the tasting glasses, some saltines, and a piece of cheese from the refrigerator. "We'll start with the Chardonnay," he said, "that being the lightest, and we'll work up to the Cabernet Franc. Grab a chair, everybody."

It tasted like wine to me; that much even I could tell. I smacked my lips appreciatively. "Mm, good," I said, not being up to phrases like bouquet, raspberry aftertaste, and lingering sense of oak.

Harriet murmured something similar.

As Don rinsed the glasses before the next tasting, and we took some cheese and crackers to clear our palates (Hah!), I said, "You going to take time off and get yourself some venison this year, Don?"

"Depends," he said. "Depends on how the business is going. I may have to stick close to home this year, especially now that things are beginning to look up."

"You men are so bloodthirsty, going after those beautiful creatures with your revolvers," Harriet said.

Tupper and I both laughed. "Revolvers!" I said. "You tell her, Don. She doesn't listen to me."

"No revolvers for deer, Mrs. Lorimer. Personally, I use a Winchester thirty-thirty. My dad gave it to me when he took me out hunting the first time, when I was a kid. Gave me my own rifle, my first red jacket, and my first red hat."

"Oh, you men," Harriet clucked. "Every generation teaching the next on how to kill."

"You like to eat don't you?" I asked.

"It's not that bad," Tupper said. "Sure, it's sport. It's a game of skill, but that's not all. We only shoot what we can use, and it's more than a simple macho trip. I remember that first time I brought along some beer, and Dad gave me hell. Made me leave it at the edge of the woods to pick up when we came back, and said if he ever caught me making a party out of hunting he'd take the skin off my back."

"Sounds like a smart man, your dad," I said.

"He was. And still is."

We kept a moment of silence over our second tasting, partly because I couldn't think of another thing to say after that highly original, "Mm, good." Harriet said, "Delicious," which I was reasonably certain exhausted her resources as well.

During the third wine, ("I *really* like this!" I said.) I kept the subject alive: "Well, if I'm not too busy, I expect to get into the woods, get some venison for us. Harriet's a real cannibal when it comes to deer meat." She shot me a venomous glance; I smiled at her, innocently. "I hope you got yourself a license, in case you get a chance yourself."

"Oh, yes. I keep up with it. Someday, I'll let my staff of hundreds do the heavy lifting, and I'll be out in the woods or off on the yacht somewhere. You can bet your sweet life on it. I'd love to get out with Dad again, and I know it'd make him happy, just like the old days. Still keep up with the hunt club, too."

"I'm sure you'll make it," Harriet said, "and I hope the time isn't too far off."

"Amen to that, Mrs. Lorimer. Amen to that."

We left. We had found out what we wanted. Don Tupper was downgraded from clearly guilty to possible suspect along with all the others. And it had only cost me a cool hundred to find out. To find out what? Nothing? As usual, I wrote up the interview, had Harriet look at it for additions and corrections, and put it away with the rest of the case for later study.

FORTY-TWO

A FEW DAYS WENT BY, during which I took care of the rest of my life, like trying unsuccessfully to balance my checkbook for the first time since the previous July, restocking my beer cellar (I don't believe in wine cellars), washing the car, and sticking the summer clothes that had been glowering at me for a month and a half into the cardboard box that slides under the bed. I sprinkled them with mothballs certain to give me headaches during the night for at least six weeks. Why is it that old shirts and pants reach the maximum of comfort and softness at the same time they begin to get holes or come apart at the seams? (I put them away anyway; they were old friends who had stood by me, and now I'd stand by them.)

I did, however, attend to duty sufficiently to review all my notes on the case. And something stood out. A brand new idea. I buzzed Harriet. "Listen, sugar, I've got a new angle on the Beasley business I want to try out on you. You feel like the grilled shrimp at Tamah's Tavern tonight?"

"Sure. Though the last time we were there I thought the oil she was basting with was rancid." (Harriet always made them use oil for us—none of that lethal butter, I regret to say.)

"You're probably right, but I think it'll be okay. She generally switches to winter-weight oil this time of year. Pick you up at seven?"

Tamah's is the last eatery in the area to call sherbet sherbet instead of sorbet and jacking up the price by half a buck. We lingered over our orders—I had gained a little weight, Harriet claimed, and wasn't allowed to order pie. Not even à la mode-less pie. "You see?" I said. "Both times, that's what Timmy was saying. At his house and then again in the hospital. First time, when we were both there, the phone rang and somebody tried to sell him some bonds. We thought he was repeating himself. The second time, when I saw him in the hospital, I interrupted the boy and when he started again I didn't catch on to what he was saying."

"You could be right," Harriet said, "though I hate to think so."

"Me too. But now the thing is, how do we find out? There isn't a shred of evidence. And without evidence, you've got to find a way to help people trap themselves."

"Meantime, why don't you look in on Timmy and check this idea out?"

"I was planning on that," I said, "and I think I'll trot on down to Florene's end of the road while I'm there. I've got a couple of questions for Cynthia Parker again. Speaking of which, if you're interested, I've got a little job you can handle better than me."

"'If I'm interested'! Of course I'm interested."

"Okay. Try to find a handful of people who grew up around here and went to the local schools. People you judge to be around forty, forty-five. Don Tupper's age. This is what I need you to ask about, anyway you want to do it." I told her the plot and she agreed. "When I get done at the Parker place, if I hear from her what I hope to hear, I'll be off somewhere else for at least a couple of hours, so don't expect me back anytime soon. Okay?"

"Okay. I understand. Incidentally, don't forget that the wine tasting is on for Saturday afternoon. I'm charging a fiver for admission, and it's open for all to meet the candidate. Twenty people makes back the cost of the wine, and if you figure one bottle for more than four people, it'll take less than five bottles to cover costs."

"Plus a few bucks for potato chips and things."

"No, no potato chips."

"Why not? Potato chips are a natural. And they're cheap."

"Potato chips are too salty. They'll only encourage more drinking, and that's not what we want. I want leftovers. We'll pick up something unsalted, some kind of cracker or other. Salt-free popcorn, maybe?"

"Lorimer," I said, "you're a crook."

"I can but try," she responded modestly, "though I have to confess to some small success."

"Let's get out of here," I said, "unless you can think of a way to avoid paying."

"You might try saying there was a bug in the sherbet."

"Not a chance. You did that last time."

"I'm only human, Hugh."

"Now there's a confession I've been waiting for for years."

She hit me with her pocketbook and we left, pleased with each other and with the plans we had made both on behalf of her candidate and our murder case.

The next morning I drove out to Timmy Young's. I knocked, and when the door opened I had three shocks. It was Florene who opened the door; she had a broom in her hand; and she was wearing makeup and nail polish, each reasonably applied and each on the appropriate parts of her anatomy. "Florene?" I asked weakly.

"Yeah," she responded. "Yeah, mister detective." She laughed, but pleasantly, clearly in a good humor. "Who'd ya think, Minnie Mouse? Come on in, no point standing outside." She smiled a warm, inviting smile, and I knew, for heaven's sake, that she really wanted me to visit.

Inside was the fourth surprise, a domestic scene. Timmy was on the floor playing with the baby, the two older kids were putting together the tracks for a set of electric trains, and the whole picture was bound together by the thick, warm scent of something pungent on the stove. Timmy looked up. "Hi, Mr. Morrison. You want to play with some electric trains? We just got 'em."

I'm afraid the shock showed on my face. Florene was embarrassed. "So I moved in for a couple of days," she said. "What's the big deal? The place needed some cleaning up." I refrained from observing that the same courtesy could well have been extended to her own cave, unless it had changed substantially since I had last slogged through it. "And he looks after the kids while I go shopping."

I didn't know what to say, which the woman took for criticism. "Don't look at me like that, Mr. Morrison. I'll be going home in another day or two. Judge not or something, like the Bible says. Honest," she muttered, "some people!"

"Sorry," I said. "I was a little surprised to see you here. That's all." How did this lamebrain manage to get me on the defensive? "I need to talk to Timmy for a couple of minutes and then I'll be off."

"Suit yourself. I'll be in the kitchen, you want something." She walked out, her waddle still apparent, but less ducklike, a touch of alley cat having been injected into the mix.

I turned to Timmy. "Timmy," I said, "I wrote down all the names of people you said went down the road back then. Here it is, just like you said it." I handed the paper over. "Now, is there anything wrong with this?"

He frowned over the paper, painfully reading what I had written. "No, nothing. That's what I said, all right."

"How about these two names. Was I right to put them down like that?"

"Sure," he said, surprised by my denseness. "They was both down there, the two of them. That's why I said it. Is there something wrong?" He looked anxious.

"Not at all, Timmy," I said. "Just the opposite." I could feel my excitement rise, and I knew my face was starting to flush. "I'll be on my way now. 'Bye, Florene," I called out. "I'll be in touch. I think I'll have some news for you soon."

She stuck her face into the room. "Good. Hey, you wanna stay for lunch? Or maybe a cup of tea?"

The smothering odor of incipient domesticity was heavy in the air. "Thanks. I'll take a rain check."

As I walked out, I heard Timmy ask, "What's a rain check all about, Florene? It's not raining, is it?"

"Nah. He's nuts, that's all." They both giggled.

I continued on to the Parker place, still excited by the first fresh idea I'd had in weeks. There was no answer to my knock. Since my retirement I sometimes forget that other people go to work; it seems such a peculiar thing for sensible folk to do. Swallowing my disappointment, I drove home and drummed my fingers on the desk, the walls, my bald spot, and the refrigerator, and dialed the Parker number for what was probably every two minutes on the half minute.

Finally, the right half minute arrived and my call was answered. "Hello, Mrs. Parker. This is Hugh Morrison."

Her reaction was cautious. "Yes. Did you want something?" she asked.

I told her I was still working for Florene, and that I was convinced not only about my client's innocence but about her father's as well. She told me that the police had let her father go, but she wasn't so sure they were finished with him. Also, he had promised her to take his retirement as soon as he could do it without seeming unreasonably frantic, and that he had joined a support group to help him kick the habit. She also told me, though I think I could have figured it out for myself, that "poor Florene" was by way of becoming the ideal neighbor now that the bad influence had been removed.

A decent interval past, Cynthia Parker sounded sufficiently relaxed for me to spring my crucial question. Her answer was what I wanted. "Why, yes!" she said. "For weeks? Didn't Elroy tell you that?"

"No, he didn't. Neither one of you did."

"You know, as I think about it," she said, "it's got to be because it was almost like part of the scenery. It was there because it was there, like when you take a snapshot of the cliffs at sunset and you forget about that power line stretching across the view. You know? It's so much of a fixture that you don't see it anymore until it turns up when you get the prints back from the store."

"I get you."

"Yeah. Like the paint stain on my front steps. It's something I never notice anymore except when a visitor mentions it. Gee, I'm sorry we didn't tell you. Of course I couldn't tell you who it was because we never saw who was running it. Is it important?"

"No harm done." I didn't say it was important. Why upset the woman for an honest oversight? And after all, it wasn't important. It was more than important. It was the whole damn case, clear as crystal and spread out before me like a kid's picture puzzle where you can only find nine of the ten cats and dogs hidden in the landscape until you suddenly spot the tenth one and wonder how you possibly could have missed anything so obvious.

I drove to Middletown and headed for St. Sebastian's Hospital, giving the replacement car I had acquired after my insurance on the old one had come through its first real high-speed workout. While it would never replace the old dynamited sweetheart in my affections, it earned my total respect for its performance.

Inside the hospital, I worked my way through half a dozen assistants and finally landed the chief administrator. I explained what I wanted, and got the answer I expected.

"I'm sorry, but hospital records are confidential. There's really no way I can help you."

I explained again, this time dramatizing the importance of the information for Florene's future, and stressing my own sterling character as a former police officer.

Nothing worked. The administrator, a Ms. McGuffey, was adamant.

I tried a two-pronged approach. "This girl, this woman, for years had been abused by her husband. A battered wife. Because of that alone the police are trying hard to find her guilty of her husband's death." Ms. McGuffey looked concerned. I tried the second prong. "I appreciate your inability to open the records completely. Could you at least let me know, in all confidence, if he was admitted to the hospital back then, and never mind either the reason or the length of his stay?"

She chewed the end of a pencil, and when the eraser came off, she looked at it sharply, stood up, and said, "Wait here. I'll be a few minutes."

She reentered, sat behind her desk, cleared her throat, and announced, "No patient of that name was admitted to this hospital either the year you inquired about, or for three years before or after that."

"Oh, thank you, Ms. McGuffey. You can't imagine how much you've helped. Could you also let me know whether—"

"No, Mr. Morrison, I could not. I don't know what else you want, but the answer is no. I'm glad to have been of help to your client."

I thanked her again and left, driving home even faster than I had come. The car and my spirits had taken wing.

FORTY-THREE

SATURDAY. The day of the wine tasting. Mid-fall in the valley is without a doubt the best time of year, but it's not what anybody could call completely reliable. The air was fresh and clear, as promised in the travel ads, and the trees still had most of their leaves—orange, red, purple, yellow, brown. But the clouds were climbing over the cliffs, and a threat of the season's first northeaster was drilling icy passages into the bones of everybody over thirty-five. The candidate, Lena Mae Hollander, had tacked up notices on every bulletin board in the area—at the school, the ShopRite, the Grand Union, the discount department store, the deli, and the hardware store—thus guaranteeing herself an enormous crowd despite the threatening weather. She omitted the liquor store, for reasons unknown.

Since Harriet took in over three hundred bucks, there must have been over sixty people present either to judge the wines or the candidate, but fortunately their arrivals were staggered according to local custom. The locals, those who had lived in the area for most or all of their lives, considered promptness to be the essence of good manners. They, therefore, arrived at two, the hour designated for the start of the festivities. Their menfolk wore cotton flannel shirts, generally plaids, and cotton chinos in various hues, while the wives came in either woolen slacks or dresses, depending on what their figures could reasonably accommodate; many sported cardigans in modestly dull colors.

The retirees up from New York City, according to their citified conception of proper manners, arrived between two-thirty and three. The men, out to prove their total assimilation into the countryside, showed up in blue jeans, preferably faded, and in the case of the wealthier ones, slightly torn, while the women again were in either slacks or dresses; male and female alike displayed expensive woolen sweaters with vaguely Norwegian motifs. A few among both sexes needed a shave.

Last to show, somewhere between four o'clock and closing time at five, was the college faculty, their late arrivals signifying that while they were certainly *in* the community and *with* the community in its search for good government, they were nevertheless not *of* the community, being themselves descendants of a higher mammalian order. The men tended toward turtlenecks and tweed jackets (a few with leather elbow patches), while the wives again were in slacks or dresses, and frequently wore brooches, pins, or rings that needed no label to make clear their origin in the workshops of interesting young designers whose creativity demanded support.

Those of the faculty who were in the Arts department could sometimes be counted on to stay after the closing bell, as long as there was still a popped kernel of corn or an open bottle of wine to be snuffled up. These were the ones who had, in their youths, tried to make it without teaching, going hungry in Soho or the East Village, and the principle of staying put as long as anything for ingestion remained available was burned into their souls. The last of these was gone, however, by six-thirty.

It had been an eventful day. Lena Mae Hollander's hair, normally pulled back tight in a bun, had flown apart in the crush. Harriet had exhausted herself walking a fine line between making the supply of food and drink look generous and holding back as much as possible, especially as regarded the hooch.

I had been assigned the duty of keeping people from standing silent on the sidelines and talking up Lena Mae as the best hope Appleboro had for honest governance. Since I knew little or nothing about the woman, and since I was enough of a patriot to believe, like all good Americans, that those not in office were automatically better than the incumbents, I wasn't overburdened with facts, and the assignment was pleasurably easy. It also gave me the chance to talk to my latest suspect.

Don Tupper had brought his old dad. "I hope it's okay," Don said. "If I've had any success with the vineyard a lot of the credit goes to dad. He's been with me, helping and backing me up every step of the way. Sometimes I think his heart's been in it more than mine. So for my first tasting, and in the old hometown at that—what the hell, I couldn't do it without him here to celebrate."

"Harriet would have been furious if you had left him out," I said. "And speaking of which, he's looking lost over there on the sidelines. Why don't I go over and cheer him up?" With Don's agreement I did just that.

"Hello, Mr. Tupper," I said to the old man. "You should be pleased. This is your day."

"Don's day," he said. "Not mine. And sure I'm pleased. The boy's been working like a dog the past couple of years, and maybe now folks around here will stop their sniggering when they see the land go into something besides corn and onions."

"Come on, now. You were right there with him. Everybody in town knows it."

He dismissed the notion. "What the hell. Sure I helped. But you know what? I was against it at first, wanted the boy to go in with me, take over the construction business when I phased out. But that's how it goes. The young ones go their own ways no matter what."

"Sure," I said. "You did too when you were a kid. So did I. It's only right."

He grinned, a wry grin with his eyebrows raised, and he looked at me for the fool he saw me as. "Bullshit," he decided. "He'd be better off today if he'd gone in with me. Money, security. A going business. But maybe it'll work out okay now." He canceled the grin and tilted his chin in my direction. "Listen," he said with a hint of defiance, "ain't you gonna ask me what kind of gun I have, how's the hunting, crap like that?"

"I don't know," I said. "Am I?"

"You been asking Don. You been asking half the people in the goddamned town, is how I hear it."

I wasn't ready for this, but I didn't see what choice I had. "Sure. I wouldn't leave you out. I'm asking."

"I got a Winchester thirty-thirty. I hunt deer regularly every year. I got my licenses for the last quarter century in the bottom drawer of the dresser unless my old lady trashed 'em. I'm in the hunt club. And in a couple of days, by God, when the season starts, I'll be out there popping at the mothers. Anything else you need to know?''

Before I could frame a reply he was off again. "Oh, yeah, if the cops want to match my rifle against the markings on this shell I hear you found—they can be my guest. And no, I didn't kill your professor or his neighbor or take any shots at Timmy Young. If I'da wanted to, I would've done better than wing him in the shoulder, I can tell you.''

I felt slighted that he had neglected to include the dynamiting of my car in his denial. I needed time to think. "Look, Mr. Tupper, I'm not sure this is the best time for us to go into this. I've got to go around and talk up the Hollander woman with the voters. If you want, why don't we get together later and go into things? It's up to you. I mean, how can you be sure I was going to ask you questions anyway? You want to talk more, okay we'll talk. You don't like the idea—well, hell, then we forget it. Your choice.''

He hesitated. I tried to look calm while I bombarded him with thought waves and prayer to push him the way I wanted. I won. He couldn't resist the chance to find out if I knew anything or was only guessing blindly or even if I was guessing at all. "I tell you what. I've got a job on next Wednesday over in Ellenville digging a foundation. First decent job I've had in a couple of years, since I got sick. You want to come over we can talk in the truck. You don't want to come, we forget the whole thing. Meet me at the barn where I've got my equipment: no need to go up to the house.''

There was nothing in the world I wanted less than to be stuck in Ellenville for a day while the man dug holes, but he had me dangling. It was take it or leave it. I took it. I'd be out to his barn at seven-thirty Wednesday morning and we'd drive off in his flatbed truck wagging heavy machinery across the cliffs to Ellenville. It did cross my mind, somewhat more than fleetingly, that meeting him at the barn would mean nobody else in the household would know I'd be riding with him, but nothing ventured, nothing gained.

FORTY-FOUR

GOING TO ELLENVILLE means taking Route 44 across the Shawangunk Cliffs from our valley to theirs. And the cliffs are something very special in our little world. Eons ago, in the last ice age, when those diamond-hard chunks came thundering out from the North Pole, they flattened everything in the way, or, if they couldn't flatten it, they smoothed it down and rounded it off, like some sort of cosmic sandpaper. That's what made the elegant rolling hills of the Catskills, which we can see, hazy blue in the distance, from the Shawangunks.

Our cliffs, however, are another kettle of rock, made of the toughest mixture of quartz and other things this side of the nose cone of a space rocket. No glaciers could tame them; all they could do was leave scratches on the rock surfaces from north to south as they passed over, like outraged pussycats. (In fact, to this day if you're lost in the local wilds what you do is look for the scratch marks. Then the only problem is to figure out which the hell way is north and which is south, and you're home free—if you guess right.)

Well, there I was, sitting in the cab of old Tupper's truck, crawling around horseshoe curves, the cliffs dropping off precipitously first on one side and then the other, one of them the tallest sheer drop this side of the Far West. Sometimes they rose above us as we continued to twist and climb on the narrow road.

"Nice day," I observed by way of making fascinating conversation.

"You could say that," Clarence agreed, and we drove on in silence.

I spotted a couple of hawks circling—below us; in another season I might have seen a plane down there dusting an apple orchard. The threatening storm of the day before had passed over, and the wild north winds had taken possession. Fallen leaves were doing somersaults along the way, and the tall pines and hemlocks were swaying. Before the day was over, one or more of those pines, too big for their shallow roots, would have come crashing down.

The tension was as tough on him as on me, and neither of us was about to start. Clarence gave way first. "You know," he said, "you shouldn'ta done that."

"Done what?"

"Morrison, my kin been around here since before the Civil War. There's nobody in town more than twenty years that I'm not related to by blood or by marriage. Nieces, cousins, brothers, great grandnephews—you name it. You think nobody could find out about the phoney story you planted in *The Clarion?* Think again. Good gossip don't set quiet. I got a cousin with a boy on the force and he told us. Told the whole family about this so-called trap you set yourself up for somebody to ditch his Winchester, lie about being a hunter."

He stopped talking as he maneuvered the long flatbed around a curve on the narrow road. We were going faster than we should have, and I was pressed against the door of the cab. "Only thing the boy didn't tell us, I already knew. You were fishing for me, wise guy, weren't you?"

Now who was doing the fishing? "Maybe," I said. "Maybe not."

I looked at him. Several times his mouth opened to say something but then shut again. The muscles in his cheeks flexed and unflexed, and the stubble on his face stood out or lay flat as his expression changed and changed again. He wanted, needed, to find out what I was thinking, or better yet, what I knew—or thought I knew. My guess was that he was afraid that with too many questions he might give too much away, too much that I might not really know, that I might only suspect.

I had to help him, make him think I knew things when I was only wondering about them. I went for broke. "I know what a bastard Beasley was, Clarence. I know he was blackmailing you, or trying to. Maybe I'd have done the same as you in your place."

A closed-mouth smile, a smug smile, spread across his face. "You don't know shit," he said.

He was right. Blind alley. He figured me for stupid. What else could I try? I wanted to save my zinger for last, to see if he'd tell me himself. I could tell he was tensing up; his hands were tight on the wheel and his foot pressed harder on the gas. The tires squealed as we negotiated a turn. The wind moaned its fury and sent gusts to slap at the cab. This was my only chance. If I lost him now, I'd have lost him—period. I chanced it. "It was Betty Ann, wasn't it? You knew she was going to those parties Beasley threw. You were afraid for Don's sake, weren't you?"

"You're guessing, mister. Lot of hot air."

I had to go on. "So you went to Beasley. Maybe you threatened him. Maybe he told you Don was a big boy and you should let him look out for himself."

"Come on, cut that bull, okay? It was Timmy told you I was down that road, wasn't it. Nobody's about to believe what that dimwit says. And you know it, man."

"You know, when we first met, when you told me not to take any stock in what Timmy said, I thought you were protecting Don. But you were protecting yourself, weren't you. Yes, Timmy said Mister Tupper went down the Swamp Bottom road, and then he said it again. *Two* Mister Tuppers, and one of them was you."

"Of course I was down there. For weeks. I had a job to do, building a pond for that scum. So what?" Just like Cynthia Parker had told me the other day when she said that if something's around all the time, in this case Tupper's heavy machinery, you simply don't see it anymore unless there's something to force it onto your attention. And since most of the time he was in the cab, working the machinery, she and her husband weren't that much concerned about squinting through the glass to see who the operator was.

"Uh huh, and what was he paying you with, gratitude? He didn't have a damned cent to his name. But he had his brains. And while you were warning him off Betty Ann he remembered that Clarendon was going broke, that it was second best to DeWitt."

He sat quiet, rigid as a board at the wheel. I was thrown against the side of the cab again, and as I put my hand out to brace myself I realized that the handle was off the door. I was locked in. No exit. I had to go on. "He made you an offer. He could help Don out by putting Clarendon on top, by seeing to it that DeWitt would slip from first, didn't he?"

"I told him I didn't want to know about it." He was snapping his words faster now; we both were.

"Yeah, but you were interested. You didn't want to know about it, but you wanted it to happen, right? He suggested a swap—you build him a nice little pond, and maybe there'd be an accident over at DeWitt's. And for good measure, he'd let Betty Ann alone. I should have known it weeks ago, when you showed me your shiny gear in the barn."

"You think so, do you?"

"That's right, I think so. Because when you slapped a fender, a lump of mud fell out, mud that had been thrown up when you were digging Beasley's pond. You told me your machines had been in the barn for years, and I was too dumb to realize right off that you'd had it out and operating. There's no way mud could've hung there under a fender for two years and still come off in a soggy clump." He stayed silent. I went on. "You never should have lied about that, Clarence. If you'd said you were building a pond, I wouldn't have thought twice about it. But when you try to hide something, I have to wonder why, don't I?"

"I don't know, do you? You been telling these crazy stories to anybody else? I hope not, for your sake. There's these libel laws I keep reading about in the paper. Could get you in trouble."

"Get one of us in trouble, anyway."

I didn't like my own story about Betty Ann. It left too many holes, too much unexplained. Besides, not even a macho type like Clarence would kill a man because his son's honor had been besmirched by his woman's minor sin. I had to look further.

"You know," I said, "you kept warning me off talking to your boy. You said this was a make or break time for his business, and you didn't want him upset."

"At least there's something you remember right. But it didn't do no good, did it? I told you about his breakdown; I told you he couldn't take another shock like that, didn't I! But it never got through your thick skull, Morrison. Like talking to a god-damn wall.''

"It got through, all right, mister. And I'll tell you a couple of other things that got through. St. Sebastian's over in Mid-dletown has no record of any Don Tupper in their loony bin twenty-five years ago. And nobody in Appleboro ever heard of a girl jilting Don Tupper, ever. In fact, I hear that he was so busy jilting the ladies that he never got around to shifting gears and marrying one until a couple of years ago.

"And I'll tell you something else," I added. "You weren't protecting Don at all. At first, you only wanted me to stay away in general, but then you realized that nobody had told me you were building Beasley's pond. What a break that was for you. You figured maybe you could keep it that way, that if I didn't talk to Don maybe I'd never find out you were dredging for that pond. No, sir, if there was anybody you were protecting it was yourself, not your son.''

He shook his head in disbelief, and turned his head briefly from the road. He stared at me in disgust. "You're one stupid son of a bitch, man," he announced.

Maybe needling the man would boil something interesting out of him. "Me? I'm stupid? Hey, with your equipment stored in a barn half a mile from the house, Don would never have known you had taken it out. In fact, since the doctor had side-lined you, you even kept your son from knowing. You sneaked it out and over to Beasley's when you figured nobody'd be around to see.''

The main effect I had on the man was for him to go a little faster, gripping the wheel as if it were the safety bar on a roller coaster starting its first big descent. We had reached the crest of the road, and the sky and the next valley were spread out before us, the Catskills hazy on the horizon, white fair-weather clouds racing south and east in front of the north wind. The trees, now fully open to the elements, danced and swayed more crazily than on the ascent. The valley below, off the edge of the cliff, was an unreal picture of toy houses and open fields. A wind-up toy automobile slid silently down a distant road.

"Uh huh. Still no reason why I would've killed nobody. I just hope you've kept your mouth shut.''

"That's right, no reason at all to kill until Beasley suddenly needed money and needed it real bad, and started to hit you up. What'd he do, threaten to say Don hired him to louse up the wine down at DeWitt's if you didn't pony up? The man was desperate, afraid for his life. There was a drug dealer on his tail. Talking might have ruined him, but it would have been worse for your Donnie, wouldn't it? Who would have believed Donnie hadn't set the whole thing up to knock out the competition?"

"You're nuts, Morrison."

"Not so nuts. I don't have it all in a package yet, but when I do I'll have to start talking." (That line was my mistake, and I knew it as soon as it came out of my mouth, but in no way could I cancel it, no way now I could ever convince him that I had already spoken to the police, that others besides me knew.) "Two men are dead; a woman has been accused of murder. Even if they can't make it stick, her name has got to be cleared. I've got a hunch there's a pile of money been drawn out of your bank account lately, Clarence, blackmail money for Beasley. Only it was never enough, was it? And believe me, that's something easy to check, once the police get around to it."

I felt for that missing door handle again. It was still missing. I began to worry.

Clarence looked over and grinned. "Maybe I shoulda said before, but you can't get out that way, not without somebody goes around and opens the door from the outside." He tittered. "And . . . we're going a tad fast for that." He stopped talking to negotiate a turn, largely, at the speed we were going, on the wrong side of the road.

We were headed sharply downhill and a road sign indicated low gear for trucks. We stayed in high. "I'm sorry," he said suddenly. "I wouldn't mind for myself. I killed that bastard and I had no right to. I didn't mean to, but he kept asking for money and more money. Then that day he sent that wife of his to shop in town, and there was just the two of us. He started threatening to ruin Donnie again, and I swung at him with the first thing that came into my hand, that damn pickax. Didn't mean to kill him."

He shook his head. "Didn't mean to kill nobody. I went crazy, and I was goddamn scared. Didn't mean for it to happen. Didn't know what I was doing. I started up my machine, dredged up some muck, and built the son of a bitch right into the wall of his lousy dam, wiped off the pick and got my butt out of there fast. I'd undo it if I could, but I sure as hell can't."

"I'm sorry, Clarence."

"Don't be, boy. Don't be, because I still got to take care of Donnie. Not for myself. What've I got left? Maybe three, four more years of 'Don't strain your back, Dad. Better stick to the toast, Dad, the eggs, the steak, is bad for you. Don't this, don't that, just die nice and quiet, Dad.' Screw that." He snorted. "Look. I tried to warn you off, didn't I? Mussed things a tad at the Lorimer woman's place to warn you, didn't I? Only reason I didn't do more is because I like the woman. She's an old bag now, but she used to be a hot little fox, and I never in my life hurt a good-looking woman—" he laughed "—unless she asked me to. Why couldn't you take a hint, man?"

The dam had burst, and it was all pouring out, so I dug for more. "Tell me," I asked, "when did you set up that bomb in my car?"

He looked as if I had just flattered him. "Pretty good, hey, wasn't it! That's why I came in late. I waited for you to pull in, and then I slapped it under your fender, soon as nobody else was in the parking lot. But if you'da behaved yourself I would've gone out and taken the thing off."

"Supposing I had agreed to stay away from Don but then I had left before you, or we had gone out together. How would you have got it out from under my fender?"

"You know, I never thought of that." He put on a happy face. "But I would have been very sorry. Would have sent flowers." He even screeched at the best joke he had heard in years.

I began to get the idea, and I didn't much like it. "Let's not do anything rash," I said. "Easy does it, now. Let's think it over."

"I already thought it over. That's why that handle's off the door. I'm sorry for you, mister, but it's got to be this way. Not for me, but for my boy's sake. Donnie's got to have his chance.

Can't have those DeWitts suing his ass off, can I." I realized, a bit late, just how demented the man was.

We were damn near flying down the road, and a sharp curve to the left lay dead ahead. I knew in one hideous moment that Tupper's plans failed to include that left-hand turn. Straight ahead led off the cliff and into the toy valley below. I tried to take control. God knows I tried, but I failed. Ever reach over to push up on a steering wheel when a madman at the helm is pushing down with all his strength? Don't bother. It doesn't work.

The road turned. We didn't. I banged on the door as we bumped over the rock-strewn verge. I hammered on steel and glass and it didn't feel a thing. We headed, we flew, toward the edge. Unthinking, I strained back in the seat as if to keep myself from sailing into space, and my hands were braced against the dashboard.

I don't really remember going over. It's vanished from my mind. But go over I did. Clarence, me, and the flatbed truck.

FORTY-FIVE

AT THIS POINT, I'm afraid I have to stop and go back for another lecture on the geology of the Shawangunk Cliffs. With a little botany thrown in. I'll try to be brief. I've already said that the Shawangunks are harder than your everyday rock. As a consequence, time and erosion and acid rain and the gnawing away of lichens have done relatively little to grind them into soil. Many stretches are treeless, though the cliffs are as old as sin, except for the spaces and cracks between the broken boulders. And it took the earth itself in violent upheaval to produce those spaces.

Over the millennia, seeds and dirt and bird droppings, gum wrappers and prophylactic devices and facial tissues have caught in the cracks and decayed into a soil of sorts. And in that mean and stingy soil, pitch pines have managed to establish a foothold. They grow short, tortured, and twisted, as if in an agony of trying to wrest a living out of what is mostly unsympathetic rock. The first reaction a newcomer has on seeing them is that he or she is looking at nature's bonsai trees, sometimes only a few feet tall and bent into shapes that would certainly gain the admiration and envy of even a professional in the art of the bonsai.

Now back to the story:

When old Tupper's truck smashed into the boulders that had been placed at the edge of the drop to keep sightseers from falling over, it flipped up and over. Hikers told us that later. And my door sprang open, launching me into space in a manner less like Superman than some old rooster that had latched onto the foolish notion that it could fly.

I came earthward precipitously, off the edge of the cliff, and when the hikers rushed to peer into the abyss, they saw Tupper's truck still tumbling violently until it burst into flame, and me—me about twenty feet below, my down jacket speared by the upright branch of an unyielding pine that probably considered the upset just another misery visited on it by the cold, hard rocks. I was, they told me later, dangling facedown, the tree limb through the back of my jacket, while the only sign of motion, if not life, was the occasional dancing through the air of the feathers that were escaping from the torn jacket. (Every Mother's Day since, I march to the edge of that cliff, toss my own special pitch pine a handful of fertilizer, and wish it well.)

When I came to my senses and looked down—at space—I froze. That was, however, all to the good, as people were yelling at me not to move and that help was on the way. Soon I heard sirens. A bit later a rope was dangling next to me. It was a sort of a sling arrangement. I had seen others like it many times before when I was on the force, and knew, fortunately, what to do. I grabbed it, and since no bones seemed to be broken, I was able to twist myself into it by carefully easing out of my jacket and at the same time into the loop of the sling.

People kept shouting, "Easy, now! Easy, now! You can do it!" I kept wishing they'd shut up and stop making me nervous. It was like telling someone to be careful after he had already fallen down two flights of stairs. I had no intention of taking it anything but easy and all those shouts about what I could do were making me doubt that I really could. But I did.

When I got to the top they helped me out of the sling. I stood, but my legs gave way and I fell. My hands were bleeding, and there was something trickling down my face that I doubted was resin from my very favorite pine.

At that very moment, Harriet's car squealed to a stop. Pinky had called her. She came running over and tossed aside half a dozen cops and medics to fall weeping next to me, her arms clasping me. A little kid came over, a little golden-haired kid who looked like one of those urchins who's supposed to break your heart in a second-rate movie. He said, "Don't cry, lady. That man's okay, lady."

I said, I'm afraid, "Beat it, kid. The lady wants to cry, you let her. This is my party."

Then I think we all started to cry: Harriet, me, and the kid.

I woke up again in the emergency room, where after X rays and doctors saying, "We're not worried one bit," (Why do they always talk in the plural, those bums?) they sewed up a gash in my back, gave me a tetanus shot, antibiotics, pain killers, and advice, and let Harriet take me away that evening.

FORTY-SIX

"I EXPLAINED IT down at the station," I told Harriet while she was changing the dressing on my back, "and they'll go along with it. They don't like it, but they don't have much choice."

"Mm," she said, "you're going to be left with one big scar when this is over with."

"Heck, that's all right. I'll say it's my duelling scar. I got it at Heidelberg."

"On your back?"

"Of course. Running away, like any sensible young boy."

"What do you mean, they don't have much choice?"

"Clarence is dead. They can't prove anything now, and it isn't worth the effort to try. So they'll put Beasley down as an unsolved crime and let Florene all the way off the hook. And Don Tupper never need know, though I suppose it'll all leak out in another ten years or so. The cops are kinda mad at me, though."

"That's great. The cops don't like it, that's tough. Poor old Clarence. I suppose it's all for the best."

"It better be. There's no alternative." I sat up and slipped back into my shirt; it hurt when I raised my arm. "You know, Harriet, the old boy was joking about being buried in his backhoe, and he damn near made it, by the time they finished sifting through the wreckage. I feel sorry for him."

"Myself, I'm not so sure about that."

"I know. He did bad things, but from his point of view, he got sucked into it. Look, when he wanted to frighten me off the job, he trashed your place, but gently, as if he was saying he didn't want it to be any worse and please don't make him do it. It's crazy, but there it is. The man was in a trap. Sure, he set it himself, but he never meant to." I wondered if that sounded lame.

"If you say so." She shrugged, unconvinced; girls are tougher than boys. "Let's not talk about it anymore."

"Okay," I said. "Okay. But I can't help thinking. There were so many hints along the way. Maybe I should have figured it out before."

"You mean like Timmy saying 'Mr. Tupper' twice."

"That, of course, but other things too. Way back, John Mittleman said there was a backhoe down at Beasley's. It should have been obvious to me that digging out that pond called for somebody's heavy equipment to be on the scene, and I should have asked myself how come it had been taken away before the job was finished. Besides that, there's that car bomb. How does an ordinary Joe get hold of a couple of sticks of dynamite? I'll tell you—he doesn't. But Clarence was in the construction trade, or had been. It would have been easy for him. He may even have had some lying around, waiting for the day he expected to get back to work."

I shook my head, annoyed with myself. "Then the Parkers had told me Beasley was very careful about the property line. He kept to his side and squawked when they crossed over theirs. Yet the pond strayed over onto the Parkers' land, and I never asked myself if somebody who didn't know where the boundaries were had been at work . . . Damn!"

"Such a waste." Harriet sighed. "So much hurt, so much death. Especially the Parker boy. I keep thinking about him. A decent young fellow, a wife, a child. Such a waste."

"I know," I said. "That night at Carrie Nation's, Clarence heard Parker and me talking about getting together for something he wanted to tell me. He wanted me to know about his wife's father, old Fabian Cribbs, that he might have been involved. But Clarence figured he was going to tell me about the man who was digging the pond, and he thought he had to stop that. The boy's death was needless, even from Clarence's crazy way of looking at it."

I shifted in my seat; my back was healing, and it itched. "Another big mistake was deciding right off that old Tupper was stonewalling me because he wanted to shield his son. It took me too long to realize that he was worrying about somebody else's hide, namely his own."

"Oh, stop it, Hugh," Harriet said. "Stop blaming yourself. You did real good, and I'm proud of you, even if...."

"Even if," I echoed. "There's always an 'even if,' always something to realize too late, which is what I hate about this game."

FLORENE DROPPED IN a few days later. Her clothes were clean, and since she was alone there was no need to peer through several layers of kids to locate the body. "I'm getting my insurance money," she said. She touched her hair with a preening gesture, as if to assure herself that every strand was neatly and most unusually in place. (It was.)

I waited for her to express her gratitude and even cross my palm with a few pieces of silver. "You know," she confided, "even though you didn't exactly find out who killed Al, I guess you did a lot of good. The police, they said I'm in the clear, which is what those insurance crooks wanted to hear." She blushed and looked down as she handed me an envelope. "I owe you something for your trouble. Thanks, Mr. Morrison." She turned clumsily on her heel and beat a rapid retreat out the door.

Harriet and I looked at each other in disbelief. I opened the envelope. There were ten neat, clean, crisp, pretty hundred dollar bills in it. I looked at Harriet. "My God," I said. "I'm overwhelmed. I wonder how she can afford this."

"The rich are always stingy. If it had been Elsie Delavergne it would have been even less. Take it and be grateful."

"The rich?"

"That's right. She's got the insurance money, Beasley's pension fund from the school, and I guess something from Social Security. Plus now that she and Timmy have combined households, they're probably better off than we are."

"Combined households? That's terrible! Suppose they— What if— Look, Timmy's a healthy young man, and God knows that muttonhead is capable of mass production if the opportunity arises." The more I thought about it the more agitated I got. "Listen, that's got to be stopped! For the future race if for no other reason."

"Oh, relax. Nothing's going to happen. You're just an old blue-nosed Puritan at heart. I always suspected it, and now I know."

"What do you mean, nothing's going to happen? I'll bet you this envelope that before nine months is up— What a horrible thought!"

"Of course things will happen. But not babies. Timmy's father thought ahead about that, too. I thought you knew. Timmy had that operation. No babies. Fun and games, yes; babies no. I think it'll be great. He'll have the kids to play with, Florene will have a house to keep for the lot of them, and Timmy will help with the heavy work. There'll be great pots of stew on the stove, and clothes drying on a line stretching from Swamp Bottom to Main Street, and everything'll be as near to perfect as those two can possibly have it. And you know what? I think you've got to take a chunk out of that thousand bucks and buy them a—what should I call it?"

"A nonwedding present?"

"Right. A nonwedding present."

"I think I'll go back to bed," I said. "I'm weaker than I thought, and I'm glad."

A FEW DAYS LATER, I was as good as new. Better, because I had shed nearly fifteen pounds and I didn't have to suck my stomach in and look like a shell-shocked penguin when I walked. Well, not very much, anyway. I studied myself in the mirror on the inside of the closet door. Then I went over to Harriet's for dinner. She'd been feeding me regularly while I was working my way back to normal, chicken broth at the ready each evening at seven.

"Baby doll," I said, "I've got the figure of a twenty-nine-year-old man." I turned sideways to let her admire the outline.

"Uh huh. You better give it back. You're getting it all wrinkled."

I went on stubbornly. "I deserve a present. If Florene gets one, then me too."

"With that I can agree. You deserve a present. What'll it be?"

"I want a thick steak, a thick, bad-for-me steak. Rare. Baked potato with sour cream and chives. No grass and vinegar. Maybe green peas. And I want to finish up with a hot-fudge sundae with vanilla ice cream and whipped cream and nuts."

"You've earned it. But just this once. Should we eat in or go out?"

"Out. Except for one problem. I'd like you to make the hot-fudge sundae here at home, if you know how. They don't make it right in the stores these days."

"How so?"

"Well," I said, my voice getting soft and dreamy, "When I was a kid, my folks lived in Chicago for a couple of years, on the South Side. Sometimes, Saturday nights, we'd go to a movie downtown. We'd take the I.C.—the Illinois Central to you—down to, I think it was Rush Street but I'm not sure. And we'd walk to the Loop. We always stopped at . . . was it Walgreen's or was it Leggett's?—and had a hot-fudge sundae. The fudge, oh, the fudge!"

I was choked with emotion. "The hot fudge was the kind that you could carve your initials into, practically, and when it hit the cold ice cream it turned to rock. Wonderful, glorious rock."

"I'm feeling faint," Harriet said, "but go on. The suspense is killing me."

"Oh, Harriet, then when you sank your teeth in, right up to the gum line, it was damn near impossible to pry them apart again without that fudge pulling your fillings out." I was crooning, and my eyes were closed.

"Huh, these days it'd be your upper plate that'd get pried loose."

"I've been dreaming about that stuff for over half a century; nobody can do it anymore, and I want it."

"Nonsense. I can do it. There's an old cookbook by Rombauer that's been in my kitchen since I was a young bride. The secret's there. You have to boil the sauce for ten minutes and after that, it turns to concrete, the way you like it."

"Oh, Harriet, that'd be heaven," I breathed. "I may weep."

"Oh, Hugh, heaven can wait; it's your turn to do the dishes. Get going, lad, and weep later if you still feel like it."

A RECONSTRUCTED CORPSE

SIMON BRETT

A Charles Paris Mystery

First Time in Paperback

A STIFF ACT TO FOLLOW...

If playing a dead man could be called a role, Charles Paris has sunk to new lows when he agrees to play missing Martin Earnshaw on the true crime TV series "Public Enemies."

The show has all the hallmarks of a hit: a vulnerable, tearful wife, a sexy female detective and, best of all, dismembered limbs probably belonging to Earnshaw turning up each week just before airtime.

As viewers shudder gleefully and ratings soar, Paris discovers there's more to the whole production than meets the eye...and the climax is a killer.

"A perfect vacation read."   *—People*

Available in March at your favorite retail stores.

CORPSE

GRIZZLY

First Time in Paperback

CHRISTINE ANDREAE

A Lee Squires Mystery

FAIR GAME

English professor Lee Squires is spending Easter break in
Montana as cook for the J-E dude ranch, where friend and
owner Dave Fife is hoping that some Japanese investors—
plied with home cooking—will pour cash into the
struggling J-E.

Lee has come ready to whip up hotcakes, biscuits and
chicken fried steak—but not to wrestle her libido over Dave's
brother, Mac, a tireless bear activist...or to find a dead body
with missing parts.

Another mangled body later, officials are hunting a bear.
Lee doesn't buy the theory—but in tracking the truth, she
comes face-to-face with a human killer who is nothing
short of...grizzly.

**"Good character interaction, great sense of place, and
steady suspense."** *—Library Journal*

Available in May at your favorite retail stores.

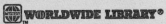 **WORLDWIDE LIBRARY®**

GRIZZLY

Dreaming Back
M. E. Hirsh
A New Mexico Mystery

First Time in Paperback

PATH OF DEADLY RESISTANCE

Boston artist Leigh Haring arrives in northern New Mexico
to claim the body of her sister, Leni, found with a cache of
exotic drugs on the scene. But straight answers are not
forthcoming and Leigh must draw her own conclusions.
She suspects that Leni's doctoral research on the history
of visionary drug use has somehow cost her her life.

As she is drawn into the complex web of Leni's life, Leigh
encounters secrets involving sacred Indian ceremonial
grounds and CIA experimental drug use—and the mystery
that has haunted her own family since childhood. But in
getting to the truth, she finds that Leni's tragic fate may
also be her own.

"A compelling plot..."—*Los Angeles Times Book Review*

Available in March at your favorite retail stores.

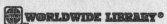

THE POISON POOL
PATRICIA HALL
A Yorkshire Mystery

First Time in Paperback

CLOSED RANKS

When old Tom Carter is found bludgeoned to death, Inspector Alex Sinclair makes quick work of arresting the only suspect, Joey Macready, a young man living with his mother.

Social worker Kate Weston is convinced that Joey is innocent and persuades Sinclair to probe further. But queries are quickly stonewalled by his superiors. Worse, he's accused of accepting bribes and is suspended from the force.

Together, the two discover a dark conspiracy deep in the tightly knit Yorkshire community. Closing in on its dangerous secrets, they must challenge an invisible enemy who is implacable and desperate enough to silence them forever....

"Auspicious debut..."   —*Publishers Weekly*

Available in April at your favorite retail stores.

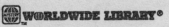
POOL